URBAN

Real Life Street Niggaz!

Nyamekye Shakur

Urban Genocide - Real Life Street Niggas
©2018 Nyamekye Shakur

Melanic World Publishing

ISBN 9781948708265

Printed in USA
10 9 8 7 6 5 4 3 2 1

For Worldwide Distribution

Urban Genocide

Chapter 1

The thick clouds of smoke from the marijuana had the Monte Carlo stuffy. It was 2:30am and the club has just let out. The street was quiet besides the coughing in the Monte Carlo. The driver opened his car door and puked, then I heard six shots.

Pop! Pop, pop...!

The driver's body laid slumped outside the car. The passenger pushed his legs out and then pulled off. I jumped out of my car to see was there still help for the young man. My boys were telling me to come on because we had enough artillery to be the Taliban Fighters so I jumped back in the car and pulled off.

I couldn't sleep much that night. After dropping my boys off, I went home devastated. I sat down on the couch watching BET. *How did cuzz get twisted up in that bullshit?* I rolled up a blunt, smoked half of it then went to sleep. As always, the weed plus a 5th of Remy took a toll on me.

I woke up just in time to watch the 11:00 o'clock news. I wanted to see who got killed last night.

Searching for the remote, I found it and turned it on to Flint's channel seven. I caught the news just in time. There was a picture on the screen of the boy who died last night. He was twenty-three years old. The police said it could be a gang related shooting and they had no suspects in custody.

I smelled food so I went into the kitchen. I lived with my mother and she was a master chef.

"Hey Mama," I said.

She turned around with tears rolling down her cheeks. She was watching the news. I hated to see my mother cry. I didn't know what was wrong with her. She would usually tell me to come to breakfast but today she didn't. I all of the sudden lost my appetite.

The phone was ringing in the living room. I didn't want to bother my mother so I answered it.

"Hello."

"Hey, Travis. Where yo' Mama?" It was my Aunt Francis.

"Hold on," I said. "Mama, telephone. It's Aunt Francis," I yelled.

My Aunt Francis lived on the north side and had recently moved to Flint from Chicago. I would usually go check on her but for the past couple of months, I was trying to stack my chips to cop this house on Paterson Street. I had a job working in

6

this factory but they fired me for lying on my job application. It was hard finding a job in Flint after the shops closed so I had to lie or it was back to the block. I knew my mother and Aunt Francis would be on the phone talking for hours so I got dressed and hit the streets.

It was July 16th and the sun hit my eyes like a chest ache that only lasts for a minute. Pulling out my keys, I hit the car alarm and remote starter. I had a gray Grand National with twenty-inch rims on it. The females loved it but the niggas hated it and me. I learned that envy and jealousy was a part of life so I wasn't trippin'. Niggas knew how I brought drama and they didn't want no part of it. I jumped in my ride and turned up the music. I was listening to Skanbino Mob, *Mob Affiliated*. It was nice outside so I went to the car wash. I knew it would be off the hook and it was.

Since I lost my job, I went back to my old business. It was a risky one. I never knew if one day I would become a victim of this business. I stayed strapped or my job would turn into something else if I wasn't careful. I stayed prepared just in case.

When I got to the carwash I thought I saw the car from last night. This Monte Carlo had hubcaps, the other one had rims on it. I parked and got out. It was too hot to be sitting in the car plus I saw this female from high school parked next to me. I got out and hollered at her. I left my gun on the passenger seat with the window rolled down just in case I had to grab it. I understood life was a precious gift and you only live once. I knew niggas hated me and my hood from what they heard, and from what some had felt the wrath of. There were no chances to be taken.

After talking to the female, I saw a spot to wash my car. I took advantage of the opportunity. I hadn't ate yet and my stomach was letting me know what time it was. I sprayed the car, threw some Armor All on the tires and cleaned the rims. I hadn't washed it in a week. It looked brand new so when I pulled out, I was hurting the game. The carwash was getting jammed packed and I wasn't gon' put myself in a fucked up situation. I knew it was time to go.

The guys in the Monte Carlo was leaving too but I took the lead. It was three of them in the car acting all rowdy. I knew they had to be young or either looking for trouble. I usually carried a .45 automatic. I still had the Mac 10 in the car from last night. It was fully loaded with thirty-two shots. I knew I couldn't ride around with it all day. When I left the carwash, I headed toward the Steak and Onion restaurant. I had to smash something.

I pulled in and got out of the car. I saw them three dudes in the Monte Carlo riding slowly pass the restaurant. The driver was pointing his finger at me nodding his head so I threw my hands up like "what's up" but they kept going. I was trippin' then for two reasons. One was that I couldn't bring the Mac in the restaurant without the waist strap to carry it, and two, I didn't have a spare shoe string to use. My stomach was still growling so I ran in and ordered my food. While waiting for my food to come up, I called to my right hand manz.

"What's up my nigga," J.B. said.

J.B. was my nigga. I stayed messing with J.B. back in the day, he was like my blood brother. We done been through it all. I told him about my unknown admirers in the Monte Carlo. He told me he had been trying to call me so I can call my ole miss and see what's going on because she had been looking for me.

I told him I would be by his house in a minute. When I hung up the phone, my food was ready. When I walked out the restaurant I just knew someone would be out there waiting on me, but to my surprise, no one was. If it was me on the other hand, the story would be different. Wondering why my mother was looking for me, I went home.

I figured it wouldn't be good, especially after this morning. My mother was my father also. My ole man passed two months before I was born so the streets taught me how to be a man, and a soldier. I couldn't quite put together the mystery of why my mother was crying earlier and now she wanted me.

I made it home and saw my Aunt Francis' car was still in the driveway. I pulled my car in behind hers. I took a couple of bites of my steak sub before I made it to my room. Yelling my name, I headed toward the living room.

"Tra," she yelled.

"Yeah, Mama. It's me," I responded.

When I got into the living room, my aunt was sitting there teary-eyed. My mother looked grief stricken.

"What's wrong Mama?" I asked.

My Aunt Francis got up and hugged me. I was never the emotional type but I couldn't hold back the tears. My mother told me to sit down. My aunt told me her son got killed last night. He had only been in Flint from Chicago a couple of days. She said he had a greenish car with some rims on it. I was hurt as she told me the story. She said the police had not found the car or the killer yet.

"I wish he could have gotten to meet you Travis," she said.

"I wish he did too, Auntie," I said as I walked back to my room.

I was salty from what went down. That was my cousin and we never got to kick it. Plus, I witnessed the whole thing go down. I called J.B. and told him that I was on my way over there. I sat on the bed thinking while I finished my sub. I knew that this day would be ugly.

I grabbed my .45 and an extra clip. It was empty but I had plenty of bullets for it over at J.B.'s spot. In the concrete jungles of Flint you never know who's out to kill you. I did a few hits for niggas so I knew money was involved but it didn't make sense to me. *What was cuzz doing up here?*

I got to J.B.'s crib and this nigga got Pit Bulls everywhere like the fucking dog pound or something. It was so many dogs and he swears they are all killers.

J.B. was a cold hearted nigga. This one chick tried to set him up but the plot fell through. J.B. called the female over his house and like a fool, she came. After he had fucked her she was lying in his bed butt naked and he sent five of his dogs in the room on her. They fucked her up and we ain't seen her since.

"Who is it?" J.B. yelled.

"ATF nigga!" I yelled back. Then I heard a lot of commotion inside the house. I guess that nigga was trying to get rid of stuff.

"J.B. its Tra nigga. I was just playing!" I yelled. Then things got quiet and he peeked out of the blinds.

"Man, open up the door!" I yelled.

When J.B. opened the door I was laughing so hard. He was scared to death. He had the whole house smoky. J.B. was on some *Cheech and Chong* type stuff. This nigga has a house full of naked females, dogs, and smoke.

"You play too much nigga," he said.

"Shut up nigga," I said dropping the Mac on the couch. "Let me hit that weed nigga while you get dressed. We can talk about that later."

I waited almost an hour for him to get dressed. That nigga acted like we were going to the club or something. Finally he was ready to go and we left.

I broke the situation down to him about my cousin and them niggas I saw at the carwash. Me, J.B., and Tye was out there last night when that nigga killed my cousin so he knew exactly what I was talking about. J.B. knew what I was thinking already, especially after I stopped at the store. I got some Remy and a couple of blunts.

"Tra, you know I'm with you no matter what!" J.B. said.

Me and J.B. was well respected gang members back in the day but we grew up and started getting money. Killing niggas over colors was stupid so we started doing hits for the cheddar, besides, it was well worth it.

I pulled up in front of Tye's crib and J.B. ran in and got the waist strap for the Mac, and a couple of bags of weed. I guess Tye's baby mama, Shante was there because I didn't see his car in the driveway. We was all like family so J.B. got the weed and came back out. I threw him the blunts and he began to roll them up.

I circled the hood a few times, threw it up to some young G's and rolled to the north side. I was looking for that Monte Carlo. I knew I would see it sooner or later and I did. It was parked right there on Foss Street. I knew that whole neighborhood like the back of my hand. I pulled down the street about ten houses and parked. J.B. passed me the weed and I passed him the empty .45 clip. I told him to put it in the glove box. I planned on waiting for the driver of the Monte Carlo all night but patience is the virtue I didn't have. I knew that nigga would slip up sooner or later. There was no doubt in my mind that I would be there to catch them.

Chapter 2

Two days later I was chillin' over my baby mama house and J.B. called me about a hit on some out-of-town nigga that had a spot on the eastside. The Big Homey wanted us to get rid of the dead weight. I knew this was serious cause I haven't heard from the Big Homey in a minute. I told J.B. to come get me and hung the phone up. I was ready to leave anyway. I often crept with my baby mama and last night she called me with a lame excuse to come over. I told her to come pick me up because I was too tired, high and drunk to drive. I knew she just wanted to make love. I hadn't seen my daughter in two weeks and I needed to spend some time with her anyway. I didn't want my baby mama to get any ideas so I knew it was time to go. I heard loud music and knew it was J.B. pulling up so I kissed my daughter and walked out the door.

I still had on the same clothes from yesterday so I had J.B. take me home to change. When I made it home my mother wasn't there. J.B. came in and immediately turned on the video game. I put my clothes on the bed and got in the shower. I thought about making J.B. wait for me like he made me wait for him but business comes first so I hurried up.

I put on a baby blue Nike velour outfit with some gray, white and baby blue Air Force Ones. I put up the .45 for the mission and grabbed a box of 357 mag bullets. I didn't have the weapon in the house though. I tried not to keep too many guns in my mother's house because she liked to clean up my room a lot. Plus, I feared the police raiding and finding a murder weapon. I tried to be as smart as possible so I kept the weapon in the garage, in a toolbox along with a pair of leather gloves.

Riding down Dupont Street, I was loading up the weapon and J.B. had his music banging hard. He had a 1987 Caprice. It wasn't fancy but it was clean. I tried to buy the Caprice from him a few times. I knew the car had potential and I wanted to be the person to bring it out the right way.

Murder was something that I could never take lightly. In the beginning I had nightmares and my

15

hands would always sweat but soon my feelings became neutral. I always thought about leaving Vehicle City and move out somewhere far but my hood made me feel safe.

J.B. gave me the details about the outsider we were plotting on. It was only him and his girl that was supposed to be in the house. I knew this would be easy because she would be used as a bait. I told J.B. to turn the music down as we approached the eastside, we could not risk getting pulled over by the police. They would have a field day plus the weapons we had would give them a reason to shoot us. J.B. had two .38 specials for the mission and with my .357, we were like the revolver twins.

As we rode passed the house, the information looked correct. J.B. hit a U-turn at the corner and parked down the street. I got out the car and walked down to the house. I wished that I wore some more pants. The gun was slipping down and I had to keep my hand in my jacket pocket. I knew the out-of-towner was gone to meet the Big Homey so I wasn't worried about him. Taking advantage of the female would be real easy. I knocked on the door.

As I knocked on the door, I heard a dog barking inside the house and it made me scared. I knew it was too late to choke up. When the door opened I saw a beautiful, red bone female standing there in her nightgown. My heart dropped from her looks.

"How you doin?" I said.

She smiled and before she could respond, I had the .357 in her face walking in the house. From the living room I could see the barking dog was chained up by the back door. I wasn't worried about him though.

"Please don't kill me," the girl kept repeating.

She was pretty and I didn't want to kill her. I told her to be quiet. When J.B. came in he tied her up and sat her on the basement steps. The dog was now quietly laying on the floor. J.B. started laughing at the dog. I guess it wasn't his breed.

I started searching the house for drugs and hopefully a safe. I found a P95 Nine Millimeter Ruger under the bed and a pistol grip Mossberg gauge in the closet. I knew that there was some money in the house somewhere and I was determined to find it but J.B. beat me to it. J.B. found thirty-two thousand dollars under the couch in the living room. I never did think to look there but I was glad he found it. Now our only problem was waiting for the out-of-town nigga to come home. The Big Homey was meeting him to sell a couple of bricks of cocaine. Our mission would be complete once he arrived.

Me and J.B. stayed in the bedroom waiting. He finally pulled up. I was ready to get back to the west side of town so when he came in, me and J.B.

stood ready waiting. Soon as he walked in the door I hit him over the head with the .357. I snatched him up and made him tell me where the kilos were. He said they were still in the car under the backseat. I left J.B. to finish the job while I got the bricks out of the car. As I shut the car door I heard shots and J.B. came walking out of the house. We both ran to the car and smashed off. We didn't talk much on the way home. I had a lot on my mind. I couldn't stop thinking about the female and how she looked with her night gown on. J. B. interrupted my thoughts with laughter. That nigga was crazy.

"Man, what the fuck you laughing at?" I asked.

J.B. looked at me and said, "Nuttin' man," with a grin on his face.

I turned on the music and continued to think. My thoughts went to the Monte Carlo and my cousin's murder. I guess them niggas thought they got away with it but I had other plans for them.

I was ready to chill now. We had thirty-two thousand dollars, two and a half bricks of cocaine, a new 9mm, and a pistol grip 12 gauge. We went back to J.B.'s crib and broke bread, sixteen thousand dollars apiece. We sold the bricks back to the Big Homey for fifty thousand dollars. I kinda felt like he got over on us but then again, he put us up on the lick.

Me and J.B. smoked about three blunts and drunk a six pack of beer while counting the money and waiting for the Big Homey to arrive. The Big Homey had money, long money at that. He basically raised us. Back in the day, he got popped by the feds on some conspiracy shit and did seven years in the joint. He just came home last year. He knew how it was in the hood so he started paying us to kill niggas who owed him money or was steppin' on his toes.

The first mission was crazy. I had to stay under this nigga's car for hours until he came out of the house. J.B. usually came in on missions after me. I would tell him to do the messed up stuff. He knew I wouldn't kill any kids or females unless it was mandatory but it rarely was.

After the Big Homey left, J.B. dropped me off at home. When I went in the house, my mother was cooking. It smelled like chicken. I hadn't ate much all day. Me and J.B. had smashed a big bag of chips from the out-of-town nigga's house but that was it. I was hungry so after I put up my stuff, I went in the kitchen where my mother was sitting down watching television.

"Hey, Mama," I said.

She smiled and said, "Hey, boy."

I was happy that she felt better. I loved my mother to death. She was all that I really had. I reached for a plate and asked her what all did she cook but she didn't say nothing. I turned around and she was glued to the television. There was a picture of the out-of-town nigga's house on the news. I almost dropped the plate. The news reporter relayed the news that a multiple homicide took place and that the Ohio natives, a male and a female were shot to death in the house along with a dog. They located the female tied up, fatally shot in the basement and the male was naked in the bedroom shot to death. My heart sunk after hearing that. J.B. was wild as hell for that but I didn't have the guts to kill the girl. She saw our faces. She had to be killed. I put the plate back up. My mother just looked at me shaking her head. I grabbed a piece of chicken and went to my room.

Even though I was freshly dressed, I had to change clothes. I couldn't take the chance of blood or gun powder being on me. After changing I put the .357 back in the garage. I ran in the house and grabbed my trusted .45, jumped in my car and pulled off. I intended on just riding around for a while to clear my thoughts but I stopped in the hood to holler at my niggas. My hood was known for gang banging. We all lived and died for that stuff at one point, however, the young folk were still doing they thang. I couldn't blame them. They were only repeating what they saw, just like any other kid would do. I had mad love for the shorties. One time a older nigga was trying to bully one of the shorties and he asked me did I have a gun he could use. Although I didn't want to give it to him, I thought about it and decided to go ahead and help him out. Later I found out the shorty shot the nigga seven times putting him in critical condition. A few weeks later the shorty tried to give me the gun back but I told him to keep it. I told the young brother that if he got caught, remember, he didn't know me.

I went over my mans Tye's house to get some weed. I needed to smoke. When I went in the house his kids were so happy to see me. That brought a smile to my face.

"Hey Uncle Tra," they said in unison.

My nigga Tye had did a couple jobs with us some months back but he flipped his money with dope and weed. Me and J.B. were tired of hustling off the block. We wanted that fast money and figured out a way that was better. I got three sacks for twenty from Tye and left. I was going to ride around and get high. I knew just where to go. I figured J.B. was at home smoking his life away. As I think about what happened, that nigga J.B. was silly.

I got some blunts, sat at the store and rolled one up. I wanted to see had my cousin's car moved since a couple days ago so I rolled down Foss Street. I saw a nigga and two females walking in the house so I parked down the street and fired up a blunt. So many thoughts went through my mind. I had the radio down low and my ears were wide open as my mind roamed. All I could hear was the rattling of my trunk from the music. I coughed as the weed hit my chest. When I looked in the rearview mirror, my eyes were so dilated. I knew I had to make them niggas come get me or at least try. I jumped out of my car and started walking towards the house. I felt light-headed as hell. That weed was some fire. I hit the blunt a couple more times and threw it before I walked on the porch and knocked on the door. I pulled out the .45 and took it off safety.

Someone came to the door and yelled, "Who is it?"

I opened the screen and shot in the house ten times. I ran back to the car and drove off.

I wouldn't know the outcome of the shooting until the news came on or my cousin's killer retaliated. So I had to wait. I pulled up at J.B.'s crib and parked. I needed some more bullets so I grabbed the empty clip out of the glove box. Although I still had six or seven more shots in the clip, I could never settle for that being enough. I was too deep in the game. I knocked on the door and J.B. let me in. J.B. kept some females at his house. I thought he was trickin' half of the time but you never knew with J.B. He was something different.

"Where them bullets at?" I asked.

"Come holler at me," he said as he walked towards the back of the house.

"What's up Tra?" he asked. "I know you nigga. You ran into those niggas didn't you?"

"Not really," I said. "I had to make them niggas come out of hiding."

I believed that J.B. got the picture. I loaded both clips, threw one in my pocket and went back into the living room. I was tired so I sat down on the couch and started conversation with one of the females. She was beautiful. She had a caramel skin complexion with long hair. Her name was Tanisha. I called her Nisha. We had fucked around a few times before. She was best friends with J.B.'s main girlfriend Teresha.

"What's up for the night?" I asked her.

"What you mean what's up for the night Tra?" she responded.

"Let's go somewhere," I said as I stood up. She grabbed her coat and told her friend Teresha that she would be back.

"Get at me if something jump off," J.B. yelled as we walked out of the door.

I had probably about four hundred dollars in my pocket so I went to the store and got some more

Remy and a blunt. Nisha didn't smoke weed so the blunt was personal. I took her to my house. My mother was still at work. When we walked in I could still smell the chicken.

I put my gun, money, weed, and the things I purchased from the store on my dresser along with the .45 clip. As I sat down on the bed, I pointed to the kitchen told Nisha to get us some cups. I was high already but I had a lot on my mind. I turned on the television and waited for her to return with the cups. I was diggin' Nisha but my baby mama was so jealous. She was constantly trying to stop me from being with anybody. I had to slap her once for threatening this female I was messing with. I didn't want to put Nisha in the middle of that bullshit.

I put in a DVD and poured us some of the liquor. This was Nisha's first time at my house so she was relaxed. Then out of nowhere she turned to me and started talking.

"Tra, you be on some bullshit. I be keeping it so real with you and you ain't even tried to let me be with you. Tra, you know how I feel about you. Do you got a woman or something?"

I just sat there looking at her for a minute. Then I said, "You know, Nisha dig, a nigga would love to make you my woman but right now, I'm trying to do a lot and there's a lot going on in my life. But I'll tell you this, I'm feeling you like a muthafucka but I don't want to hurt you either. Just give me some time. Do you feel me?"

Nisha shook her head yes in response. I leaned over and kissed her and that kicked everything off. Nisha started unbuttoning my pants, then pulled off my t-shirt and began kissing my chest. I told her to take off her pants and she did. Nisha was thick just right. I pulled down my pants and she locked her mouth around my dick and automatically my head went back. We made love for hours and eventually we went to sleep.

Chapter 3

I woke up exhausted the next day. I was so tired I could hardly get out of the bed. Nisha was next to me still sleep. My cellphone was ringing like crazy. I picked it up and the number was J.B.'s.

"What's up Tra, can I speak to Nisha," Teresha said.

I had to shake Nisha a couple of times before she woke up. When she opened her eyes, I just smiled and passed her the phone.

I went in my mother's room to check on her. When I peeked inside, she was still sleep, too. It was still early in the morning and she had just got off work at 5:00am. I wasn't going to wake her up. I knew she needed the rest so I went back to my room.

Nisha was still in the bed when I walked in. She looked good, even in the morning. *Maybe she is ready for me to take her to the next level.* I got my clothes out for the day and we got into the shower together. Her body was beautiful. I washed her from head to toe. She enjoyed every minute of it. I was intended on making sure she would always be down for me. I posted her up under the water and she wrapped her legs around me as I slid my dick in her. I had to put my hand over her mouth because she would have woke my mother. Our sexcapade lasted about forty-five minutes. We washed up again and got out of the shower.

Once I got dressed, we left. I took Nisha to get some breakfast then I dropped her off at home. We made plans to go to the movies that night at 10:00pm that night. I promised her I wouldn't be late. I still hadn't heard anything about what happened to them niggas and I had planned on giving J.B. some space for a few days. I needed to take care of some business. My mind was on Nisha and what my next move would be. I had close to one hundred thousand dollars. I knew one day I would have to chill from thuggin' and Nisha made that thought more clear.

I picked up my phone and called one of my old connects. It was a Jamaican who used to sell me guns back in my gang-banging days. This Jamaican had come to Amerikkka and came up. He owned a couple of businesses and houses in Flint. I knew that he had the plug for me.

"Yeah," he said answering the phone.

"What's up man? This is Tra. How you doing?"

I told him my motive and he told me to come by his house. I told him to give me thirty minutes and I would be there. I headed to the north side. *Damn, this nigga live far as hell. He come up off them guns and moved out of the hood. That was a super smart move cause niggas would have tried to kill that nigga for a few pennies.* I felt the day wouldn't be right without some Remy so I went to the store and got a pint and two blunts. I knew the Jamaican had plenty of weed.

I got to the store and got out. The north side was grimy. It was niggas standing outside the store. I guess they were hustling but you can never tell with these young niggas. They smoking dope at seventeen years old. I walked pass 'em and went in the store. Usually the Arabs owned all the stores in the ghetto but this was a black owned store. I had come to the store a few times before when I was on the north side. It was this bad ass female who worked the counter but today she was off.

I paid for the stuff and headed toward the door. Something told me to put my gun in the bag. The pistol was a nice size. You could barely find one like it, especially a seventeen shot. I looked up and them niggas in the Monte Carlo was riding pass the store slow. I figured they noticed my car and at that moment, I knew it was going to be some shit. I took the gun out of the bag and walked out of the store with it in my hand. Soon as our eyes met, they pulled off. I guess they seen the gun in my hand. I walked to my car looking around the area. The streets were crowded with killas like niggas at a Tyson fight. When it's like that, any nigga can get it.

I got in my car and pulled off. I had my gun on my lap. I was upset I didn't bring my extra clip but I didn't know something would jump off. I rolled through some neighborhoods by the store hoping to see what house those niggas went to. Niggas was outside everywhere. Families were barbequing and it was a street full of niggas playing basketball on the corner. I had my music beating a little bit listening to my theme music *Killas on Yo Team* by MOB. I came through the crowd and niggas stop balling to let me through. When I got to the corner, a nigga came out a backyard bustin' at me! All I seen was him running with the gun. My music drowned the shots then a bullet went through my back window shattering it. I smashed off. I was in shock for minute that I just kinda looked at the niggas. I got down the street and felt a burning sensation in my stomach. I knew I was shot. I looked down and blood was spreading on my t-shirt. I knew if I panicked I would die so I turned down the music and headed toward the hospital.

I was doing about 50mph in a 35 zone. I called J.B. and told him to meet me at the hospital because I had been shot. When I hung up the phone with him, I called my mother. I didn't want to tell her but I knew I had to, so I dialed the number. After the third ring she picked up.

"Hello," she said sounding irritated.

"Hey Mama. I'm on my way to the hospital. I got shot but I'm alright. I'm in my car right now and I'm almost there."

My mother didn't take it lightly which I already knew she wouldn't. Who would? I was her only child.

She said, "Tra, I'm leaving right now baby. I'm on my way."

I was weak as hell. I lost so much blood it was ridiculous. I made it to the hospital finally. I threw my gun under the seat and got out. I looked at my car and the driver's side had about eight holes in it. I was mad as hell. I ran in the hospital holding my stomach. My t-shirt felt like wet tissue. When I made it to the desk, I was immediately checked in.

I woke up naked with a needle in my arm and a hospital gown on. All I could do was smile. Not only because I was alive, but because my mother, J.B. and Nisha was standing over me smiling too. My mother kissed me on my forehead and told me she loved me. I could tell that Nisha had been crying because the tears left a stream down her face. When our eyes met, she was acting shy.

"Come closer," I said to Nisha.

When she came, I kissed her on the lips like a true solider. My mother and J.B. was just looking at us kiss. J.B. didn't say much, he just kept looking at me shaking his head. I knew what he was thinking but I was in too much pain to go there. Plus, I wasn't trying to spoil the moment with my mother and Nisha.

My mother and J.B. stayed for a while. We talked and they went home. I wanted to go with them but I couldn't. Nisha stayed with me that night. I wanted to take her down through there but I knew I would be in too much pain afterwards. We talked for a while. I told her that I did not know who shot me and actually, I didn't. All I knew was how he looked. We watched television and eventually Nisha fell asleep holding my hand.

I couldn't sleep though. I had too much on my mind. The nurse came in my room and gave me a blanket for Nisha. I covered her up the best that I could and continued to watch television. I heard my cellphone ringing but it was in my pants pocket. I knew I couldn't make it over to get it. Nisha looked like she was sleeping good but I had to wake her up. Nisha was a deep sleeper and it was hell waking her up. When I finally did, my phone stopped ringing but she got it for me. I kissed her and told her to go back to sleep. I looked on my phone and it was J.B. I called him back. As soon as he picked up the phone I could hear his dogs in the background barking.

"What's up nigga? I woke you up?" he asked.

J.B. seemed to be wide awake. I told him that I couldn't sleep and he busted out laughing. He said that after leaving the hospital, he rode down the block where we first saw the Monte Carlo parked and the house was lit up with the car in the driveway. He said he parked down the street and walked back down to the house with the Mac and threw a cocktail bomb through the picture window then ran around the house busting the Mac. I started laughing. That nigga was wild but that's my nigga. He told me to get some rest and he would be up to the hospital to see me the next day.

I sat back and recalled how I almost became another dead nigga. I slipped hard trying to catch them niggas. I thought about my car and the damage done to it. I was thankful that I made it out alive. I turned off the television and feel asleep.

The nurse woke me up a few hours later with breakfast and a shot of morphine. The food didn't look right so I didn't eat it. I was still sleepy but my stomach was empty. I wasn't gon' be happy until I got some real food. I woke Nisha up and told her I was hungry. Thank God she had her mother's car or I would have been out of luck because I couldn't let her drive mine. Laying there, I had forgot that I never rolled up my car windows so I asked her to do it for me and to grab my gun from under the seat on her way to get us some food.

I turned on the television and started watching an old episode of *Sanford and Son* when the nurse came in. She was cool. She looked down at the hospital food she brought me and asked me why I didn't eat my breakfast. I told her that I couldn't stomach it. She started laughing. She was a young, white woman. She looked around twenty-seven years old. We talked and I asked her how long would I be in the hospital. She told me I took a bad shot and I lost a lot of blood. She said I was smart not to panic because I would've lost my life. Then she took my temperature and left.

Nisha showed up just in time to take my mind off of death. She brought me a hotcakes, eggs and turkey bacon meal. She also handed me the .45 which had blood stains all over it. I wrapped it up in a towel, placed it under my pillow and began to eat breakfast. I felt Nisha looking at me but I didn't want to look back cause I didn't know what to say. I was hurt physically and mentally. I finished my food and laid back. Nisha said she was gonna go home, check on her mother and she would be back.

I laid there for a minute and allowed my wondering thoughts to put me to sleep.

Chapter 4

I stayed in the hospital about a week and a half. Every day Nisha was there by my side and I loved every minute of it. I was happy to be home. Me and Nisha's relationship grew stronger as the time passed. I was healing slowly and able to help myself again but my mother and Nisha babied me to the fullest. After a month in the house, I finally went somewhere. It felt good to see the smiles on the faces of my family and friends.

I didn't feel safe driving my car. It was shot up so I put it in the shop to get the bullet holes repaired and get a paint job. I had to change up the game so I painted it canary yellow. I couldn't wait to get it out.

I called and explained the situation to the Jamaican. We made plans to meet up in two days. I was ready to get my own house. I was afraid of someone seeing my car outside my mother's house and putting her in danger. Shit was getting deep and I knew it was going to get deeper.

I called J.B. and he came to pick me up. I got fresh for the occasion. I hadn't seen him in a few days but he called every day. He said that he got hot after he shot up that house. Apparently someone noticed his car leave the scene. After the shooting the police rolled passed his house looking at the Caprice. He said a female got shot in the chest that night so he wasn't moving too much. He had been riding around in his girl's car and that's what he was in when he picked me up. I refused to get caught slipping again so I went everywhere with my gun close in hand. The thought of dying helpless haunted me. I knew life had its' ups and downs but I was in it for the long run.

Me and J.B. went to the hood for a while and chilled. Niggas was shocked when I got out of the car. Rumors had spread that I wasn't gonna make it. I laughed but deep inside it hurt. I wondered what God had in store for my life and why I was still living. I knew only time would tell.

It was still early and I was ready to get into something so me and J.B. left. I called Nisha and told her to come over to J.B.'s house in an hour so we could go somewhere. I still had some healing to do. The bullet really messed me up and made me reflect on all the people who were shot by me.

I knew I couldn't hang out like I wanted to. I had J.B. stop at the store and I went in to get some blunts. It was time to get high. I was in pain and J.B. knew it. I got back in the car and we pulled off. I could tell my nigga anythang. We had been through so much together. He was always there for me.

After we were riding, J.B. broke the silence. That nigga was ridiculous. I was rolling up the blunt when he began to talk.

"Nigga, I thought you wasn't gon' make it either dog. I wouldn't know what to do if you died on me," he said.

I rarely heard J.B. get deep like that so I played it off and told him to shut the fuck up. Usually J.B. was on some funny shit or on some straight killer shit. To hear him talk serious about my situation made me think. I fired up the blunt and turned up the radio. I was happy to be alive but most of all, I had a chance to get revenge soon.

We pulled up at J.B. house and his girl, Teresha and Nisha was sitting on the porch. My baby was looking so fine, too.

"How you doing Tra?" J.B. girl said. Teresha was cold as far as looks go but not like Nisha.

"I'm straight Teresha. How you doing?" I responded.

Nisha got up and gave me a hug and kiss. I wanted to go out and chill but J.B. wasn't that type so I sparked up the invitation.

"Let's go to the club or somewhere tonight y'all. What's up?" I said. I knew Nisha was down but I had to get J.B. out of the house.

Teresha spoke up. "Yeah, baby. Let's go somewhere tonight," she yelled at J.B.

"Fuck it. My mans wanna go to the club we in that bitch!" J.B. responded. He was turned up.

"Yeah nigga. We out tonight fuck what ya' heard!" I told J.B.

J.B. was down so we made plans to go to the Beavers, a local night club. I had to get fresh for the occasion so me and Nisha went to the mall. I only had about two hundred and fifty dollars so she took me home first so I could get more money.

When we pulled up I ran in the house. My mother was in the crib chillin' watching soap operas. I kissed her and went to my room. I took eight thousand dollars, ran back outside and jumped in the car.

"I'm ready," I told Nisha and she pulled off.

I put my gun on my lap. Nisha looked at me and shook her head smiling. I pulled out my cellphone and called the repair shop to see was my car ready. The repairman said he was putting the finishing touches on it and I could pick it up in an hour. I was smiling thinking about my car as I hung up the phone. I looked at Nisha and nodded my head. I was feeling it. It was Saturday and the mall was packed. I usually went to Detroit to buy my clothes but I didn't feel up to taking the trip, plus I didn't have my car.

Nisha was looking good. I walked behind her through the mall looking at her booty. I believe she knew it because she kept smiling. I got a couple outfits and two pairs of Air Forces and one pair of boots for the night. I bought Nisha two pair of Capri pants and some boots. We walked through the mall and I stopped at a jewelry store. I tried on a five karat bracelet. It was tight but I didn't buy it. I saw Nisha over by the female rings, trying on a ring and talking to the female employee. I walked over to see what the ring looked like. It was beautiful. It had a platinum band with a heart formed in diamonds. It was four karats. Nisha turned around and saw me standing there and asked me was I ready to go. She gave the ring back and we left. We were on our way out the door. I knew Nisha was feeling that ring so I told her I left one of my bags and I would be out to the car in a minute. I had to make up an excuse. I ran back to the jewelry store to buy the ring. They wanted thirty-five hundred for the ring but I talked the owner down to twenty-seven hundred.

I knew that I had to play it off so I stopped at another store and bought an Iceberg sweater. I made my way out to the car. When I got to the car, Nisha was laid back in the seat listening to this song called, *Nothing in the World*. That was our song. I love to see her smile so I started messing with her. She started the car and we left. *What would be the coldest way to give her the ring?* I knew whatever I did, it would have to be memorable.

We had spent at least two hours in the mall so I knew that my car had to be ready by then. I asked Nisha to take me to pick it up.

"So you about to act up tonight huh Tra?" she said.

"And why would you say that?" I asked.

"Because I can see it in your eyes from when you first brought the issue up about going out." I

38

just smiled and laid back. I knew she was about to be shocked.

We got to the car shop and went into the garage where my car was. I could see it from outside but only the top. I never told Nisha I was getting it painted so she couldn't tell what I was looking at outside. The repairman said I made it just in time cause he was headed out the door for lunch. He put chrome panels on the bottom of the doors for free. Shit, I paid him six thousand for the paint and the bullet holes. Nisha was looking at my car like, *damn*. I asked her did she like it.

She looked at me and said, "Boy, you know you wrong. I know why you were smiling earlier now. You are a trip."

I jumped in my car and started it up. I missed my baby. The garage door let up and I told Nisha to follow me home.

It felt good to be back in my car. My mind flashed back to the shooting and I put my gun on my lap. I turned up the music and started fooling. All I saw was niggas in their cars stopping and looking. I was the only nigga with a canary Grand National with chrome siding and twenty-inch chrome blades.

I was swerving side to side fooling beating that Skanbino Mob. I slowed down and Nisha pulled up on the side of me. I told her to go over to my house and I would be there in a minute. I made a left on Lawndale and grabbed my cellphone. I was coming towards J. B.'s house so I dialed his number and turned down the radio.

"What's up?" he said answering the phone.

"Nigga this Tra. Come outside. I'm riding down your street right now." By then I was in front of his house with the music beating. He came out the house foolin'.

"J.B., these niggas ain't stopped nothing baby. It's going down tonight," I yelled.

I pulled off knowing I was hurting the game. I pulled up next to a Cadillac truck on twenty-twos. I guess the nigga had the A.C. blowing because he rolled down the window smoking a blunt. He nodded his head and told me that I was killing the game.

I pulled up at my house banging the music. My mother and Nisha was sitting on the porch smiling. I jumped out the car like; *they really hate me now.* I noticed my next door neighbor's daughter standing in the doorway looking. She was about eighteen years old. I would often catch her looking at me. I figured she had a crush on me but she was too young for me and I was too much for her.

Nisha told me that my bags were still in the car. I reached in my pocket and got the box with the ring in it and placed it in her glove box. I grabbed my clothes, hit the car alarm on my National and went in the house. I went to my room and Nisha was right behind me. I put my clothes down and shut my room door. I sat on the bed.

"Come here," I said to Nisha. She sat on my lap. "I got a surprise for you. I believe you gon' like it too. I mean you been by my side through all of this and I love you for that. I don't want this to end and the surprise that I have for you is the beginning of something that I want to last forever. I know that you are thinking what can it be and I'ma show you in less than thirty minutes. Just be patient with me."

Nisha put her hand over my mouth and said, "Tra, I love you and I don't want this to end either, I swear."

I wanted to make love to her right there but my ole miss was in the other room. I kissed Nisha and told her to call me as soon as she walked in the door. I gave her another kissed and she left. I heard my mother yelling my name so I went into the living room. It was the telephone. I grabbed the phone and went back into my room.

"Hello." It was J.B. He was foolin'. "Nigga you got the National skanless. I know you gon' do it real big tonight. So when y'all come through, I'ma already have the Mac and that Ruger in the car. We going in my girl car just in case something jump off. We gon' follow y'all to the club. Oh yeah, Teresha wanna know is Nisha over there?"

I told him she just left and we will be over there at ten o'clock and hung up the phone. It was late already so I did not have long to get ready. I needed my hair braided so I asked my mother to do it. My mother was really the only person that I would let braid my hair unless I found a female that was cool. I wondered if Nisha knew how to braid.

I sat in front of the television and my mother started braiding my hair. The phone rang. My mother answered and passed it to me. She rarely got phone calls so I guess she figured it was for me anyway. It was Nisha and she had made it home. She called like I told her to. I made up a little lie and told her I had left something in her glovebox and asked her to get it for me. She told me to hold on for a minute while she went out to the car. I turned the T.V. to my favorite channel, BET as I waited for her to come back to the phone.

"Tra, what are you up to?" my mother asked.

"Nothing Mama, I'm chillin'."

Then I heard Nisha screaming. I knew she got the ring. I let my mother hear the screaming. She just shook her head and smiled. I knew Nisha would be foolin'. She just kept saying, "Tra, I love you."

Nisha was the only female, besides my baby mama, that I ever bought something for. I have smoked weed and drank with females but going out to a store to buy something...that was different. I told Nisha I was getting my hair braided and once I got ready I would be over there to pick her up.

Chapter 5

It was 9:50pm and I had dapped on some cologne. I was running late but I was fresh. I had on a gray, black and white Iceberg sweater, some black Iceberg pants and my gray Rockport boots. I wasn't obsessed with jewelry but I wore my Rolex link and a Rolex watch with diamonds in the face that I robbed a nigga for back in the day. I grabbed twelve hundred dollars to spend for the night then snatched up the .45, the extra clip and walked out of the house. The night was just right. I hit the car alarm and jumped in. Breaking down a blunt, I hit the remote control starter and emptied the bag of weed inside the cigar and turned up the music. I flipped the blunt and pulled off.

Saturday nights was always live. It was late and people were everywhere. On my way to pick up Nisha, I saw my baby mama in the car with some lame. If she would have saw me, she would have been sick. I played it off and kept going. The police had niggas stretched out on almost every block. I turned down my music and changed my CD. I was in a relaxed mood so I put in this Ginuwine CD that this one female bought me a while back. I pulled up in front of Nisha's house beating. I didn't even turn off the car. I got to the porch and she came to the door looking like a contestant in the Miss America pageant. She had on some blue jean stacks, blue jean Capris and a baby blue Phat Farm stretch tank top. Her hair was in a ponytail dangling to her back, nothing less than a ten piece. When she opened the door I just stood there day dreaming for a minute. She had to snap me out of it.

"Tra, you wild boy. Here I come," she said.

I walked back to the car embarrassed as hell. When she got in the car I said, "Oh, you gon' get you a man tonight, huh?"

She gave me a kiss and said, "You the one trying to take somebody home tonight!"

By me being the goodfella that I am, I said, "Yeah, if I can."

Nisha just smiled. I turned up the music and fired up my blunt. I handed her my cellphone and told her to call J.B. and tell him that we were on our way. I stopped at the drive-thru and got a box of blunts and a pack of Newports. Nisha said Teresha was on the phone cussin' J.B. out and I started laughing. I had a lot of thoughts going through my mind. I didn't talk about the shooting much to Nisha. I wanted her to forget that it ever happened. I looked at her and she was playing with the spare .45 clip. The sight made me hurt inside. My life was like a book full of drama and pain and here I had a beautiful woman playing with a .45 magazine.

We got to J.B.'s house and got out. My blunt kept going out. It was the first one of the day it seemed like because I was feeling it. I didn't even knock on the door, we just walked in.

"Look at y'all looking all cute," Teresha said.

Teresha was looking good too. She had on some tight black pants, some black stacks with a black, white, and blue Avirex shirt on with her diamond rings on her finger. J.B. was in love with that girl. He came out of the back room wearing a Roc-A-Wear sweater, some black Roc-A-Wear jeans and some black and blue Air Force Ones. This nigga had a Gucci necklace and everything.

"Nigga, you a fool. Y'all ready?" I asked.

J.B. said, "We ready nigga. Let's go buy the bar!"

That nigga was sick. Nisha was flossing her ring to Teresha doing they female thang. I told them to come on because we out. J.B. let two of his dogs run around the house. I guess they were supposed to protect the house while he was gone.

Nisha got in the car. I hit the starter button and waited for J.B. to lock up the house. This nigga was slow about everything except dropping a nigga or squeezing the trigger.

"Come on nigga what you going on a cruise or something?!" I yelled.

J.B. came out the house with the Mac and handed it to me. He lifted up his shirt and showed me the nine millimeter in his waist line.

I grabbed the Mac and yelled, "Man, you be on some bullshit!"

When I got in the car I put the Mac in the backseat and covered it up. Nisha was looking at the Mac probably thinking this nigga bringing all these guns. I pushed the mute button on the music and asked that slow as nigga J.B. did he have some weed.

Hanging out of the window smoking a blunt he said, "Fo' show."

Man, I was mad as hell. I sparked up my blunt again and pulled off.

"What's wrong? Why are you so mad?" Nisha asked.

I told her the real. "That nigga was supposed to been had that gun in Teresha car. I can handle my .45 but I can't shoot that gun right now. You know I got these staples in my stomach. It ain't nothing really just that we talked about it already. But fuck that shit. We gon' go in here and have a good time."

I hit the weed a couple of more times and threw it out of the window. I knew that I needed to clear my thoughts before I made it to the club cause I would be destined to get into something if I didn't. I slid my hand down Nisha's pants. She jumped as I fondled her clitoris. I started talking stuff then.

"I'm killing this tonight baby for real. I hope you ready cause its going down!"

Nisha was moving around in the seat like crazy. She said, "Tra, you gon' make me cum on myself."

I said, "So what? Do you love me?"

"Tra, you know I love you. You gon' make me cum. Please stop," she begged. I pulled my hand out and licked my finger.

"Boy, you nasty," she said laughing.

I started laughing, too. I was fooling. We pulled up at the club and traffic was bumper to bumper. I found the perfect parking spot. I parked on the side of the club behind a Ford Explorer truck. I put my gun under the seat and we got out. I saw J.B. park like three cars behind mine. Me and Nisha went ahead in the club. I wasn't the ID carrying type so I had to pay extra. I gave them a fifty dollar bill for me and Nisha and walked in.

As soon as I stepped through the door they was play the shit, that Lil Jon and the Eastside Boyz. "Bia" niggas and females was staring hard at me and Nisha. We took our table and waited for J.B. and Teresha to show them our table.

J.B. and Teresha was coming through the door. I asked Nisha what did she want to drink and told her that I would be back in a second. The music had niggas geeked up. I walked through the club shinning. I felt niggas with their scanners on. I showed Teresha the table and me and J.B. went to the bar. I bought three bottles of Moet and two double shots of Remy. Nisha wanted an Absolut with cranberry juice. J.B. got three bottles of Moet and two Hennessey sours. We had the waitress bring us the Moet and we carried the drinks. I gave Nisha her drink and sat down at the table. I had a couple of bags of weed so I started breaking down the blunts. The club was getting more packed by the minute. The waitress brought our drinks to the table and popped the bottles. I twisted the blunt and passed it to J.B. I felt someone looking at me and when I looked up, it was my neighbor's daughter. I was shocked. I figured she didn't go to the clubs. She waved and I said, "What's up." *She gon' get her ass whipped if she come home drunk.*

It was ballers night so I got up and went over to the picture man. He had a nice lil' background for the pictures. It said, "Street Dreams." I wasn't the picture type but I said why not enjoy myself. I went back to the table and sat down. J.B. passed me the weed. That nigga was a smoker for real. He had nearly smoked the whole blunt while I was gone. I downed my Remy and hit the blunt. I couldn't let Nisha get drunk. I knew I would be faded before the night was over. Nisha still had damn near a full cup of Absolut. The time was flying. It was 12:00am already. I looked at my watch. Some young G's from the hood was in the club. They came to the table and hollered at us. J.B. took a pistol from one of the lil' niggas. He was ridiculous. It was so packed niggas was standing in front of our table so we got up.

I grabbed two of the bottles of Moet and J.B. grabbed two and we went over to the picture man. He wanted twenty dollars for big pictures and five for the little ones. I bought five big pictures and we flicked up. To my surprise, I saw the nigga that shot me in the crowd looking right at me. I was sick. I started stunting, pulling out knots of money.

"J.B. look at this nigga dog. These bustas better get money, nigga what?" I yelled.

The nigga was with two of his manz. I got my pictures and moved through the crowd. I walked in them niggas faces and pulled up my shirt.

"Let's see how many bodies drop tonight nigga!" I yelled through the club music.

As I walked off, Nisha was trying to calm me down and J.B. told me to chill out. He had never saw them nigga up close before. It was 1:15am and the club was letting out at two o'clock."

"Let's go home. Tra, you ready baby?" Nisha asked.

I saw the niggas trying to leave so I said, "Yeah baby, let's go."

I looked around to see where was J.B. and Teresha but I didn't see 'em. The little homie that J.B. took the gun from told me that J.B. was outside arguing with some niggas. I ran outside and all I saw was J.B. standing at the driver side door of the green Monte Carlo shooting then taking off running.

Damn, there is no movement in that car. Nisha had my pictures and the bottle of Moet. I had dropped the other bottle in the club when I ran out to see about J.B. The scene was crazy. Females were screaming and cars were smashing off. When we got to my car, I saw Teresha still parked, sitting in the car. I guess she was trying to wait for J.B. I told her to leave and that J.B. was probably at home already or close to it. Teresha pulled off and we followed behind her.

Police were everywhere now. Them niggas was dead in that Monte Carlo. Police was trying to pull everybody over to check their car so I had to leave Teresha. I D-b'd my way into traffic and hit the back streets. I didn't want to talk about what happened so I turned up the music and fired up a cigarette. I looked down and the light on my cellphone was on. I had the music up so loud I didn't hear it ringing. I turned down the music and answered the phone.

"What's up," I said.

"Tra, where you at nigga? Come pick me up from the store. I'm on Wade Street."

It was J.B. and I was glad to hear his voice. I told him that I was on my way and hung up the phone. My thoughts went to Teresha and how she must be feeling. I told Nisha to call her and let her know we were on our way over there with J.B.

I got to the Wade Street store and J.B. was walking down the street. I opened the door and he jumped in. Nisha was still talking to Teresha on the phone and handed it to J.B.

I put my hand on Nisha's thigh and asked her was she mad at me. I figured she was mad at me from what happened.

"What I'ma be mad about Tra? I'm just ready to go home so you can hold me," she said.

That was music to my ears. I was tired and hungry. I grabbed my bottle of Moet and turned it up. J.B. was in the backseat rolling up a blunt and talking to Teresha.

"Cuzz, y'all gon' have to buy me a battery or something for real," I told J.B.

He told Teresha to run him some bathwater with bleach and hung up the phone. I started laughing at the thought cause hot water and bleach eats up the gunpowder residue off your body. That was an old school trick that's been in the game for years. We got to J.B.'s house and I told him to give me the 9mm and take the Mac back in the house. He left the 9mm in the backseat and grabbed the Mac.

I told Nisha to drive and we switched places. I was exhausted. I laid the seat back and chilled. My thoughts wondered back to the club. Everything happened so fast. I saw my fair share of murders but I wondered what was going through Nisha's mind. She knew how our names traveled in Flint about things we did. Rumors in Flint were like cars, they went everywhere so they were hard to get around. I tried to drown my thoughts with the Moet but couldn't. Nisha pulled up in the driveway and cut the car off. I grabbed the 9mm out the backseat and my .45 and we went in the house. I was so tired, I threw everythang on the dresser and laid on the bed. I kicked off my shoes.

"Baby, you hungry?" Nisha asked.

"Yeah, you gon' cook us some breakfast or something?" I asked.

"Yeah, what you want?" she asked.

I told her whatever she felt like cooking and she went in the kitchen. I took off my shirt and turned on the television. It was 3:00am. Flickering through the channels I caught an episode of *ComicView* on BET and walked in the kitchen.

Nisha had it smelling good. She was cooking toast, turkey bacon, and eggs. I got behind her at the stove and just held her in my arms.

She said, "Tra, I want you to myself. I don't mean it like that. I mean, but, I just can't see

53

myself living without you and I don't want to lose you."

All I could do was listen because I felt the same way. I knew the lifestyle I lived would have to come to an end one day but I couldn't figure out when that day would be.

"Nisha, I'm not going nowhere and I don't want to lose you either. We just gon' take this one day at a time, you feel me? But I promise you, I'm not going nowhere," I told her.

I sat at the dinner table and Nisha gave me my food.

"I didn't know you was cold on the cooking tip. You shouldn't have let me tasted yo' cooking. You done messed up," I said to a blushing Nisha.

We finished eating and went back to my room. When I sat on the bed Nisha pushed me back and took off my pants.

"Now you know you can't handle this muthfucka. Why you playin'?" I said.

She took off her Capris and pulled down her panties. I was smiling like crazy. She had on a baby blue thong. I immediately turned off the television while she took off her Baby Phat shirt and bra. I just let her do whatever she thought she was ready for and I laid back on the bed. Nisha pulled off my boxers and got on top of me. She grabbed my dick and put it inside of her and began passionately riding me up and down. The juices flowed on my dick like the Nile River. I laid her down and put her legs on my shoulders. Nisha begged me not to stop as I gave her every inch of me. It was so good it made me beat that pussy more. She was moaning like crazy. I didn't want nobody to get suspicious so I put the pillow over her face, letting her legs down I grinded her slowly, in and out. My bed sheets were soaking wet and she was moaning so sexy.

"I told you didn't I?" I said enjoying every minute of our lovemaking. Her body shook as I went in and out gripping her booty, pounding that pussy like a true trooper. We made love til 4:30am and fell asleep.

Chapter 6

The next day I woke up to the rings of my cellphone. Nisha was sound asleep. *I knocked that ass out.* I grabbed the phone.

"Hello."

"Tra, this is Teresha.

Teresha was crying and I knew something was wrong. She said the police kicked in the door and arrested J.B. for what happened last night. She was crying her heart out. She said that they took the Mac, the pistol grip gauge and ten thousand dollars out of the shoe box. I told her to calm down, I was on my way.

I was hurt. I woke Nisha up and we got dressed. I had to be smart about the situation. I put the guns I had in the garage and we jumped in the car.

It was only ten o'clock in the morning. I could not believe what was happening. J.B. was my nigga, my brother. I was driving faster than I was when I got shot. The loud pipes hollered as I circled around cars. I pulled up and noticed the screen door laying on the grass. We ran in the house and found Teresha trying to clean up the mess and we assisted her in the tragedy.

When we went to the police precinct they said J.B. was charged with three murders and his bond stood at $50,000. I knew I had to get my nigga out. Teresha said she could get $20,000 out they bank account. I put up the difference. We drove back to the house and I gave Teresha the money and dropped her back off at home. She said she was about to go get him. I was happy to see her smiling again. I told her I would holler at J.B. later.

I couldn't imagine what my nigga was going through. I spent three days in the county jail for a dope case but they dropped the charges. It was hell sitting in the bullpen. Niggas came in and out all night long.

I looked at Nisha. She looked so innocent. I knew she was tired because we only got maybe five hours of sleep. I had an appointment to look at a house at two o'clock so I had to get a few more hours of sleep in. We went home and got back in the bed.

I got at least fifteen minutes of sleep before my mother came busting in the room.

"Tra, what's going on? Who James done killed? His picture is all over the news. Was y'all together last night?" she asked.

As calmly as I could I said, "Mama, J.B. got into an argument last night in the club and somebody shot the boy he was arguing with when the club was over."

My mother looked at me, spoke to Nisha laying in my bed then went back into the living room. I was trying to hide my anger but Nisha started laughing.

"Why you laughing? I can't get no sleep for nothing."

"Ah you poor baby," Nisha said trying to be funny.

I looked at her and turned on the T.V. It was eleven o'clock. *What the hell. I might as well get on up.* I sat on the bed and Nisha put her arms around me.

"It's yo' turn to cook breakfast," she said.

"We can go get something to eat. I don't do the cooking thang," I said laughing.

"Why not?"

I told her the real. "All I know how to cook is eggs and Ramen Noodles."

She laughed at me. Nisha had the prettiest smile I had ever seen. She was so beautiful. I noticed that she had the ring on her finger indicating that she was married so I spoke on it.

"I see you got yo' ring on the right finger."

Kissing me on my neck she said, "I gotta put it where it belongs."

Nisha was wild. I got up and looked through my closet for something to wear. I took out some black jeans and a plain white t-shirt and sat it on my bed.

"Come get in the shower with me," I told Nisha.

I washed her body from head to toe and she did the same thing to me. I knew Nisha was getting the royal treatment but I was a special kind of nigga. I knew that she deserved the best.

After we got dressed, Nisha went into the living room with my mama and I went into the garage and got the .45. As I was letting the garage door down someone called my name. I turned around and it was the little girl from next door. She was standing there in her night gown with some big ass teddy bear house shoes on.

"What's up," I said.

"I didn't know you be going to the club," she said.

"I don't mess wit' it like that. I go every once in a while. I was surprised to see you there. Do you go all the time?" I asked.

"I go every Saturday," she said. "I saw you and yo' boy get into it with them dudes. The one with the Avirex jacket on tried to holler at me."

Laughing I said, "Oh for real."

As I started walking toward the door she said, "Tra, was that yo' girlfriend you was with last night in the club?"

"Yeah, that's her."

"Oh," she said and walked in her house.

I went into the house thinking about the young lady. I was positive she had a crush on me then. She was cool and I hoped that I didn't hurt her feelings.

I walked in the kitchen where Nisha and my mother was eating breakfast.

"Nisha, you straight now." I told her.

My mother just had to say something. "Boy, I cooked enough for you too.

I took a couple pieces of bacon and went into the room. Looking at my watch it was almost 12:30pm. I went back into the kitchen and asked Nisha was she going to wait until I got back. She said she would. I kissed her and my mother started laughing. I looked at her and walked out the door.

It was a hot day. The little girl from next door was sitting on the porch when I came outside. I looked at her and got in the car. I forgot I left that Moet in the car last night. It was still basically full. I picked it up and took a sip. It was flat and hot so

I opened the door and poured it out. The little girl was just staring at me. I took out the Ginuwine CD and put in this rapper from Sacramento, California and pulled off.

I was thinking about J.B. so I called him. The phone rang twice before Teresha picked up.

"Teresha, this is Tra. Is J.B. there yet?"

"Yeah, Tra. Here he go," she said.

"What's up nigga?" J.B. said answering the phone.

He sounded sad so I told him to come outside. I hung up the phone because I was almost at his house. I pulled up and he got in the car.

"I got something to tell you Tra. Pull off, let's ride," J.B. said.

Wondering what it was, I pulled off and he continued.

"Man, big homie was in the county with me. He got caught with a pistol and we was kicking it, know what I'm saying. I told him what I was in there for and the nigga looked sick when I said it. He said them was his lil' dogs and he would holler at them to do lil' jobs and stuff for him. Cuzz, to make a long story short, he paid that lil' nigga to kill yo' cousin from Chicago. He said yo' lil' cousin was up here selling heroin and Big Homey said he was taking food out of his mouth."

"What J.B.? This nigga had that nigga kill my cousin?!" I yelled. J.B. nodded his head.

I told J.B. the real. "Man, fuck Big Homey nigga. I gotta have that now! I was thinking about getting him anyway."

"Baby I took a loss. I gotta get a lawyer and everything. Let's go get his bitch ass. That nigga got bonded out yesterday." J.B. said.

We made plans and I dropped J.B. back at his house. I had twenty minutes to get to my appointment. The house was in a nice neighborhood so I had a little ways to go. I took out the Cali music and put in my homeboys, the MOB. I needed some murder music. Song fourteen was exactly how I felt. I fired up a half of swisher from last night and sang along with the music. *When thugs collide somebody they gotta die. Mama's gone cry when the bullets start to fly, when thugs collide.*

I was hurt because I knew that plenty of niggas died because of Big Homey and fifty percent of the time we did the killing for his fat ass. That nigga was too heartless and greedy for his own good. The worst type of nigga was Big Homey. He was a by-product of urban genocide.

I got to my appointment to see the house and it was beautiful. The Jamaican was walking in the house with a white couple. I tucked the foe nickel under the car seat. I couldn't take it in the house cause I had on a white t-shirt and they would be able to see it. I got out of the car and walked up to the house, the Jamaican met me at the door.

"What's happening Tra mon, you feeling alright, yes?"

"I'm straight. How you doing?" I responded.

He nodded his head and I walked in the living room. The kitchen was huge. It had granite tops and wood cabinets. I asked how many bedrooms and the Jamaican said three upstairs and two in the basement. He then pointed upstairs.

I went up the carpet steps and in to the bedrooms. The master bedroom was big. I began visualizing the work I could do with it. I pictured mirrors on the ceiling and me and Nisha making love in a king sized bed. I fell deep into my day dreaming until the Jamaican interrupted me.

"Tra mon, you like it?" he asked with that funny Jamaican accent.

"Yeah, what's the ticket on it?" I asked.

"Seventy-five thousand and it's yours."

"Damn, J man, you trying to break a nigga. But I want it man. I'll have the money for you tomorrow," I told him.

We shook hands and I left. The white couple and the Jamaican was walking out of the house before I pulled off. The couple looked disappointed. I turned up my music and skirted off. I was making plans for the house already. I had fifty-three thousand at the crib. Now I had to come up with the rest. I turned down the radio and called home.

"Hello, the Turner residence," my mother said answering the phone.

"Mama if you don't stop it," I said.

"What do you want boy?" she asked.

"Let me speak to Nisha."

"Hello," Nisha said.

Nisha even had a sexy voice. "What's up baby, what you doing?" I asked her.

"Nothing. Just helping yo' mama clean this fish."

"Chill out. No you not," I said.

"For real. She cooking fish and spaghetti. What you doing?" she asked.

"I'm on my way home. Do you want something before I get there?"

"Naw," she said.

I told her that I would be there in a minute and hung up the phone. I grabbed my strap and tucked it in my waist. I stopped at the store and got some blunts and some Remy. Coming out of the store I saw Tye pulling in. He was right on time.

"What's up nigga," I said.

"What's up man? I saw J.B. on the news this morning, where he at?"

"He's at home," I responded. "I went and got 'em this morning."

"That nigga!" Tye continued. "I didn't know you painted the National. I saw you flying down 5th Street this morning. You hurting 'em for real now."

"Nigga you silly. Let me buy some weed."

Tye pulled out three fat bags of some lime green looking weed. I gave him twenty-five dollars and told him I'll get at him later on. Tye's baby mama was sitting in the car. I waved at her and jumped in my ride. That nigga's baby mama was always looking at me. I had plenty of opportunities to take her down through there but Tye was my nigga and I wasn't gon' mess up the love over a female.

I started my car up and sat there rolling up a blunt. Tye came out the store and told me to stop by his house later. I sparked up the weed and pulled off. I started thinking about the Big Homey and decided to ride past his house on the way home. There was a Sebring parked in front of his

Jaguar. I figured it was his girls' and him but he still could get caught slippin' though.

I pulled up at my house, sat in the car and finished smoking my blunt. I knew Nisha was gon' love the house and my mother, too. The neighborhood was just right. Nisha came to the front door then came outside and got in the car.

"You gon' take me home so I can get some clothes Tra?" Nisha asked.

"You staying a night with daddy again?" I asked her. She smiled. "Yeah, I'll take you home cause I got something to show you anyway."

"Hold on, let me go tell yo' mother I'll be back."

I sat back and inhaled the weed. It made me cough and my eyes watery. My throat instantly got dry so I cracked the Remy and took a sip. When Nisha came back out I told her to drive. She moved up the seat and pulled off.

"You can't handle the National baby, you been trying though," I told her.

She said, "I can handle you can't I?"

"Be for real. You know the deal on that tip."

"What you got to show me Tra?" she asked insistently.

"I'm about to show you. Turn right here."

I gave her directions to the house. When we arrived I told her where to park.

"I don't got no clothes on to be meeting anybody Tra."

"Just come on," I said.

When we got out of the car I pointed at the house. "Look!"

"Who house is this?" she asked.

"I'm about to buy this tomorrow. That's where I went this morning. It's out cold in the inside too," I told her.

We walked around the house to the fenced backyard. It was a nice size. I thought about buying a pit bull and putting him back there. I asked her did she like it.

"Tra, I love it."

I continued. I grabbed her by her hand, looked her in the eyes and told her the real.

"Man I am trying to take us away from all this bullshit. So much has happened lately. Nisha, look sweetheart, I love you and I never thought I could feel this way about another female after my daughter's mother and this is the only way I can tell you this. But if I can't have you like I want you, and need you, man, I don't even want to waste any more time."

When I turned around and walked back to the car Nisha was still standing there. I was hurt because I loved Nisha and I didn't want nothing to come between us. I was ready to live life and be happy. I rolled up another blunt and started smoking. Nisha got in the car crying. I was really sick then because I wasn't trying to hurt her. I just sat there. I felt awful. Love is so painful. Nisha had her face in her hands.

I put my hand on her thigh then said, "Nisha, do you understand how I feel?"

She wiped her eyes and said, "Yeah, Tra." Her voice was cracking. "Tra, I love you, too. Man if I didn't want to be with you I wouldn't do the things I do. I don't want to get hurt either. What do I have to do to show you that I love you?"

I put the blunt in the ashtray. I looked at Nisha and said, "Will you marry me?"

She looked at me as the tears rolled down her face and said, "Yes Tra, I will marry you."

I wiped the tears from her face and kissed her passionately. She wrapped her arms around me.

"Tra, please don't leave me."

It was a moment to remember. We rode to her house talking. I told her I would take her and my mother inside the house the next day. She held my hand as I drove to her house. I backed in her driveway and went inside. Her mother was sitting on the couch watching soap operas.

"How are you doing Miss Washington," I asked.

Tuned into the television she said, "Oh, how are you doing Tra? Are you hungry baby?"

"No thank you. I'm alright," I replied.

Her mother was cool. Nisha's father divorced her mother and married a white woman that was crazy. Nisha's mother was fine. I often wondered what was wrong with her daddy. Maybe it was a money thang.

Nisha came into the living room with her clothes in her hand ready to go. We both kissed her mother and walked out the door. My heart dropped when I got to the car. The police was riding down the street slow. They made me paranoid. I guess my conscience haunted from getting away with so much stuff. I wasn't trying to take a chance so I told Nisha to drive.

"Boy, you need some gas," she said.

She drove to the gas station and I got out.

There was a female working behind the counter that I messed around with a couple times coming from the club. She was alright but nothing to take home. I waited in line as she handled a customer. I wished that Nisha would have picked a different gas station but I wasn't trippin'. She was old news.

When I got to the counter she said, "What's up Tra."

"How you doing? Let me get twenty on pump seven and a pack of Newport shorts," I said.

She was looking out the window as I was handing her the money.

"I see you painted the National. Who is that, yo' baby mama in the car?"

Looking at her I said, "Naw, that's my wife!"

Rolling her eyes, she gave me my change and my Newport's. I walked out the door laughing. I never understood how females can get mad about a nigga being with another female especially when they have a man.

I filled up the tank and we pulled off. Nisha asked me why I was laughing.

"People a trip now-a-days," I said.

We made it home and I laid down. It had been a long and painful day. I received an overwhelming amount of bad news. I was high, tired, my head was messed up and it was only five o'clock. I couldn't imagine how my aunt Francis was feeling. I wanted to call her but I couldn't stand anymore pain. Nisha laid her head on my chest and we feel asleep.

Chapter 7

"There can be no love lost when there's no love shown it's a cold world."

My eyes opened around 9:00am. I was hungry so I went in the kitchen and threw a couple pieces of fish in the microwave and sat down at the dining room table. My mind had totally slipped my plans so I called J.B.

"What's up," he said answering the phone. He had the music beating in the background. "What's up nigga, you getting' out tonight or what?" he yelled.

I told him that I would be over his house in a minute and he told me to bring some blunts. I laced the pieces of fish with hot sauce and went back in the bedroom. I woke Nisha up and told her to get under the covers and that I would be back. She nodded and went back to sleep.

I smashed the fish, grabbed my pistol, and stormed out the house. I went to the garage and got my gloves, the nine millimeter and the .357 Mag. Although Teresha never said anything about the police taking his .38's during the raid, I brought the extra pistol just in case.

I jumped in the car and put the .357 and Ruger on the passenger seat. I fired up the rest of my blunt and started up the car. Before driving off I realized that I left the extra .45 clip in the house. I needed it but I wasn't about to wake Nisha up. I knew she had wanted me to stay home so I said fuck it. I kept the music at a low tempo. I had too many guns to risk gettin' pulled over and I wasn't in the mood to be running. I wanted to complete the mission and make it home in one piece. I hit the weed a few more times and tossed it. I picked up the still reserved bottle of Remy from earlier and hit it hard. Memories flowed about all the hits we did for Big Homey. I was sick not only about my cousin's death but also how greedy Big Homey was. I figured one day he might send somebody to kill me.

I got to J.B. house and tucked the .45 on my waist. I put the other two guns in my pockets then downed the remains of the Remy. I got to the door and he let me in. The nigga was walking around the house naked and I was mad as hell! Teresha was in the kitchen cooking tacos and she had the house smelling good. I went in the kitchen and gave her a hug. She fixed me two tacos while I waited for J.B.

"Where's Nisha?" Teresha asked.

Teresha busted out laughing when I said, "She over my house sleep. I had to knock that ass out before I left."

I finished the tacos and went into the living room. J.B.'s pit bulls were laying on the floor in front of the television. The jello man was on and it seemed like the dogs were watching it.

J.B. came out fully dressed smoking a blunt. He passed it to me and went in the kitchen. I smoked so much weed I felt I was hanging with J.B. cause he was a true bud smoker. Once he was ready I offered him the nine millimeter. He lifted his shirt exposing the .38's. I handed him the blunt and we left.

I rolled up the windows on my car while J.B. started the Caprice. I knew I couldn't drive my car. I was the only person in Flint with a canary Grand National. I left the .357 in my car and carried the two automatics. I hit the car alarm and jumped in with J.B.

I told J.B. off the back, "Cuzz, I'm coming in shooting."

He didn't say nothing in response, he just pulled off. J.B. wasn't a flossy nigga at all. He was strictly about the money and getting high. I knew he had a lot on his mind cause we both had mad love for Big Homey but for me, the love was lost. When we pulled up to the house it was now a white Navigator parked in front of the Jaguar.

"I wonder who is that," J.B. said.

"I don't know and don't care," I responded.

J.B. parked in front of the house and I got out first. Someone looked out the blinds and as I approached the porch the door opened and Big Homey stood there.

He said, "What's up Tra baby," and let me in the house.

There was a nigga and two females sitting around the table. Big Homey turned around heading back to the table and I gave his bitch ass a dome shot. Blood splattered everywhere. The females scream uncontrollably. J.B. ran in and immediately shot them. The nigga made a run for the kitchen. He was helpless for two reasons, it was a two story house and he missed the stairs. He stood in the kitchen pleading. He threw his money and jewelry on the ground. He even mentioned he just bought some dope from Big Homey that he had in the Navigator. I guessed J.B. figured that it was too easy. He shot him point blank range.

J.B. grabbed the money and threw me the jewelry and car keys. Big Homey laid on the floor, brain fragments were on the wall and the couch. J.B. ran upstairs and I went in Big Homey's pockets, retrieved two Gotti knots and ran upstairs. J.B. was stuffin' money in a pillowcase. I found two SK assault rifles in the closet and four shoe boxes of cocaine. I put the shoe boxes in a foot locker bag and J.B. grabbed the 2 SK's and ran downstairs. I followed suit. I put the bags in the Caprice and jumped in the Navigator. I pulled off and J.B. followed.

I was nervous as hell. My clothes and gloves were bloody. I parked at a high school and searched the truck. The nigga had six twelve inch speakers. I wanted to be greedy but I knew time wasn't on my side. I found five kilos and jumped in the Caprice with J.B. leaving the Navigator abandoned.

Riding home J.B. looked at me and said, "Damn nigga, you got blood everywhere. Now I'ma have to clean this bitch!"

I couldn't say nothing. I was bogus. We got to his house and ran in and opened the back door. I couldn't go in the front because of Teresha. She would have flipped on us. We took the dope and money in the basement and broke bread. We counted $120,000.00 in cash, not counting the knots we took. We spilt it 50/50. I knew he needed a lawyer so I let him get down on the cocaine. He had three kilos, two boxes of cocaine. I had two boxes and two keys.

I took off my shirt and gloves and threw them in the furnace. I wasn't about to get in the National like that. My head was messed up. I guess it was after play. I was ready to get back to the house before the police got to circling the city looking for suspects. J.B. walked me to the back door and told me to take the SK's home just in case the police wanted to raid again looking for the Ruger. I put the SK's and the dope in the trunk and told that nigga I would holler at him tomorrow.

I put the pillowcase in the front seat with me and peeled off. I rode home in silence. I couldn't understand how J.B. could kill females so heartlessly. I wondered did he look at them as niggas. I guess not having a mother made him not care but my heart is too big. I made it home and backed up in the driveway. It was too late to be opening the garage so I left everythang in the car except the .45 and the money. I went in the house and as soon as I got in the room, Nisha woke up. I felt kinda stupid standing there with no shirt on and a bag in my hand.

"Why you didn't tell me you was going somewhere?" she asked.

I sat the bag in the closet. "I did tell you. You was sleeping so good you musta' didn't hear me."

I had blood spots on my arm but Nisha seemed not to notice. I went in the bathroom and ran some bath water with extra bleach. I wondered what she thought when she seen me. I put the gun on the sink and got in the tub. The water was scolding hot but it had to be. I couldn't get all the gun powder off me in warm water. Nisha stood in the bathroom door in just her panties and bra. She kneeled beside the tub and gave me a kiss.

"What's up baby?" I asked.

She said, "Lay back and let me wash you up."

I leaned back and let her do her thang. She scrubbed my body to the fullest. It felt so good I didn't want to get out the water. I scrubbed my hands extra then she handed me the towel and I got out. I didn't bother putting any boxers on. I dried off and got in the bed. Nisha put her arms around me and I went to sleep.

Chapter 8

Life is crazy and you never know what to expect. I was happy to be alive and still free.

I woke up to breakfast in bed. Nisha stood in front of me with a plate of pancakes, eggs, and bacon. She was not only beautiful but she was sweet also. I didn't have a appetite really but I ate the food anyway. It was only 10:30 in the morning and I had been sleep for five hours. I was still tired.

Finishing my breakfast, I laid back and thought about what happened last night. My stomach dropped at the thought of leaving the Navigator without burning it up, just in case. I was not the spiritual type but I was praying deep inside. I wondered did God hear those kind of prayers. I knew if I continued to think like that my whole day would be messed up. I got up and took a nice hot shower with Nisha.

I was in a zone that whole day. Nisha sensed that something was wrong. After getting out of the shower Nisha broke the silence.

"Tra, what's wrong? You haven't said anything to

me all morning? You didn't even touch me in the shower. What's the matter?"

I had so much on my mind I was unaware of my actions. I told Nisha I just had a lot on my mind and was still tired. I rolled up a blunt, slipped on some shorts and went to my car. The day was beautiful so I started the car and rolled down the windows. Nisha came outside and sat on the porch. My mind had totally forgot what I was supposed to been doing until I looked at Nisha and remembered what I had said to her yesterday.

I turned off the car and told Nisha to come in the house for a minute. When she got in the room I closed the door and locked it. She sat on the bed as I went to the closet and grabbed the pillowcase. As she looked at me, I dumped the money on the bed and asked her to help me count it.

"Damn Tra," she said.

I puffed on the blunt a few more times, put it out and started counting money. My hands got weak when I noticed blood stains on some of the money. I was surprised Nisha didn't notice it. I grabbed the stained money quick and counted it. I always felt life was for the living and for a black male growing up without a father, I accomplished a lot.

It was around 1:30pm when we finally got to twenty thousand dollars. I knew for a fact I still had a least forty-five thousand more to count. We stopped at twenty.

I put on my clothes in a hurry. The Jamaican told me he would be at the house until two o'clock so I didn't have much time to get super fresh. I threw on some Guess jeans and a plain T-shirt. I took Nisha home and headed to my destination. To my surprise, I noticed I was being followed by two white men. My first thought was they were the police. I wasn't in the best situation to be gettin' harassed by two hillbillies. Besides that, I had a murder weapon, seventy-thousand dollars in cash and two assault rifles in the trunk. My heart probably had indictment all over it. I turned in someone's driveway and went to the door. Within seconds, a female was standing at the door in her panties and bra. I had to think fast.

"Do you need your grass cut?" was what came out of my mouth.

The woman looked at me in amazement then shifted her attention behind me as I turned around to see what caught her attention. I saw the two white males riding pass slow.

"Come on in," the lady said.

I walked in and shut the door. I exhaled long and hard. The lady told me to have a seat. I sat down and she went in the back room and put on a robe.

"What did you do?" she asked.

I knew she peeped the entire play and I was happy that she was willing to help me. I felt obligated to tell her some of the truth. After explaining my situation to this very attractive woman, I thanked her and left. My body was telling me to holler at her but my heart loved Nisha too much to allow myself to fall short. I was practicing monogamy plus I had to finish my mission. I got to the house at 2:10pm and caught the Jamaican pulling out the driveway. He smiled when I got out the car. Hell, I would have smiled too knowing that I was about to be handed almost one hundred thousand dollars. I handed him the pillowcase and we went inside the house.

All I could smell was weed inside the house. The Jamaican loved his weed. I guess he enjoyed the last moments of being in the house from the way the house smelled. After he left, I sat there and drifted into deep thoughts. I wondered was I moving too fast with Nisha and how much did she love me. I was falling too deep in love with Nisha but I couldn't help myself.

I had been with so many different women, I thought I could never fall in love. I was dead wrong. My thoughts led to tears thinking of all the murders and wild shit I was doing. I got up and left with tears rolling down my face. I drove back home in silence. I was experiencing something so special, unique and rare. I needed to get my head right so I went to holler at Tye.

I didn't see his car but the front door was opened and his kids were outside playing. I got out the car and as always, his shorty's ran up to me. I gave them a dollar a piece and walked in. As I figured, Tye was gone. His baby mama was watching television. She smiled when she looked up.

"What's up Tra," she said.

"Let me get three for twenty-five," I said.

She nodded and went into the back room to retrieve the weed. I was sitting down when she came back in the living room. She had changed her clothes from sweatpants to a skirt. I thought about her actions and dismissed them until she sat down across from me with her legs open. I noticed that she didn't have on any panties and the sight made my nature rise. She sat there looking at me staring between her legs then threw the three bags of weed to me. When I stood up to leave she stood up, too. I knew that if I stayed any longer me and her would be going at it. As I turned to leave she grabbed my arm and led me into her bedroom.

As I was trying to persuade her to think about Tye she said, "He gone to Detroit to re-cop so he won't be back until tonight. Tra, I need this!" She pushed me back on the bed and closed the bedroom door.

"Chill out, Shante," I said.

Yet, I found out trying to sound demanding wasn't working. When she pulled off my shirt, she paused for a minute when she saw the .45 on my hip. She then grabbed the gun and put it on the floor. I was trippin'. *Damn, if Tye come home, somebody gone get killed.*

Shante took off her skirt and I was in a daze. She was so thick. I didn't want to do my nigga Tye like that but I was tired of wrestling with her and I was hard as a rock. She pulled out that long awaited prize and held it gently like a priceless statue. I moaned as she stroked it up and down with her soft hands. The anticipation was killing me. My little head took control of my bigger one when I led her on top of me. Shante was positioning my dick to enter her wetness when one of the kids knocked on the door. I threw her off me.

I was dead wrong and the thought of what I almost did made me mad. I got myself together and grabbed the .45 then walked out of the room leaving Shante sitting on the floor with her mouth wide opened. The oldest kid was looking at me in amazement as I walked out the house. I knew he wasn't stupid. I dropped my head and got in the car. I had come so close to doing something I would regret. I looked up and Shante was standing in the door as I pulled off. I was hurt thinking about what almost happened. I had totally said fuck Tye, and most of all Nisha.

I went to the store and bought three blunts. I called Nisha.

"Hey baby," she said picking up the phone. The joyful sound in her voice made me more depressed.

"What you doing?" I asked her.

"Nothing right now. I am supposed to go with my mother to the grocery store. Do you want something? I was thinking about buying something to cook tonight. Is there anything you want special?" she asked.

"Yes, can I have you?" I asked.

Nisha giggled and said, "Yes, when do you want me?"

"Now baby," I whispered in a low tone voice. Without giving her a chance to respond I hung up the phone. I sat in the store parking lot rolling up my medicine. I was in a different type of pain and I needed that sticky help.

I parked in front of Nisha's mother's house with the AC blowing and the windows up. I was smoking like a chimney. The weed took away all the thoughts of my stressful day. The site of Nisha made me remember why I couldn't let her go. *I have everything I need.*

When Nisha got in the car we went to my house. I was about to show my mother the house. When I pulled up in the driveway, my baby's mother pulled up with my daughter. I was happy to see my lil' princess. I got caught up in the streets and wasn't going to see her like I usually did. My baby was happy to see her daddy, too. She jumped out of the car and ran to me. I picked her up high in the air and she gave me a kiss.

As Nisha was smiling, I looked at her and said, "I told you I got an angel."

I told my daughter to go say hi to her granny. When my baby mama got out of the car, Nisha went in the house. Hating to see me with another female, she got out of the car looking stupid. I knew she was gone do something crazy and she did. She sat on the hood of her car with the music turned up. I went in the house leaving her outside by herself. I knew she was sick seeing Nisha at my house so I picked up my daughter and walked out to the car. I looked at my baby mama and I could tell she had been crying by the crusty streaks coming from her eyes. I tried to speak but she started shaking her head.

"Naw Tra, you know it's funny. I thought after all this time I could accept you being with another woman because we been separated for so long. Anyway, I just stopped by so you could see Janiah. I am happy to see you alright. I couldn't see you in the hospital like that. I just couldn't."

I wanted to find the words to comfort her but I couldn't. I gave her three hundred dollars and told her to go and buy my daughter some clothes and I will be over later.

All kinds of thoughts were going through my head. I sat on the porch thinking about stuff until my mother came out on the porch and sat beside me.

"What's up Mama?" I asked kissing her.

"Boy, Janiah is so smart and getting so grown. She like Tanisha, too. I want you to bring her over here tomorrow so she can spend the night. I have the day off."

"Mama, get your car keys so we can drive your car. I want to show you and Nisha something."

I sat in the backseat. I had my pistol on me. When we got to the house, my mother was looking confused. I lived in a better neighborhood than her.

"Mama, I just bought this house," I said.

"Boy, quit playing. Who house is this?" she asked.

I took out my keys and walked in. She was looking crazy.

"Tra, you are serious ain't you boy?"

"Mama, I've been saving for this house a while now, "I said.

That "yeah right" look was on her face and Nisha started laughing. We walked around the house talking and laughing. When we finally left, I guess my mother was tired because she asked Nisha to drive back. As we were approaching the house, I saw Tye's car pull in our driveway. I had a feeling that some bullshit was in the game. As soon as I saw the look on his face I knew it was, plus, he never comes to my mother's house. I got out of the car and my mother and Nisha went into the house.

"What's up," I said.

"Nigga you already know what's up. You tried to holler at Shante. Nigga she said you was trying to say I was messing around on her and everything nigga! That's what's up!" he said.

"Dawg, if you wanna live pass today, you betta gone somewhere coming over my ole miss house with that bullshit. Nigga you know me. I don't want yo' baby mama nigga! You on some stupid shit. Don't get killed over yo' emotions," I responded clutching the .45.

I walked in the house and left that clown outside. Five minutes later I heard his tires squealing going down the street. I was mad as hell because Shante lied and Tye bought that nonsense to my OG house. My pride wanted murder but my heart didn't. Tye was my mans but his girl wasn't right and I knew it would take a war for him to see the light. I told Nisha what happened outside and as always she wanted me to chill and leave it alone.

My mother told me to call my Aunt Francis. I didn't want to but I knew I had to face the music sooner or later, so I called.

After three rings I was just about to hang up then a man answered the phone. I knew I dialed the right number so I figured Aunt Francis had company. Then she got on the phone.

"Hey Aunt Francis, who was that?" I asked.

"Oh baby, that's one of my nephews from Chicago. Three of them just popped up. I want you to come meet them Tra. When can you come over or are you busy?" she asked.

"No, I'm not busy. I'm just chillin'. I'll be over there in twenty minutes. Do you want something from the store or anything?" I asked.

"No thank you baby. Auntie alright," she said happily.

After we hung up I told my mother about Aunt Francis' nephews and that I was going to meet them. I told Nisha I would be right back. Her and my mother started cooking and told me to be careful.

I pulled up to the corner and as I was changing the CD, I looked up and there was Tye parked down the street like he was waiting on me to leave or something. I grabbed my strap and kept on going like I never seen him. I looked in my mirror and no shit, he was still following me. *Fuck 'em. If this is how he wants it, I'ma give it to him.* I called J.B.

"What's up, who dis?" he asked.

"This Tra. Dig this cuzz, this nigga Tye trippin'. His girl done told this nigga some bullshit and I checked him for coming to my mama's crib with that nonsense. So now I'm on my way to go holler at my family from Chicago over Aunt Francis house and I see this nigga parked down the street waiting for me to leave. I guess he got his strap. I wanna show this clown who he fucking with so grab the Mac and post up on Paterson in the alley. When this fool get to the alley, spray his ass cuzz."

"Tra, I'm on my way right now," J.B. said and hung up.

I turned up my music and fired up a Newport. That nigga was probably messed up. He wasn't peeping the play. When we got to the alley, I looked out my rearview and J.B. was standing in front of Tye's car shooting the Mac. I just kept going on my mission to Aunt Francis house.

When I pulled up to the house, there was a gray and white Excursion truck sitting in the driveway. *It ain't no telling what they got in that big boy.*

Aunt Francis greeted me with a hug and a kiss. As I walked in the house, my folks from Chicago was dressed like mob figures, wearing Dobbs hats and suits. I was tripping cause I was a sophisticated thug nigga myself but Dobbs hats and suits wasn't me. These niggas was on some real militant type shit. I stayed over Aunt Francis house for about two hours just kicking it. I had to leave once they started talking about my cousin's murder. I didn't want to hear that shit. I had enough problems and worries as it was. Besides, the nigga who killed my cousin was only a memory now.

Chapter 9

I rode home wondering was that nigga Tye dead. That was my manz but the power of pussy is sometimes stronger than love.

I sparked up a blunt and went over J.B's house and just walked in. As usual, wasn't nobody in the living room but his dogs. I wondered if I was a stranger what would they do. I walked through the whole house and to my surprise, nobody was there so I left.

I made it home to a nightmare. My mama's house was surrounded by police cars so I hit a couple corners to get rid of my .45. I couldn't let my mother and Nisha sit there suffering because of me. I pulled up and the police rushed my car ordering me to the ground. I looked up and my mother and Nisha came out of the house crying. I was sick as hell looking at their faces. I couldn't even get a word out. It was like I was mute but I guess there was nothing I could say.

I got to the precinct and the police interrogated me for what seemed like forever. They were trying to link me to numerous murders, including the one pending on J.B. They showed me pictures of different dead bodies stretched out on crime scenes. I was a soldier about it but my stomach dropped at the sight of the gruesome photos and different thoughts went through my mind. I knew that they were only fishing for information and that was something I couldn't help them with.

I was released a few hours later. I called home but no one was there so I called Nisha's house. I was glad to hear her voice. I told her to come pick me up. I always talked to Nisha about how I felt. I had learned that the best way to make a relationship work was by communicating. We talked the whole ride home. Nisha said that my mother was mad at me so she went to work early. I was hurt that my mother was mad at me because I allowed the police to come to her house looking for me. I told Nisha that I was going to stay at my house tonight so I grabbed a change of clothes, all of my guns and put it in my car. Nisha told me to follow her home so that she could take her mother's car back.

I really didn't feel comfortable that night but I followed her home anyway. I was a young nigga trapped inside a life of crime and the drama was making me tired. I was ready to die but I couldn't kill myself and I couldn't see some hoe ass nigga doing it either. Me and Nisha made it to the house and just chilled. I had furnished the house and everything but I still stayed with my mother. I knew it was time to move out.

I sent Nisha to get us something to eat and laid back. I had a passion to change the game for good but there was always a roadblock in front of me and that was something I couldn't escape.

We stayed up for some time and finally after hours of talking and doing other lil' odd things around the house, we went to bed.

The next couple of days were exhausting. J.B. had court dates and a lot was on the line. Luckily, he had got a solid lawyer who gave us all of the witnesses' addresses who were supposed to come to court. Most of the witnesses were female but I knew that my nigga's life was on the line.

I recall one situation where I sat outside the house for three hours and when the witness left I followed the car. It hadn't dawned on me until the car pulled up to the club that it was a Saturday night so I went back to the house and broke in. I was trying to make it as easy as possible. I was what some people would call a heartless muthafucka. I ate leftover chicken and other shit like it was my own house. It was almost 2:00am when I heard a car door shut. The witness came in the house and I guess she noticed the smell of chicken and remembered that she did not eat any cause she ran out the house. I came out of the bedroom gunning after her. I didn't know it was a female until I caught the smell of her perfume. When I did, I stopped. It wasn't until I heard the car door again that I continued my mission. It seemed like a Jason movie cause she was trying to get the car keys in the ignition when I shot through the window.

Life was crazy. I went home to an empty house. I told Nisha that I had some business to handle. When I got home I had plenty of voicemail messages from her. When I caught the news the next morning, the police said the gun was so powerful that one shot nearly took the girl's arm off. I told myself that I would leave the female killing to J.B. but my nigga needed me so I swallowed my feelings.

Shit was getting worse though. J.B. started acting funny and I was being watched. There were days when I would sit on the porch with Nisha and undercover police would ride pass my house smiling at me. The shit fucked me up because I moved where the white folk lived and only a few people knew where my house was.

My love for the streets was dying and I was trying to stay low-key.

January twenty-third was my true falling point. Me, J.B. and his two cousins went to this hotel room. J.B. claimed that he had some hoes that was trying to fuck. I never met these hoes so J.B. and his cousins went inside to see what was poppin' with the females. I stayed in the car. After sometime, J.B. came back out and two white females pulled up to the hotel room and went in. J.B. said the females wasn't talking about nothing and they had some niggas already in the room. I was ready to leave. I got out the car to go get his cousins and when I got to the room, they had guns everywhere. The two hoes were on the bed, there was two niggas in the bathroom and I'm snapping.

Soon as I opened the door to leave, the police was pulling up so I shut the door. J.B.'s little cousins began to panic. They went to throwing shit everywhere. Then I heard three knocks on the door. It was the police. My heart dropped. One of the cats in the bathroom ran out and opened the door for the police. I laid on the floor as the police piled in the room. The only thing I could think about was why the fuck was I in this room and where the hell was J.B.

We were all arrested and taken downtown. The dudes in the bathroom, the white girls on the bed, and J.B.'s cousins all said I had something to do with the robbery gone bad. I was sick.

I was later arraigned on armed robbery, home invasion, and some weapon charges with a seventy-five thousand dollar bond, no ten percent. I knew that with time, I could get the money but sitting up in jail wasn't my thang. I did a couple months for some petty shit but that was it.

When Nisha came to see me, it brought a sense of ease to my mind. When we embraced each other, I could tell her body yearned for mine because I felt the same. It was the first time in nearly a year that we spent time apart and I regretted every second.

"In the case of the People of the State of Michigan versus Travon Turner, docket number 10-02-1800. The defendant is charged with Armed Robbery, Home Invasion…"

It seemed like the court clerk went on for hours. I looked behind me and there was my mother, Nisha, my baby's mother, and Aunt Francis waving at me. It had only been a couple of days but to see them all there supporting was encouraging. I plead not guilty and my lawyer requested a lower bond. When the judge allowed me to pay ten percent on the seventy-five thousand, I smiled. I turned around and told Nisha to go to my house and get the money.

The sheriffs placed me in the bullpen and all I could do then was wait. The county jail was full of all kinds of cats, killers, robbers, thieves, and rapist. I bumped into one of my old partners from my gang- bangin' days. He walked in the bullpen looking crazy as hell. I didn't even recognize him. He had O.G. status back in the early nineties and I used to look up to him. He allegedly was involved in a triple homicide where some young kids were tortured. They say he put cigarettes on a young dude, stuck a broom stick in his ass, shot him in the face, and finally pushed him out of a rolling car butt naked.

"What's up Tra?" he said while walking towards me.

"What's up boy? Long time no see!" I replied as we showed love. *Damn, G look bad like he smoking crack or something.*

He said that the streets were saying that J.B. set me up but I didn't believe him.

"You know big homie the streets have been known to say too much," I said forcefully.

Me and J.B. had broke into the big homie's uncle house back in the day and his uncle knew who J.B. was so they have not seen eye to eye in years. I knew the homie still had hard feelings towards J.B. I felt myself getting mad so I was thankful when the sheriff's came to take me back to the floor. I pounded fist with the big homie and walked out.

Chapter 10

I went back to my cell and laid on my bunk. I couldn't help but think about the big homie's words. My bunkie came in the cell crying about his time. As usual, he didn't help the situation. He was a young cat, about twenty-five years old, locked up for Home Invasion or some shit. He was serving eight months straight county time. These young muthafuckas nowadays are ridiculous. I'm laying there looking at him go on about his girlfriend and how he should be on the trustee floor.

I couldn't help but tell him, "Man, shut the fuck up and sit yo' young ass down somewhere. Don't nobody wanna hear that shit!"

The young brother was my lil' manz but today was not the day for me to play big brother. I was dealing with my own problems.

The sheriff was clicking the cell door. I jumped down off the bunk and stuck my head out the door. "Turner, get your shit man, you been bond out!"

That was the best news I had heard. I grabbed my shit quick and headed out the door. My bunkie was looking crazy as hell when I left. I couldn't get outside quick enough. My mother and Nisha was right there.

I thought about all the work me and J.B. had put in together, from back in the day to the play we laid down on Tye a couple weeks ago. I made it home and immediately called him. After maybe seven rings, J.B. finally answered the phone.

"Hello."

"What's up!" I said.

"What's up G, I see you made it outta there," J.B. said.

"Yeah though, I gotta holler at you though. Meet me tonight in the hood on Paterson," I said.

"No doubt," J.B. responded.

In a way I felt I was wrong for even thinking that J.B. played me but I remembered what an old head told me, "Milk can spoil overnight." Loyalty means the world to me and the mere thought of my closest homies setting me up or just being on some slimy shit was not sitting right with me. I took a hot shower and sat in the living room talking to Nisha and my mother until moms went to work. Nisha went into the kitchen and started cleaning up. I sat there and exhaled. I was happy to be home and in a position to tighten up all the loose screws to avoid doing a long bit in prison.

When I walked in the kitchen, Nisha was washing

dishes and she was looking good. I walked up behind her and wrapped my arms around her. She smelled good, too.

"Did you miss me?" I asked her.

Turning around and hugging me she said, "You know I did Tra. This shit is getting worse every minute. There is always something going on."

She was crying so I just let her vent because she had endured so much with me in such a short time. She told me that it seemed like every since she started kickin' it with me her life had changed completely. She explained how I was the first man she really loved and that the thought of losing me was hard to bear.

I kissed her passionately as I led her to the bedroom. I had missed her, too. The thought of incarceration was a reality and I had been trying to live semi-right. We made porn love that day and went to sleep exhausted. I woke up to the ring of my cellphone. It was J.B.

"Tra, what's up nigga? Where you at? I'm in the hood waiting on you!"

I forgot that I was supposed to meet J.B. "I'm on my way right now cuzz!"

I went to the bathroom and got myself together. I grabbed the .357 in case something popped off. It's best to be safe than sorry. The fact that I was already on bond entered my mind and vanished just as quick. I lived a dangerous lifestyle and I knew that if I intended to make it home that night, I better prepare for the worst.

When I pulled up on Paterson, J.B. was sitting in his Caprice. J.B. was so black that the only way I knew he was in the car was I saw the ball of fire from his blunt as he hit it. I walked up to the car and he got out and hugged me. I couldn't do anything but smile. It was the same ole J.B. He smelled like weed, cigarettes and dogs. I sat down on the hood of his car and he passed the blunt. It had been a while since I smoked some weed. Those days in the county were a relief in a way because I was able to get high without smoking as much weed.

We talked and smoked for what seemed like hours. I knew I would have to address the rumors surrounding J.B. As much as I hated to confront my dog, I had to. Just as I began to speak, J.B. interrupted me.

"Tra, look man, I already know what you are about to say because I expect you to, but bro, you know me better than anyone. These muthafuckas just love to talk. You know that. When the police pulled up to the hotel I pulled off. What was I supposed to do, get out of my car and come to the room door? I'm already fighting murder charges and shit cuzz. As I look back, there is probably something I could have came up with but I was high and trying to get the fuck on."

All I could do was listen to him. This is my family is all I thought about. I just told J.B. he was absolutely right about what he did considering his situation with the murder case. I would have probably done the same thing but we still had to deal with his rotten ass cousins.

I made it home around 2:30am. I peeked in the room and Nisha was watching television.

"Hey baby, what you watching?" I asked as I walked in the room.

"BET Uncut. I couldn't go back to sleep and this is the only thing on," she said with the sweetest innocent look.

I took my clothes off and got in the bed. Nisha got on top of me and said, "Where have you been mister?" in a seductive voice.

"I been out messing with J.B." I replied rubbing her ass.

"Tra, you can't be sneaking out the house at all times of the night. You be having me worried. You might be trying to give away my stuff."

"What stuff?" I asked her.

"This stuff!" she said as she grabbed my dick and put it inside her.

"Oh, that stuff."

Nisha was the total package. Beautiful, smart, sexy and her sex game was on another level.

She was out to prove a point that night and her message was getting through to me for sure. She slid up and down slow on me and I couldn't do anything but fight off exploding. It felt so good I wanted to stay right there. She got up just in time and she immediately cleaned up the mess while looking at me. I knew what she was saying to me. It was very clear.

I woke up the next day feeling good. Good sex always does that to a real nigga, especially if you know you took care of your business. I had been out for a couple of days and I knew I had to go see my daughter. After getting myself together, I jumped in the National. I hadn't drove my car in weeks and the tank was damn near empty so I stopped at the gas station. I pulled up and there was Tye's car. I cocked the .45 and got out the car. I walked right in front of his car and looked in the window but he wasn't in there so I went in the gas station. I got my hand on my pistol and I'm looking for him but it wasn't him. It was his rotten ass, baby mama, Shante. She looked at me and rolled her eyes. I walked straight over there gun in hand. When I saw her with the children, I put the gun up.

She started yelling, "What you gone do Travon Turner, kill me in the store in front of my children? You already tried to kill my baby daddy!"

I looked around the store. The clerk and a few customers were looking right at me.

"Alright bitch. You wanna play games. We gone play!" I said.

I turned around, walked to the counter and told the clerk, "Twenty on the yellow Grand National."

I was mad as hell that bitch Shante was trying to set me up using all those people as witnesses. A good day was ended down the wrong path all over some bullshit. When I made it to my baby mama house I just sat in the car for a minute then called her.

I would hate to come over there and she had some strange ass nigga around my daughter so I always called to make sure everything was straight. It took a minute to answer the phone and I begin to doubt they were there. If I hadn't seen the car I bought her some years back parked in front of the apartment, I would have left.

"What's up Tra? When you coming to see yo' child? You been outta jail all this time and you ain't been to see yo' damn child yet!"

"Man shut the fuck up and come open the door!" I yelled in the phone.

"Where you at?" she said. I could tell she was smiling so I just told her to open the door.

When I walked in the house my daughter ran up to me and jumped in my arms. There are no words to properly express the joy a real father has when seeing his child. I sat down on the couch and my daughter ran and got some of her toys. My baby mama was standing there staring at me. I knew it wouldn't be long before she got started. I just exhaled and prepared for the worst.

"I hope you stay out of jail Tra cause I'm not going to be bringing her all over the state to see you," she said.

I just looked at her. It was clear that she was trying to get a reaction outta me by the look on her face. I leaned back on the couch and waited for my daughter to come back. She brought damn near every toy she had and we played for a while. My baby was growing up. She was counting good and everything. I gave my B.M. some money, kissed my daughter and left. I noticed how my B.M. kept going to the back room every time the phone rang. Females are wild. I expected a call from her real soon.

I couldn't stop thinking about Shante. That bitch was as crazy as they come. I couldn't understand how we had gotten to this point. I had known Shante since the early eighties. Me, Shante, Tye, J.B. and Teresha all went to the same elementary school together. In fact, I knew her parents, too. But this bitch was on bullshit. First, she tried to give me some pussy, then she geeks up Tye like I tried to holler at her, and now she playing games like she wants me to kill her.

I rode home in silence. I had to make sure my next move was the best one. What was painful was I felt I couldn't holler at J.B. about the shit. I saw the game unfolding before my eyes and there was no room for mistakes either. I would play the game by the rule or allow the new rules to place me in prison. That was not an option to me.

I made it home and backed all the way up behind my house. I didn't want anybody to see my car. I walked in the house and Nisha was on the phone. I kissed her and went in the basement. I was watching T.V. when Nisha came downstairs and told me she had to go to California cause her favorite cousin, Rico got killed. I held her, kissed her forehead, and told her I wanted to go also. I didn't care about anything but making sure my baby was happy. I didn't have to be back in court for weeks so I figured a vacation may be what I needed.

Chapter 11

I walked through the airport relieved to be on solid ground. We landed in Oakland, California on June 6, 2007. I had never been a fan of flying but certain situations have made me do it. Back in the day, me and J.B. used to take trips out to Cali for the big homie. We would meet these old school Crips in Watts and they would give us missions to go on. These were our early days of killing. The big homie always told us them Cali boys don't know us so we could put in work and be gone before the bodies were found. We would stay in Cali for a couple of days and then a few hours before our flight was scheduled to leave the Crips would strap bricks of cocaine or heroin on to us for the big homie.

In those years we were young niggas having grown money. We were getting spending money to go to Cali then we were getting five thousand dollars apiece for the murders. The big homie was giving us thirty-five hundred a piece for bringing the bricks back. Those were the days.

So me and Nisha driving through Oakland headed to her aunt's house and I'm just looking at the conditions of the neighborhoods. There was trash everywhere, abandoned houses, and gang graffiti spray painted on every corner. *Damn!*

When we pulled up to Nisha's aunt's house there was a bunch of niggas standing in the front yard. I assumed they were bloods because they all had some form of red clothing on. I can't lie, when I got out of the car I felt vulnerable in front of all them niggas. I was in a foreign territory with no pistol and then I was wearing blue from head to toe. I was good though. They looked at me, I looked back at them and walked in the house. I had never met Nisha's aunt Shirley but she was cool. In fact, she opened up her house to us. I couldn't do it though. We ended up getting a room in the Holiday Inn. I just didn't feel comfortable.

Nisha's aunt told us that everyone was saying that her son Rico was killed by a crackhead named Jody. Apparently this Jody cat had just got out of prison a couple months ago and got desperate. Aunt Shirley said that the niggas outside of her house were Rico's homies and they were always standing out there. I immediately started thinking where the hell was they when her son got killed by that fiend. Luckily the funeral was only a couple of days away because I felt some bullshit coming. I have done so much wrong that I didn't want these gang-bangin' ass niggas to get me confused with someone else.

The next day we went over to Nisha's aunt's, I decided to go outside and find me some weed to smoke. I hollered at one of the yard niggas about some green.

"Hey cuzz, I'm tryin' to find some tree," I said to one of the yard gangsters.

He looked at me in disgust and said, "Ain't no tree around here blood."

I immediately thought about what I had said to him. There I was standing in the front yard with eight gang bangers all wearing red from and to toe and I called him cuzz. I started to tell him that I wasn't with that bullshit but it was too many of them niggas out there. I knew I was out of place.

I went in the house and hollered at Nisha's aunt. "Aunt Shirley, I'm trying to find something to smoke."

"Baby, what you tryin' to get some weed, crack, cigarettes, what?" she asked.

So I went in. "Aunt Shirley, I'm looking for some weed," I responded.

She said, "Holler at one of them niggas in the front yard."

I told her I already hollered at one and he said he didn't know where it was.

"How much do you want?" she asked.

"Just enough to last while I'm out here so maybe a couple of ounces," I replied. Unaware of the Cali cost, I gave her two hundred dollars and sat on the couch. Nisha stood in the kitchen doorway laughing as her aunt stormed out the front door. I couldn't do nothing but smile.

Within a few minutes Aunt Shirley came back in the house and threw the two ounces in my lap. Now Cali was beautiful, especially on the weed tip. Those two ounces looked like four in Flint. It was lime green and crunchy. I was happy as hell. I started rollin' a blunt then heard about seventeen shots. I dropped the weed, the blunt, and got on the floor. Nisha's aunt ran to the door like she was bullet proof and went outside. *This woman is crazy!*

"Yeah baby, it's time to go to the hotel room," I told Nisha.

Aunt Shirley came back in talking about them fools out there shooting in front of my house talking bout they seen Jody drive down the street. I'm sitting there trying to revive my blunt trippin'.

"Auntie, I will be back in a couple days," Nisha told her Aunt Shirley.

"Baby, why you leaving?" Aunt Shirley asked. "I told them clowns to get out my yard and they gone now." She was trying to convince Nisha she was straight.

Nisha said, "My man can't be around this shit. We just came from the same shit in Flint. He fighting all kinds of cases now and I can't jeopardize his freedom like that. So I will see you in a couple of days."

Aunt Shirley said, "Tra baby, I'm sorry. There has just been so much going on around here since my son, you know."

"Auntie, it's not your fault and we will be back in a couple of days. If you need anything just call," I said jumping in. I hugged her and walked out.

I understood exactly what she was dealing with cause just a couple of months ago Aunt Francis was suffering the same way when my cousin from Chicago got killed. I sparked up the blunt and leaned back in the car seat as Nisha pulled off.

For some strange reason I didn't feel comfortable in Cali. It was probably because usually when I went out of town, J.B. was with me. I was scared something would happen on the mistaken identity tip so I made sure Nisha always drove and my seat was back.

When we got back to the room I called J.B. and Teresha answered the phone.

"What up Tra! So how is California?" she asked.

"Oh, it's straight out here. Just these gang-bangin' muthafuckas out here go so hard it's crazy," I told her.

"So what they be saying in the movies and shit is true about the gangs?" she asked.

"Hell yeah!" I responded. "Me and J.B. used to come out here many years ago. Speaking of J.B., where is that lame at?"

"Hold on. He's in the backyard," she said. "J.B., Tra on the phone. He wants you."

I hear her yelling for him to come to the phone. Nisha came in the room and sat next to me. "Who you talking to?" she asked.

"I'm waiting on J.B. Hold on, here he go," I said.

"Hey, what's up boy?" J.B. said excitedly.

"Aw man this shit ain't right without you nigga I swear. Nisha got me all around these blood niggas. They shooting at muthafuckas and everything."

"What!" J.B. said as he busted out laughing.

"Yeah, this shit crazy out here. I was thinking about taking the trip down the way," I said.

"Oh yeah! Damn you make me wanna come out there. I had forgot all about the homies. It's been so long," J.B. said.

"Yeah, I might have to make that trip though. I'm not sure yet," I told J.B. and hung up the phone.

It had been over ten years since the last time me and J.B. went out to Watts. I was much older now and knew those Crips were also. But I was tired of sitting around Nisha's aunt's house so I decided to go.

Chapter 12

I started to drop Nisha off over to her aunts' but I thought about those wild ass blood niggas standing in the front yard. I knew I would not be able to forgive myself if something happened to her over there. I told her I would be back later and left her in the hotel.

When I got to Watts I was fucked up. The city looked worse than Oakland. You could definitely tell the difference from the gang territories also. The Crip graffiti is everywhere, on cars, stores, houses, stop signs and even house roofs. When I was in Oakland, it was only on stop signs, abandoned houses and a few buildings.

When I made it to the O.G. Crip house, that was exactly the same as Oakland and Nisha's aunt's house. There were about fifteen Crips in the front yard. Again, I felt vulnerable and started to pull off until one of the Crips said, "What's up cuzz, you lose something around here?"

"Naw loc, I'm looking for the big homie, Capone. This is lil' Tra from Michigan," I yelled back.

One of the younger Crips came to the car with his pistol in his hand. He looked in the car and said, "Yeah, the homie in the house. Come on in loc."

I was a little spooked because the homie had his pistol out and shit. I felt like if I got in the house there may be no coming out. I made up my mind that if everything went well, I was not leaving that house without a pistol.

I walked in the house and there were more Crips sitting around with pistols on the table, smoking weed, and playing video games. Then Capone stood up.

"Tra, what's up lil' loc? Come over here!" Capone snatched me up as we hugged.

"Yo loc, this is one of the young niggas from Michigan I been tellin' y'all fools about. This family right here cuzz!" Capone said to the other Crips.

I felt right at home though once I saw Capone. I started thinking about all kinds of old shit me and J.B. did out there.

"So where the other lil' nigga at cuzz? What's the loc name?" Capone asked.

"J.B." I said.

"Yeah, young ass crazy J.B. What's up with the loc? Where he at?" Capone asked.

"Oh, the homie at home. I talked to him last night about coming out this way," I told him.

Me and Capone went in the backyard and kicked it in private.

"So what's up loc? What brings you out west?" Capone asked.

I explained how I was in Oakland with Nisha for a funeral and all. When I told him about the bloods out there he flipped out.

"Aw cuzz, them slobs out in Oakland is soft as hell. They know better than to come to Watts. They will definitely get smashed out here," Capone just kept going. "Dig loc, you know you shoulda' brought the young Cripette with you. Don't be having her around them soft ass blood niggas."

"Capone," I interrupted.

"What up Tra baby?" Capone stopped and looked at me.

I said, "Cuzz, you know that love runs deep and everything and after this funeral me and lil' queen might come spend a couple nights out here before we jump on that flight. But dig, I'ma need some work on both ends, how we used to do it."

"You already know what it is Tra. You family baby," Capone said. He began to walk in the house and I stopped him.

"Hold on cuzz, I'ma need a strap, too. I'm out in Oakland feeling vulnerable than a muthafucka," I said.

Capone laughed and said, "Come on cuzz."

When we walked in the house I sat down and pulled out some weed and a blunt.

One of the younger Crips said, "Man what's that?"

I threw him about a quarter ounce of that weed Aunt Shirley got for me. The lil' homie started laughing uncontrollably then passed the weed to the big homie Capone. Capone chuckled and threw the weed back to me.

"What's this, some Michigan shit?" Capone asked.

I said, "Naw, this that Oakland."

He responded, "Man cuzz, you don't gotta smoke that shit. I got you. Matter ah fact, cuzz, go get me a couple zips and one of them .45's out the backroom." Capone looked at me and said, "I told you I got you loc."

The lil' Crip came back and threw the shit in my lap. I've had plenty of .45's, it's nothing new to me but this weed looked like it came straight outta cotton factory. There was so much white crystal looking shit on it."

"Man, what the fuck is this? I asked. The whole house started laughing. I chilled with the homies for a couple more hours and got back on the highway.

I pulled up to the hotel about 11:00pm. I called Nisha and told her I was on my way upstairs and she said okay. I was so high that I got on the elevator and went to the wrong floor. When I finally made it to the room, Nisha said she wanted to go get something to eat. So instead of going in the room and laying back, I went with her.

We went through the drive thru of some little fast food spot that was ghetto as hell. Then while Nisha was ordering the food, some clown bumps the back of the car. I immediately opened the car door to see what's up and Nisha grabbed my arm.

"No Tra, please don't feed that clown," she said.

I couldn't do it though. I got out the car and the dude did too.

"Man, what's taking y'all so muthafucking long," he said.

And before he could say anything else, I shot him in the chest with the .45. His passenger tried to get out and run but I shot him in the back of the neck. I took off running leaving Nisha sitting in the car. I learned a long time ago to never run back to a parked car and drive off because people have a tendency to get your license plate. I hit about seven blocks and called Nisha.

"Tra, you alright?" she asked.

"Yeah, I'm straight. Baby I'll meet you back at the room," I said.

I hid the pistol behind a house and walked to the hotel. When I walked in Nisha was sitting on the couch on the phone.

"Who you talking to?" I asked her.

"Teresha crazy ass," she said.

I went into the bathroom and turned on the bathwater. I asked Nisha to go down to the front desk and ask for some bleach. After about ten minutes she came back and immediately poured the bleach in the hot bathwater.

She began scrubbing my hands and said you know the funeral is tomorrow so when it's over we can leave tomorrow night. I explained to her that we would go to Watts for a few days so I can get some things in order.

"Tra, you know I'm with you baby," she said. That was good to hear even though I already knew it.

The next day Nisha went and changed the rental car for a Cadillac Escalade. We got dressed and went to Aunt Shirley's house. When we pulled up to the house I saw all them bloods and I remembered I had to pick up my pistol. There were twice the number of bangers it usually was and no one had on a traditional suit. They all wore street clothes with one dominate color…red!

When we got out of the car Nisha went in to check on her auntie. I stood in front of the Escalade and smoked a blunt. I knew I would have to get high to be around all them cats.

One of the bloods walked over to me and said, "What's up blood, you from outta town right?"

"Yeah, what's up?" I said.

He looked at me and said, "Is there any bloods from where you from?"

I just started smiling and said, "I guess that's what they supposed to be."

He started laughing and that eased the tension. We kicked it for a few more minutes then Nisha came out.

I told Nisha to take me to this spot. I had trouble finding where I hid the pistol. When I finally did, my stomach dropped. Someone was in the backyard barbequin'. I was mad as hell because I did not feel comfortable going around all those gang-bangin' ass cats and the funeral gets shot up or one of them lames act stupid. I came up with a plan.

I had Nisha go to the fence and call the man to ask for directions. The man was around his forties and white. He looked like this dude I saw on the Amerikkka's Most Wanted. When he came out to help Nisha, I went around the other side of the house. After retrieving the pistol, I hopped the fence and came out around the corner. I called Nisha and she came and got me.

I was ready for the funeral to be over with. When we got there it was jammed packed, bumper to bumper. It reminded me of that scene in *Boyz in the Hood* when Trey and Ricky went to hang with Doe-boy on the strip. These cats were hitting switches, ghost riding, and throwing up all kinds of gang signs.

Nisha looked at me and said, "Tra, please don't start trippin'."

"I'm not," I said.

She asked me to promise her but that was something I could not do.

I must have been called blood a thousand times. The funeral service was ridiculous. One thing I must say about them California gangs, that shit was a lifestyle for them for real. Nisha's cousin Rico was no doubt a respected blood. He was dressed in a red velour outfit with a red Boston Red Sox hat on. There were bandannas, cards, money, shirts, and pictures inside the marble red casket. I thought that Flint funerals were ghetto, this took the cake.

After the funeral, we spoke to Nisha's aunt for a while then headed for the highway to Watts. I was glad to be getting' the fuck away from them niggas and that city.

When we made it to Watts we got a room and sat back. Nisha called her auntie and let her know we made it to Watts safe. And just as I suspected, Nisha's aunt said to be careful because the police was looking for a young, black woman in her thirties along with a black male who may be in his thirties with his hair in braids. She said they were wanted for questioning of a murder and attempted murder at a East Oakland restaurant a couple nights ago. I told Nisha to stay in the room and that I would be back in a minute.

I called the O.G. Capone and told him I was coming through right now. It was kinda dark so I knew I better had called. These California cats will pop off at the slightest feeling of a threat. When I got there Capone was standing outside with the rest of the front porch Crips.

Soon as he walked up he said, "Boy you keep switching rides and shit. I didn't know who you was."

"Yeah, that's what I came to holler at you about." I explained the scenario and told him I would have to come back out west at another time. I couldn't afford to get caught up, especially with Nisha as a accomplish. We made arrangements to get some of that weed sent up to Flint in a couple of weeks so I felt a sense of satisfaction.

I shot back to the room, packed everything up and we left for the airport. I made a quick stop at a sewer and ditched the .45. I could tell Nisha was ready to get home. We walked through the airport on pins and needles. I just knew that by now there had to be pictures of us floating around. That was actually the first time I wanted to get on a plane.

Chapter 13

I felt like shit when I got off the plane. I turned to Nisha and it made the situation worse. She must have felt my pain because she squeezed and told me that she loved me. Seeing my O.G. was the only reason I was able to smile. She was my world, my rock, and the only woman I could never do anything wrong to. Her and Nisha was tight. They became more like some sort of women's sorority. They immediately started talking about the trip and the funeral. I sat there in silence and reflected on many things. I had a court date in four days and I hadn't even begun to tighten the lose screws.

"Tra...Travon Turner! I know you hear me talking to you!" my mother yelled from the front seat.

"Huh," I said regaining my focus.

"Did you enjoy yourself in California?"

"Oh yeah, it was straight. Just a bunch of young and old niggas running around killing each other," I replied.

"You know your daughter been staying at my house the pass couple of days," she said.

"What for? You went to get her or something?" I asked.

"Naw, yo' baby mama got jumped on by some girl and she's in the hospital. It's nothing serious so don't start acting up," she said.

I had my mother drop me off at the hospital and told her and Nisha I would call them later. I was mad as hell when I saw her. I inquired about what happened and she said that Shante and some girl jumped her in the club for nothing. She said that she was at the bar talking to some dude and out of nowhere Shante hit her with a Moet bottle and she fell to the ground. The last thing she remembered was the bartender bringing her change back from a twenty dollar bill.

Later on that day I rode pass Shante's house and saw Tye walking in the door. I thought he was dead for sure but God has blessed many who didn't deserve it. I knew it was only a matter of time and I would clean house. As bad as I wanted to stop and holler at Tye, I knew I couldn't, but something would have to change. Shante violated all the rules and to me, Tye was her co-defendant. He couldn't keep his own woman in line.

I met up with J.B. to do some damage control with his little cousins. We went over his aunt's house to see what she could do with her sons. She said that the boys already agreed to clear me of the charges. She said that the police wanted me bad and they conspired to get me cooked. I was thankful that J.B. and his aunt was able to get the shorty's to stand tall on their own. I gave his aunt five hundred dollars and thanked her for the help. The mission now was to assist J.B. in his case. The lawyer he had was one of the best in Flint. He was a high priced, Jewish lawyer who was known for beating murder cases. The club was jammed packed the night of the murder so our only hope was that misidentification would be the key to his needed freedom.

Life is messy like that. Young warriors live like there's no tomorrow. They have to fight with every muscle to maintain their liberty. One of the victim's girlfriend was already a casualty of war and J.B.'s lawyer was now saying two more people have come forward as witnesses to the slaying. J.B. was struggling to stay afloat and the financial burden of everything was taking its toll on him. I could see it in his face. Desperation is something that you never want to see your brother suffer from. There's a old saying that goes "pressure will bust a pipe." Not to say that would happen with J.B. but I didn't want to find out. I told him to be patient and that I had a few things manifesting on the money tip. J.B. kept talking about hitting a lick and I only had one lick in mind and that was taking some muthafucking lives. I guess that was a bit selfish on my end because I wasn't hurting on the money but my homie was. I told J.B. I would be to see him in a few days.

I got the call from Capone and he told me that the city weather looked windy and everything was beautiful in the wild one hundreds. That was music to my ears. We coded everything on that tip because the cellphone game was tricky and most companies were infested with federal government task force agencies hoping to catch a Al-Qaeda operative or potential drug kingpin. Capone had the weed waiting for me in Chicago in the wild one hundred blocks on the south side. I got J.B. and a

127

couple of my old homies from the hood who were still gang- bangin' and we drove down two Chicago in a three car caravan. We used to fuck around in Chicago back in our gangsta days and although the love was still deep, we were much older and off into other shit nowadays. Them Chicago boys were wild and the only cats I knew crazier than them is them boys in California.

J.B. rode with me. I took the National down there to show off on them Chicago cats. We smoked blunts and kicked shit the whole way. It was the first time in a long time that me and J.B. got a chance to just have a man to man talk. J.B. said his lawyer wanted another thirty thousand dollars to do his trial and he just didn't have it. And on top of that, Teresha was pregnant. I felt his pain.

Once we made it to Chicago I called Capone and he led me to the destination. The homies got out and followed me and J.B. inside the house. Although Capone was like family, he wasn't in Chicago and I still didn't trust many people. We went in the basement. It was smelling good as ever, one hundred pounds of lime green cotton, as I called it.

"Cuzz, I can't wait to smoke some of this shit," J.B. said.

Rubbing his hands together and looking at the weed, he looked just like the Grinch who stole Christmas.

I loaded the weed up in two cars, the two cars that the homies drove and headed for the highway. I wouldn't dare take the chance of putting any weed in the National. That would be equivalent of walking into a police station with blood stains on your shoes. The National was canary yellow with chrome rims with a African American male behind the wheel. I would be asking them to take me to jail.

I rode back to Flint alone in the National. J.B. rode in one of the cars with the homies. My dawg would protect the goods. We took chances everyday no matter the cost. I cannot remember a time when it was on the floor and either me or J.B. did not react first and deal with the consequences later.

The ride from Chicago to Flint was three hours and thirty minutes long. Most of the ride I talked to Nisha on the phone. Nisha was home cooking me some fish and spaghetti. She thought I was still in Flint just out doing my thang. I was beginning to feel bad that I had exposed her to so much bullshit and felt that if I wanted to move on, or got caught cheating, she would definitely consider telling her story. The thought crossed my mind many times to just leave her one day and never come back but I would have to come back to see my mother. I knew she would be worried sick about me. As soon as I called her she would be calling me everything but a child of God. I was in love with Nisha for sure. I remembered all my promises to her to leave my lifestyle alone. So far those promises were nothing but empty lip confessions.

Thankfully, God was on our side because we made it back to Flint in one piece. I had the homies go over J.B.'s house to unload the weed from their cars to mine. I wasn't about to show them where I lived and taking the weed to my mother's house was not an option. I blessed the lil' homies with a pound a piece and gave J.B. twenty pounds to get his money situation together. Twenty pounds of that weed was love because we sold it for twenty-five dollars a gram. The profit was outstanding.

I promised myself that after I got my money up from this weed, I would leave the game and find something legit to do, if that was possible.

Two days later I went to court hoping everyone stuck to the script and this chapter of my life would be over with. I took my mother and Nisha with me. They were my good luck charms. To my surprise, J.B. and Teresha was in the courtroom, too. I was glad to see them both. I kicked it with J.B. while Nisha and Teresha shared giggles and hugs. J.B. being there was a kind of a assurance that his little cousins would do the right thang, and they did.

The judge dismissed my case with prejudice after a long battle of back and forth from my lawyer, the prosecutor, and the chief investigating officer. The prosecutor had a look on his face that resembled a guy on the *Maury Show* finding out that some eighteen year old child wasn't his. That was one of the happiest days of my life. Looking at my mother, I could see the relief in her face as we walked out of the courtroom.

Chapter 14

Later that night me and Nisha went over J.B.'s for the celebration. Teresha was cooking barbeque beef ribs and I was definitely in the mood for some fun. There was quite a few people over there and I didn't expect so many. The mother of J.B's little cousins was there also. She gave me a big hug and wished me luck. To me that seemed like bad luck was on the horizon. Me and J.B. smoked like never before, blunt after blunt. He seemed to be doing better financially too but I began to think about the murder still hanging over his head.

I had lost a lot of homies from the hood to the prison system but none as close as J.B. was to me. We stepped outside to get away from all the noise.

"Well homie, one down and one to go," I said.

"What are you talking about now Tra?" J.B. asked.

"I'm talking about one case gone. Now we gotta make sure yours disappear my nigga. You feel me?"

J.B. hit the blunt then looked at me. "Hell yeah my nigga. We definitely gotta knock this bullshit out the way."

Over the years I came to learn that nothing was easy as it seemed but back then I was unaware of such a thing. I thought like others that no witness meant the state didn't have a good enough case.

A few days later J.B. went to court fresh to death and high as a kite with that Kush fragrance coming off his clothes. Teresha said his lawyer told them the process would be quick and that they were only going over some motions. No sooner that Teresha had told me and Nisha the news, all hell broke loose. The judge came to the bench said something about the prosecution and then ordered J.B. to be placed in the custody of the sheriffs. It felt like a ton of bricks came down on me and the look on J.B.'s face didn't make it any better. He looked at me, smiled, then shrugged his shoulders and walked off with the sheriffs. Teresha was crying uncontrollably and all I could do was try to comfort her. I looked at Nisha and she was crying, too. At that moment I knew shit had to change. I was tired of all the bullshit and I could see the wear down in the faces of all the women in our lives.

I cannot think of anyone who has lived the life of a real street dude and is content with his conditions. A lot of the cats think they are on some real shit cause they smoke a lil' weed and probably carry a pistol every now and then but that does not make them a gangsta. Back in the day when me and J.B. first began drifting away from the gang-bangin' scene and started pursuing this money. We would go back through the hood and chill. Oftentimes we were trying to lay low and create a alibi with neighborhood people in case we got arrested.

So one day we go to the hood over one of the shorty's house and as always we just walked in. Normally there would be a house full of cats playing video games, smoking weed, and hanging out with females. But that day no one was around. So while I went through the house yelling, I see J.B. go to the refrigerator and all I could think was J.B. needs a job! I go to the bathroom and knock on the door, no one says anything. Then I tried to open the door and it's locked. I'm thinking the shorty's on some hide and seek type shit cause J.B. used to pull pranks on the homies. I kick the door in and there was one of the shorty's, pants pulled down to his ankles, stretched out in front of the toilet with a bullet in his head. I went straight into survivor mode. I started wiping fingerprints off everything I touched and got the hell outta there.

Real gangstas have seen so much pain and partook in giving so much out that it becomes exhausting for some. There are brothas who have not thought about their futures or anything like that. There are brothas who cared less if they lived or died. I was one of them.

I would not know what to do for J.B. until he or Teresha called so I sat around the house and got some things in order. The rest time was well needed. Me and Nisha painted rooms together and hung up pictures.

A couple days later Teresha finally called. She said the reason J.B. got locked up was that a old dope case that was P.F.I.'d (pending further investigation) was brought up and a warrant was issued for his arrest. I couldn't take it any longer and decided to find something to get into. Usually when I became bored that meant trouble. I rode around the city making money and smoking blunts. I felt alone. I was riding down Proctor Street and saw this pretty red bone. She was supa' thick. I initially drove pass her but something unknown to this day made me go back.

She was from out of town, her name was Pinky. I immediately thought of the porno chick but this wasn't her. I got out the car and sat on the hood of the National and continued smoking my blunt while we talked. I passed her the weed and she looked at the blunt like it was laced.

"Come on do you think I would be smoking some bullshit?" I asked her.

She responded just like I expected her to. "I don't know what you into. I don't even know you yet!"

"So you wanna change that. You can definitely find out who I am," I said. She smiled and I knew that I had her.

We made plans to hook up later that night. After we finished our second blunt I left. I felt like I had my mojo back. I hadn't messed with another female outside of Nisha except that day with Shante, but I didn't really count that.

I hit a couple more corners and ended up in the hood on Paterson. As soon as I pulled up there were police confronting a bunch of people outside a house so I drove down the street and parked. I wasn't about to let my car sit there in the midst of the camera crews and police.

When I walked down to the scene one of the females from the hood told me that the police had just chased one of the homies in the house. I could tell something was wrong because of how the police were moving. They would come out of the house, talk in a huddle and then some would go back in the house.

Apparently I wasn't the only one noticing their actions because people began yelling, "Send Marv out the house."

I could tell the shit was going to turn ugly and then the police came out with his body on a stretcher. Everybody went crazy! There were beer and wine bottles thrown at the police, bricks, and plenty of harsh words. One young homie started beating the police ass and a couple more jumped in. I started walking back to the National because I knew what was coming next and I didn't want to see J.B. that bad.

Over the years I had witnessed police kill so many black people and get away with it. I always disliked any form of law enforcement. Back in 1985 on the news, the Philadelphia police dropped a bomb on some black people who everyone called, "Move" that was one of the most brutal acts committed by the government. I had a cousin who said he wanted to be the police one day. I beat his ass the whole weekend over my grandmother's house. I was very familiar with the actions of the police and how to deal with them.

Later on I found out that twelve people went to jail behind that Marv situation. The police tried to spin the death off as a suicide.

When I made it home, Nisha had the house smelling good. Teresha was in the kitchen with her when I came in.

"What's up Tra?" Teresha said.

"Hey Teresha," I responded.

I went in the bedroom and laid on the bed. I was so high and tired I dozed off. My rest didn't last long when Nisha came in the room. When she climbed on the bed, I woke up. I am a light sleeper.

"Baby, I'm sorry I woke you up," she said.

"You straight. I was just resting my eyes," I responded lying. Every old head says that though about resting their eyes. I picked it up and was finally able to use it.

"So how has your day been?" she asked.

"To be honest, it's been long and depressing with

J.B. locked up, you know. I been by myself basically just riding around trying to find something to get into."

"So how did that go?" she asked.

I could tell that either she wanted to talk or she heard something, or maybe she was becoming jealous.

"Why, what's up?" I asked.

"Nothing, I was asking how yo' day been that's all," she responded.

I started to feel uncomfortable so I told her I was about to go shoot a move right quick and I'd be back but she stopped me.

"Tra," she said.

"What's up baby?"

"Can you drop me off over my mother's?" she asked.

I looked at her for a minute trying to figure out what was wrong with her because she started trippin'. "Yeah, you ready?" I asked.

She rolled her eyes and said, "Yeah."

As she turned to grab her coat and purse, I stopped dead. "Man sit down!" I snapped. "What the fuck is wrong with you? Before I left everything was good then I come back and now its drama. We have never dealt with no shit like this so what's poppin' Nisha? Talk to me."

Nisha sat there with tears rolling down her face. "Tra, I think I'm pregnant," she said.

"Oh," was all I could say at first. "So why you crying, you don't wanna have the baby? What's really wrong because I thought this would be a happy day for us?"

"I know," she said. "But I'm scared."

"What the fuck are you scared of?" I asked.

"I'm afraid you gone leave me raising this baby by myself," she said as tears flowed for her eyes like the Nile River.

I felt bad so I went over and wiped the tears from her eyes and kissed her passionately. "Baby, I'ma be here for you and my child. Don't worry about that," I said.

I asked her did she still want to go over to her mother's and she said no. I took off my shoes and sat on the couch with her.

"I thought you were going somewhere?" she said.

"I'll go later on," I replied.

Damn, my baby is pregnant. I knew something was wrong with her. I stayed in the house until around 9:00pm., then I made up an excuse to leave so I could go meet ole girl from earlier.

I pulled up to a red light and fired up a Newport. I could have swore I saw Shante ride pass. I immediately became so mad I decided to see was I trippin'. I put the .45 auto in the passenger seat as I trailed the car. Being aware that Shante was on some real bullshit, I stayed a couple cars behind her like they do in the movies. Once I seen the car turn down Tye's street, I knew it was her so I went up a couple streets and parked.

Shante went from sugar to shit in my eyes. I hated her for what she did, especially to Tye. I sat there puffin' on the Newport like it was weed trying to calm down. I knew now was the time to go ahead and finish the bullshit but I couldn't come to doing it. I needed J.B. now badder than ever.

After geeking myself up, I grabbed the .45 and got out the car. I made it three houses before hers

140

and when I saw her car, my stomach dropped. I couldn't do it. I turned around and walked back to the car.

It was now around 9:45pm and I was definitely late for my appointment. I needed some blunts and something to drink so I stopped at the store. I was out of bounds as far as hood territories goes. This was an old rival neighborhood, mostly bloods and vice lords were around the area.

I put the pistol in my pocket and walked in the store. There was a beautiful woman behind the counter. I winked at her and went to the beer cooler. There were some young muthafuckas standing around in the store like they worked there either legally or illegally, but I paid them no mind. I got a six pack of Budweiser and walked to the counter. One of the young cats nodded his head to me and I responded. The store clerk was really nice. When I got up close on her, I bought a fifth of Remy Martin VSOP, three packs of leaf wraps, a pack of Newport's, and a pack of Big Red chewing gum. The lil' female at the counter tried to get some conversation out of me but I was pressed for time. I would be mad as hell if I made it to ole girl's house and she was gone.

When I finally made it to her house it was about 10:30pm. One thing for certain, at least she knew what time it would be. I turned up my music to let her know I was out there. I wasn't about to blow the horn, and going up to knock on the door was absolutely out of the question. Going to a female's door or any door for that matter was a historical no-no. Me and J.B. used to get guys like that back in the day. We would have Teresha and Shante call a lame over from school and we would be inside the entrance of the door waiting on him, so I knew better.

I saw someone peek out of the window and I assumed it was her but I kept my pistol in my hand and eyes on the rearview mirror just in case. I couldn't see myself getting caught slippin'.

She came out looking good as hell. I was very impressed when she got in the car smelling good. I knew she would have some words for me.

"Damn, I thought you wasn't coming. I was just on the phone with my girls telling them we need to go out tonight," she said.

"That's my bad baby. I got caught up but you know I definitely wanted to see you again and I'm glad I came back. Baby you look good as hell," I said. She smiled. "So what's up? We going to a room or what?"

"Damn, you don't waste no time do you?" she asked.

I was turned all the way up. My game was on ten, so I shot back. "I mean, baby, I'ma give it to you straight. I'm trying to be with you tonight. I see something in you that's rare and I'm hoping to explore that."

She busted out laughing and said, "Okay Tra, you winning. And since you seem to know what it is you want, I'ma see what you talking about."

Once those words came out, in my mind, there was no use of talking anymore. I turned the music up and pulled off. When we pulled up to the Super 8 motel, I ran in to get the room. There was this cat I used to beef with on the gang-bangin' tip working at the desk. Once I saw him I just busted out laughing and he dropped his head.

"What's up Tra? Man look, I ain't with that shit no more. I got kids and shit," he said.

I said, "Jerome, it's been a long time man. I thought you were dead. I been looking for you, too."

He had a facial expression that reflected a scene out of a horror movie when the victim sees Jason staring in the window.

"Not like that man," I said. "I don't fuck with that shit no more either. I was just surprised that you weren't still trying to rep yo' shit. Anyway though, I'm trying to get a room for twenty-four hours. Matter of fact, give me something with a Jacuzzi and T.V. with cable."

Jerome said, "Damn Tra, I still see you doing yo' thang. I'm surprised you ain't locked up or dead by now."

Well, you know Jerome, it seems someone was praying for the both of us," I said.

He passed me the room key which was a card and I walked back to the car. Pinky was in the car trippin'. She had put in a R&B CD and was singing along with the music.

"Damn, you brought your own CD's and everything," I said.

She said, "This yo' CD. I got this out yo' CD case. I guess it belongs to your girl because you acting like it's not yours."

I grabbed the stuff from the store and we headed up to the room. Pinky was cold. She was five foot seven, with long dark hair and 35-25-41 measurements. I walked behind her as we walked down the hallway. Her ass was beautiful.

We got in the room and she was turned up with excitement. I was surprised at her reaction. I could tell she had been fucking with some scrub ass dudes. I put the stuff on the table, immediately pulled out the leaf wraps and rolled up two blunts. Pinky took off her shoes and walked to the bathroom. Women always go straight to the bathroom, whether it is a house or a hotel room. Maybe it's in the female handbook.

I took off my T-shirt and sat on the bed in my wife beater. I put the .45 on the side of me and fired up a blunt. Pinky came out with some boxers on and a T-shirt with her other clothes in her hand.

"Damn, I thought you were going to stay in there all night," I said.

"Shut up boy. I wasn't in there that long," she responded.

She came and sat next to me and I passed her the blunt. I saw her looking at the gun so I got up and put it on the table. I opened the Remy and poured two cups. I passed her one and turned on the television. She put the blunt in the ashtray and put her hand in my pants. She began kissing my ears and neck then she pulled off my wife beater. I was ready to get it in.

I began taking off my pants and she was quicker than me with taking off hers. I got butt naked and as I was headed for the mission, she stopped me. She put her hand on my stomach to stop me from getting in the bed. I was standing there naked, dick hard as a rock. She got on her knees and put her warm lips on my dick. (To this day she is still top five of all head doctors). I couldn't take it. I put her on the bed and got behind that big ass booty. When I saw that ass spread I said, "Damn!"

I slid in and she had some wet ass pussy and I went to work. It was super wet and tight. I tried to

145

put everything in her. Her body was beautiful. When she got on top she went up and down slow. Her titties were bouncing. They were pretty as hell. Some nice size ones in fact. I have never been a breast man but between her and Nisha, they had the most beautiful titties I've ever seen. She begged me to let her suck my dick after I busted a nut. *Damn, she nasty, too.* I tried to fire the blunt back up while she did her thang and I couldn't. She was a trooper on the dick. She sucked all the nut out of me and I was feeling weak as hell. She jumped started my dick all over again. I put her on her stomach and pounded that pussy from the back. The moans she made were so sexy. We fucked til 3:00am. I was so exhausted I finally got a chance to smoke the rest of my blunt. My beers were hot by then but I still drunk two of them.

Pinky got in the shower and I turned on the T.V. and fired up another blunt. I wondered about Nisha and began to make up a story in my head. I put the blunt out halfway and went in the shower with Pinky. I figured I might as well go all the way out since I knew Nisha would be asking questions. I washed Pinky up and bent her over the toilet. My dick could barely get hard but I made my boy perform. I didn't want to come out of that pussy. Pinky had that good-good.

I took her home around six in the morning. She put her number in my phone and told me to call her. I kissed her and she got out the car.

I put in my Bulletproof CD and drove home drinking a hot beer. It was 6:45am when I finally pulled up to the house. I parked my car in the backyard and sat there for a minute. When I got in the house, the living room lights were on. I wondered did she leave them on for me. When I went to the bedroom Nisha was sleep with the phone and a nine millimeter next to her. Once I began taking stuff out of my pocket and putting it on the dresser, Nisha woke up. I played it off like I didn't notice and went to the bathroom. After taking a leak I stood in the mirror for a minute looking for passion marks possibly left by Pinky. Females are good for that. They will have all kinds of hickeys on your body for your woman to see. I wasn't fallin' for that, not this time. I walked back in the bedroom and got in the bed.

"Baby, you just getting home?" Nisha asked sounding like she was talking in her sleep.

I said, "Yeah, I just made it home."

"Tra, will you hold me?" she asked.

I put my arms around her and we went to sleep.

Chapter 15

A couple days later, J.B. called me and I was glad to hear his voice.

"What's up my nigga? How you holdin' up?" I asked.

"Well Tra, it is what it is. This shit ain't change, the same ole story these white folks trying to take my life," J.B. said sadly.

"What's wrong? You sound sad as hell," I asked.

"Everythang. I'm in the box and I miss my visit with Teresha and I need some of the oowee," he said.

"What the fuck you doing in the box?"

He said, "Some strange ass nigga talking about he seen me out there and we did something to him and his family ten years ago. I don't even remember this muthafucka, but I beat his ass cause he was talking loud like he wanted to swing."

"Oh, that's good grounds for the hole," I said. "So how long they lay you down for?"

"Well, I been in here for two or three days now

and I supposed to do seven days so in about four or five days I should be straight," J.B. said.

"Dig, I'm give Teresha some money for yo' books and I'ma bless her with that other situation you need so badly to get you together," I said. "Oh yeah. I got this young bad muthafucka from mountain boy hood. She so cold."

"Oh yeah. What happened to Nisha?" he asked.

"Nothing, she downstairs doing something," I said.

"What happened to 'Man, J.B., I'm about to marry Nisha man. I'm tired of this shit.'?" J.B. said jokingly.

I told J.B. nothing had changed and Nisha was still in the running of being Mrs. Turner.

J.B. kept saying, "Muthafucking Tra Murda you out cold. You talked all that shit to me about these females just want to be able to say they had a gangsta. Man you crazy."

We both laughed. I believed we were laughing at the same thing but maybe J.B. was only laughing at me.

I can't lie. I was thinking about Pinky and how beautiful her body was. I had to see her again. I went over to J.B's to drop off a quarter ounce of weed and two hundred dollars for Teresha to give J.B. and things were crazy. I tried to walk in and the door was locked for the first time. So I knocked, hard. Teresha opened the door.

"What's up girl? It is 12:30pm. I know you ain't sleep," I said. Teresha was looking wore out. "Damn," I said as I walked in the house.

"What you want Tra?" she asked.

The house looked and smelled terrible. There were fast food bags on the table, sheets on the couch, and dog dodo on the floor. The curtains were shut and the house was dark. I was fucked up so I just started cleaning up. Teresha sat on the couch with the sheet and just watched me. I kinda figured she was going through a thang with J.B. locked up plus he was looking at a life sentence. Although I disagreed with how she was dealing with his situation, I understood.

After finishing what I considered J.B.'s chores, I gave Teresha the money and weed. She just looked at me. I told her I was going to feed the dogs and leave. She said okay.

Soon as I got back in the car I called Nisha and told her about Teresha and how she needs her right now. Nisha said she would be over there in twenty minutes. For me, that was a sign from heaven to go ahead and do what I needed to do. So I called Pinky.

After four rings, I heard the voice of the young lady who represented for me last night like a true G.

"Hello," she said in her cute little voice.

"What's up P?"

"Who is this?" she sounded irritated.

"This Tra. What's up? Did I catch you at a bad time?"

"Oh, what's up boy? I thought you was this nigga named Duke that keeps calling me," she said.

I started laughing. "Oh, you got it like that P?" I asked.

"Naw! I ain't never even kissed this nigga he just been on me for the past couple of days now I hate that I gave him my number," she said.

The way she was saying it was so funny I couldn't help but laugh and I can tell that by how I was enjoying myself off her situation, she began to lighten up.

"Anyway, what's up with you? I thought I wasn't gone hear from you again," she said.

"Why you say that?" I asked.

"You know how niggas is they only want…"

"Hold up." I stopped her right there. "First off baby I ain't nothing like none of the niggas you ever messed with and I want to get that straight now. I'm not pressed about no pussy or nothing. I got a woman at home that will fuck me in the courtroom if I tell her to. I'm actually feeling you and I believe you have great potential to do something."

"Potential," she said laughing.

"Yeah potential, not fully developed, qualities that…"

"Tra, I know what potential means. I'm just thrown off by you. I can't lie as of so far you have not let me down. It's like you know just the right things to say and you know how to work that thang," she said.

"What thang?" I asked.

"That dick," she said in a low tone voice.

"Oh yeah. I do what I can baby but on some other shit, what's up with you? When can I see you again?" I asked.

"Whenever you want to," she said.

"Well what you doing right now?"

"Nothing. Just laying here in my bed in my bra and panties flicking through the television," she said.

"So can I come over there?" I asked.

She said, "Yeah, if you want to."

"Stay the way you are in yo' bra and panties baby, I like my women like that."

"I'm yo' woman now," she said sarcastically.

"You are definitely working on it baby. I will be over there in about ten minutes."

I was actually riding down her street when I hung up the phone, but you can never trust these random females. I learned that the hard way. I parked in her driveway and just sat there for a minute. I then called Nisha.

"Hey baby, what's up?"

"Nothing. On my way over there," she said.

"Where, over Teresha's?" I asked.

"Yeah."

"I ain't over there. I'm out in traffic. I couldn't stand to see her like that plus I know when y'all get together it will be easier for her to feel comfortable. I mean, her seeing us together can't possibly be helpful to her. She might start feeling like the third wheel for real then and we don't need that," I said.

"You right. Well I'm here baby. I will call you when I leave, she said.

"Okay."

"I love you Tra," she said.

"I love you too," I responded.

I got out the car and hit the car alarm as I walked to the door and rang the bell.

"Who is it?" A small voice yelled from inside the house.

"Look out here and see," I yelled back.

Pinky opened the door and I walked in. She was still dressed the way I requested. I watched her ass as she walked in the kitchen.

"You have a beautiful house P," I said.

"Thank you Tra. You know Tra, you never cease to do things that make me tingle," Pinky said.

"P, what are you talking about?" I asked.

"I mean I did my homework on you and the things I heard I couldn't believe. The man that I see and hung out with last night was not the person people told me about. You are nothing like the stories. For example, you commented on my house. Don't know dudes even say beautiful no more, so I'm really wondering what's the deal? Are you this way with me or am I going to really be surprised later on," she said.

"You know Pinky, whoever tried to tell you something about me probably hasn't ever seen me nor talked to me. The way that I am with you is me every day. I'm a cool head dude for the most part. It's just the shit these cats doing is old to me. I been there years ago, you feel me?" I asked.

"Hell yeah," she said standing over the oven. "Are you hungry Tra?"

I walked over to the oven and got behind all that ass as she cooked breakfast and said, "Yeah baby. But I don't want no eggs and bacon. I'm hungry for you."

She turned around and gave me a kiss. Normally, I didn't kiss no other female besides my main chick, and the reason I kissed Pinky so freely to this day remains a mystery.

"Boy sit down let me finish cooking this shit. Are you gonna eat with me?" she insisted.

"Yeah baby, make enough for me," I said.

We sat down at the dining room table eating our breakfast at one thirty in the afternoon talking about all sorts of things. Pinky told me how she wanted to go to school to become a registered nurse and how she wanted kids. I was sitting there drinking some water when she just started giving me some head. She was looking at me in my eyes as she sucked and slobs on my dick like it was a freeze pop.

155

Then there was a knock on the door. She stopped and looked at me and her eyes got big. I grabbed my .45 off the table and sat down on the couch directly in front of the door.

"Pinky, I know you in there girl. Open the door," the male voice yelled.

Pinky put her finger over her lips telling me to be quiet. I started to say fuck that but I respected the game then the dude started trippin.'

"Alright bitch, you got that nigga in there. I'ma fuck his ride up. Gone ahead and have yo' fun. I'ma have mine on this bitch ass nigga car!" he yelled.

I told Pinky, "Look, if dawg touch my car he gone by laying in yo' front yard so I'ma tell you now, I think you probably wanna open that door and talk to him."

I am quite sure Pinky knew I was serious. She got up, opened the door and walked out on the front porch still in her panties and bra.

"Flez, you need to leave my house nigga!" I heard her yelling at that lame.

"Bitch, I knew you were in there," he said.

I got up and went to the door. He was in her face with his fist balled up like he was going to hit her.

"Bitch, I should beat yo' ass and that nigga ass," he said.

"Hey cuzz, gone somewhere with that dumb shit. I know you ain't talking about fucking with my car is you?" I said when I came outside.

He just looked at me and smacked his lips like muthafuckas did back in the day.

"Go in the house P," I said. She looked at me and walked off.

The lame said, "Bitch, you better bring yo' ass back over here!"

But Pinky continued to walk in the house. I upped the .45 and told the dude to come here. He looked at the gun and started backin' back.

"The next time I see you, I'ma kill you so be ready. The only reason you ain't bleeding right now is cause its light outside and P asked me not to murder you out here," I said.

The lame walked back to his raggedy Grand Am and pulled off. I went back in the house. Pinky was sitting on the couch looking crazy.

"Damn, where do you find these cats at?" I asked.

She shook her head and threw her hands in the air. "I don't know," she said.

"Is that yo' man or something?"

"Naw, I used to mess with him though. But that's been months ago. He would call and we'd talk on the phone but that's it," she said.

"Well you sure know how to pick 'em. That muthafucka was all the way in the way. Baby you deserve so much more. As a matter of fact, I want you to go out to Cali with me," I said.

"Cali," she said in disbelief.

"Yeah. California, Los Angeles, Compton, the West Coast. What the fuck?" I said.

"When you talking about going to Cali then Tra?" she asked.

"In two weeks. I gotta go out there and take care of some business. We gone fly out there for maybe a week or two and shoot back. By then, well in two weeks, you should have all yo' shit taken care of like who will watch yo' house and all that," I told her.

"I haven't ever been to Cali either," she said with the prettiest smile on her face.

I told her I would holler at her in a couple of days and left. I wasn't about to take a chance of having that lame, Flez, or whatever they called him, come back with some more clowns and shoot the house up with a AK or something, so I got the fuck on. I stopped at the hood store to get some blunts and Nisha called me. She was still over Teresha's so I decided to stop back over there.

"I will be there in a minute," I said.

I pulled up to one of the numerous closed elementary schools and rolled up a blunt. I didn't really need to go to Cali to conduct my business. I could just call Capone and go to Chicago like last time if I wanted to. But J.B. was gone and I figured could possibly run into something sweet out west. I decided to take the trip plus I could see what kind of woman Pinky was.

When I made it over J.B.'s, Teresha and Nisha were passing a blunt back and forth but all of a sudden Nisha didn't want to smoke anymore. She knew I didn't like her smoking unless it was with me and that was only on occasions. But because I knew the situation, I wasn't trippin.' In fact, I was happy because that meant I could enjoy my blunt.

The scenery had totally changed in the house and everything was back to normal with the exception of the pit bulls running around the house. I came in and started watching television. Then Teresha asked me about my baby's mother. I could tell the conversation affected Nisha cause she got up and went to the bathroom.

"She's straight. Just a couple of bruises," I assured Teresha.

"Tra, what did you do to Shante? She just snapped after Tye almost got killed."

"Tee, I honestly don't know. But one day, Shante tried to give me some pussy," I said.

"What!"

I turned around and Nisha was standing right there in the doorway. "So did she get what she wanted?" Nisha asked with her face tore up.

"Man you better sit down somewhere," I told Nisha.

"Why you can't answer the question Tra?" she began yelling.

I grabbed her by her arm and took her in the bathroom. When I looked at Teresha, she was shaking her head.

"You obviously got something on your mind Nisha so talk. Do not yell or I'ma put yo' head through this mirror," I said.

"Tra, you think I'm stupid. Look at you. You come over here smelling like one of these bitches out here with that stank ass perfume. Then you come home at 6:30 in the goddamn morning thinking I'm stupid," she said with tears running down her face.

I couldn't do nothing but listen. I was sick that I didn't go home to change clothes and I should have talked to Nisha that night. But how she played it, I thought we were good.

"Look, you on some bullshit man trying to find a reason to leave me or kill my baby, that's all. You know what, I'm leave before I say or do something stupid, cause you really starting to piss me off with this insecure shit," I said. Nisha stood there teary-eyed as I walked out the bathroom and then out the house.

For the next couple of days I stayed at the motel where I took Pinky. I didn't even call her or Nisha. I sat in that room eating pizza and blowing blunts. Nisha kept calling me and after the third day, I finally answered the phone.

"What's up man?" I said answering the phone.

"Hey, what's up? Why haven't you came home or been answering your phone? I have been looking for you for the past three days. I didn't know whether you were dead, locked up or what. And your mother has been worried about you," she said.

"Well, I'ma call her when we hang up. As a matter of fact, I'ma stop over her house on my way home," I said.

Nisha asked, "When will that be?"

"When will what be?" I responded.

"When will you be coming home? We need to talk?"

"Oh, I'll be there in about an hour. And you are right, we need to talk. So I'll be there in a minute."

"Okay," Nisha said sadly.

I was certain nothing I did would cause Nisha to leave me. I was not worried about her but I felt we were spending too much time together and I needed to break her from being so attached, comfortable and used to doing things. I really enjoyed that time alone in that motel. I even had that lame Jerome, bringing me packs of cigarettes and fresh tiles. But in all reality, I was ready to lay in my own bed and get some pussy.

When I pulled up to my mother's I saw the little girl from next door getting out of a Dodge Magnum. I was messed up because she was becoming a young woman, driving and shit. She saw my car pull up and waited for me to get out.

"Hi Tra," she said.

"Hey what's up? I see you riding good," I responded.

"I don't see you much no more. What, do you live with your girlfriend or something?" she asked.

The thought of her still watching me made me smile. "Naw, I live by myself," I said.

I saw her father come to the door. She obviously saw him too because she said, "Oh, I will see you around then." Then she walked in her house.

I still possessed keys to the house so when I walked in my mother yelled my name. "Tra, is that you?"

"Yeah, Mama!" I said as I walked through the living room. My mother was in the kitchen watching television. I came in and gave her a hug and kiss. Then I sat down with her.

"Boy, where the hell you been?" she asked without wasting any time. "Nisha has been looking all over for you, calling every thirty minutes. I thought something had happened to you."

It was good to see my mother. She was always a refreshing sight for me. Nisha had told her about being pregnant, our argument and my late night adventures. I knew I had to see to it that she never told my mother about petty shit like that again. My mother was excited about the child but she was beginning to question my activities and me and Nisha's relationship. I explained to her how I felt we were together too much and she told me I was being foolish.

"Boy, I ain't never heard no bullshit like that. You just wanna do what you want to. That girl loves you!" my mother said with that motherly conviction.

I told her that I was going out of town for a couple of weeks and she told me to be careful. "Travon, I'm not trying to be driving outta state to come visit nobody," she said.

"Is Nisha going with you?" she asked.

"Naw, she ain't going this time," I said.

"Well, I might ask her to come over here with me because I be needing somebody to talk to," she said.

I hugged my mother and told her I would tell Nisha what she said. On my ride home I w formulating how our conversation would go and what needed to be done to stop this new aggression in a once peaceful and loving relationship.

When I made it home and walked in the house, I expected Nisha to be right there in the living room watching television but she wasn't. When I got upstairs, she was in the bathroom curling her hair.

"What's up?" I said.

"Nothing, what's up with you?" she responded.

"Can you turn on the shower for me?" I asked her.

I sat on the bed and began taking off my clothes. The hot steam from the shower began seeping in the bedroom. It made me roll up a blunt. I reached on the side of the bed for my stash and rolled up a nice blunt. Nisha was still in the bathroom in the mirror but now she was looking at me. I looked back at her and fired up my blunt blowing the smoke in her direction. She turned her head down. I went in the steamy bathroom with her and shut the door. I stood behind her smoking and the window began to fog up including the mirror. When Nisha turned around and looked at me, I passed her the blunt. She just looked at it for a minute. She then took it and hit it about five times and passed it back. We stood there in silence passing the blunt back and forth until it was gone. I took off my boxer shorts and got in the shower.

Nisha was opening the bathroom door to leave when I said, "So you can't take a shower with me?"

Nisha pointed at her head.

"Man, you better get in this shower, let me talk to you," I said.

"Hold on," she said and walked out of the bathroom.

My mind began to wonder. She could be doing anything like getting my pistol, letting someone in my house or even boiling some grits. I didn't know.

Within a few minutes Nisha came back naked with her shower cap on. I smiled underneath a straight face. Soon as she stepped in the shower I pulled her close to me and kissed her passionately. I could feel her lips quiver as she began to cry. I lifted her up and posted her against the wall of the shower and slid in her. The hot water was hitting my back making me perform with more intensity. She wrapped her legs around me to keep me inside her. I stepped out of the shower with her still stuck to me and laid her on the floor. I pounded that pussy with each stroke. She moaned with the best of them.

I pulled out and lifted her legs in the air damn near making her feet touch her shoulders. I sucked on that pussy slow, then fast, then slow, and fast until she forced me to let her legs go. I stayed on that pussy. Nisha shook and quivered the whole time. My mustache probably looked like I had cake frosting on it. I turned Nisha over pounding that pussy from the back and she was going crazy trying to throw it back on me. We both put in work that day. She busted three good nuts and I was satisfied with my one. After getting back in the shower it was back to business. We washed each other's body, yet, still no talking. Once out of the shower I sat on the bed and put lotion on Nisha.

"Are you still mad at me," she asked. That was music to my ears. I knew once I heard that, she understood how she had fucked up big time.

"Nisha, at this point, I feel it is what it is. I can't make you understand and I can't stop you from feeling like you do. I honestly don't understand why this bullshit has surfaced but I believe it could be that we share the same space too much," I said.

"What do that supposed to mean?" she asked.

"That means by me and you being with each other every day the times that we are not, you feel I'm not with you so I'm with some other woman, I guess. But Nisha I have given you the best of me and I feel you have done the same. However, I also know that I cannot be, and will not be, disrespected by you or anyone. That shit you did over Teresha's was out of pocket and you made me feel uncomfortable. I have never thought of you in any other way than being my life line."

"But Tra…" she tried to speak.

"Nisha look, I love you to death and this past year I know has not been easy for you either. I cannot honestly say things will be different in the next six months. They got my right hand locked up for some shit he got involved in behind me so I gotta do all I can to make sure he get free. In fact next week, I'm going out to Cali to take care of some business so I don't know what's in the future," I told her.

"Tra," she said. "I have been there for you through all of this and I'm not going anywhere. But sometimes shit just does get a bit hectic. And maybe you are right about us spending so much time together. Then the other night when I woke up and you were not next to me, I began to think about all the other times you left in the middle of the night."

"Nisha, you don't have to worry about that," I said. "As long as at the end of the day I come home to you, there is no reason for you to question my commitment to you. Think about us as a whole. Look around where you at. And you got my child inside of you. There is no other woman I would rather have as the mother of my child," I told her.

Nisha began crying and I just hugged her. "Baby, we gone be straight. I promise you," I said.

Chapter 16

I spent the next week getting ducks in order. I even made the call to the homie Capone and told him I was about to fly that way in a couple of days. I wasn't about to go through the same shit as I did the last time with them young locs out there running up on my car and shit. That was crazy.

Pinky was ready, too. I had called her earlier the morning of our flight.

"Everything is packed and ready, daddy," she said. *She's calling me daddy already.*

Me and Nisha fucked like dogs that morning. She acted sad that she couldn't go but she understood it was business. I told her that my flight was leaving at 5:35pm but really it was scheduled for 2:35pm. I had to do that in case she tried to get slick and check up on me. I told her to come get my car from the airport before six o'clock. I gave her a kiss and shot out the door. I wanted to go over my daughter's mother's house before I left so I could see my daughter.

I pulled up outside the apartment and called my

baby's mother. "Hey, what's up girl? Where my daughter at?" I asked.

"She around here running around," she said.

I asked her was my baby dressed, and if so bring her outside. My B.M. seemed to change the tune of her voice once she found out I was outside. She brought my daughter out and they were dressed like twins. I got out the car and sat on the hood. My daughter ran up to me and jumped in my arms.

"Hey, what's up baby?" I asked.

"Nothing," she said.

"Have you been a good girl?" I asked.

"Yeah."

I told her that I was going out of town for a couple of weeks and I just wanted to come see her before I left. She put her head on my chest and started playing with my necklace. Most people say their kids are mama's boys or girls but my daughter was truly a daddy's girl. It made me realize how she may feel from me not coming around like I used to. I kissed my baby and told her I would be to see her as soon as I came back.

I gave my B.M five hundred dollars for my daughter and she told me to be careful. I pulled her close to me, gave her a kiss and grabbed her ass. Then her and my daughter went back in the house. My baby's mother was still one of the baddest females in the city, hands down. I always knew that whenever I wanted her she was mine.

It was 2:00pm and I was behind schedule. I called Pinky and told her I was on my way and to be ready because our flight was at 2:35pm. I was excited about the trip back to Cali. I was going now with an entirely different motive and most importantly without Nisha. I knew that if it came down to it I wouldn't have a problem leaving Pinky right there in Watts.

When I got there, Pinky's front door was opened and a car was in the driveway. I wondered for a minute was it that lame Flez again. When I got out and went to the door I could see some female sitting on the couch. I rang the doorbell and she started yelling for Pinky.

"P, somebody at the door!"

Pinky came running from the back and answered the door.

"You ready? We got like twenty minutes," I said.

"Yeah, here go one of my suitcases right here. I'm putting my hygiene products in the other one in the back," she said.

"Alright. I'm about to put this one in the car," I told her.

"Okay."

When I came back in the house the other girl said,

"So you Tra, huh? I done heard about you a lot lately. Now I finally get to see why," she said.

"I hope everything was true cause some people like telling stories on me," I replied.

171

Pinky walked up with her suitcase. "Okay, I'm ready," she said.

The other female who was called Penny said, "Damn, girl. California. I know y'all about to have fun. Why I can't never have a man to take me anywhere?" she asked.

Pinky said, "I don't know girl. I guess you don't know how to treat 'em."

"Shit, you can go if you want to. I don't give a fuck. But it's on Pinky though," I said.

"Shit, can you go girl?" Pinky asked her.

Penny looked at her and said, "Girl, I'm grown, we out! Hold up, how much is the plane ticket?"

"About four hundred dollars," I said.

She said, "Y'all go ahead. I got some money in the bank but that would take too long and all I got in my purse is a little over two hundred and ninety dollars."

"Come on, I got you," I said.

She said, "For real Tra?"

"Yeah, now come on before we miss the damn flight. It's 2:20pm and it will take us ten minutes to get to the airport." I told them.

I was speeding and shit until I remembered the damn gun under my seat. I knew that if we got pulled over, one of them girls was definitely going to have to say it was theirs. I passed Pinky a blunt and told her to fire it up.

"And you smoke weed, too?" Penny said. "You always get the good men P."

I turned the music down and said, "I don't know about her getting good men but I do know that she doesn't know how to treat a real one when he's in her face."

"Oh, I don't know Tra?" she said in a seductive voice as she put her hand down my pants.

I said, "Oh, you trying to show out in front of company? Wait til we get to Cali."

When we got to the airport, Penny and Pinky ran to the station to buy their tickets and I headed to the plane. A couple minutes later they came on the plane and Pinky sat next to me. Penny sat behind her and we were in the air.

Chapter 17

We made it to Cali in one piece. Besides, Pinky kept telling me there was some crazy looking Arabs on the plane. I was beginning to believe we were in trouble so once we got on solid ground I was straight.

I rented a 2008 Dodge Charger and we looked around Watts for a livable hotel to get for a couple of nights. It was only right that I got one at the Super 8. I got a two bed with a Jacuzzi, T.V. with cable, and a telephone. The telephone was actually useless since we all had cellphones but it was part of a package deal so I said fuck it.

When we got to the room I dropped the bags and laid on the bed. I was exhausted and even though I wanted to get at least a nap, I knew I had to shoot out to get some weed. I jumped in the car with the girls and we headed to the hood. I called the big homie, Capone and told him that I was on my way. When we pulled up, the homies were posted up as always.

Pinky and Penny saw all them niggas outside and said, "Damn, they deep out there."

I laughed because every time I came to the O.G. spot, I thought the same thang. I got out and all them niggas looked up.

Then I heard one of the shorty's say, "That's cuzz who had that bullshit weed from them Oakland slobs.

They all said, "Oh yeah, what's up loc?" and started showing me some love.

"A cuzz somebody out here for you," one of the Crips yelled. "Yo' name Tra, right cuzz?" the young Crip who brought me the weed and .45 last time said.

"Yeah, that's me cuzz," I said looking at the young homie.

Capone came to the door and said, "Come in cuzz."

I walked in the house and this time there was not only a bunch of dudes with guns, smoking weed and playing video games but this was the first time I saw some female Crips in the midst of them. They called them Cripettes.

I decided to see if I could get them to react to something I said.

"Can't stop, won't stop, can't C stop, Crip, Crip, Crip cuzz."

The whole house jumped up throwing up their C's

and even the ones on the porch was representing that big C. For some reason I always liked Crips. It probably began after I saw that movie, *Colors*. The O.G. Crip rocket was the man to me and Capone reminded me of him so much.

I bought a couple ounces from the big homie and told him I got some lil' females from the way with me.

"Oh yeah, why didn't you bring them in?" Capone said.

I just looked at him. When I came out of the house one of the Crips was in the car window talking to the ladies. When he saw me he said, "Alright loc."

The girls said they were hungry so we rode around looking for a spot to stop at. I gave them the game on how to talk out there and the neighborhood gangs.

Pinky wanted some Pizza Hut and Penny wanted some McDonald's, so we got both. I really didn't care what it was, I just wanted to get back to the hotel. We stopped at this liquor store in Watts that was ghetto as hell. I needed blunts, liquor and other small nick-nacks to take us through until the next day. I told Pinky to drive so I could chill plus I didn't feel comfortable just driving around for nothing. We had a destination and I could tell her how to get there from the passenger seat. I had the chair laid back chillin' when Penny caught my ear and began asking me questions and shit.

"So you seem to know your way around here pretty good. Are you originally from out here?" Penny asked.

I laughed. "Naw baby. I used to come out here a lot though when I was younger," I said as I looked in her eyes.

"Oh, you was a block burner huh?" Penny said.

I sat up in the car. "What you know about a block burner? Where you from?"

"I'm originally from the east side of Detroit but I moved to Flint ten years ago," she said.

"Turn right here," I told Pinky.

"Where you at on the east side?" I asked her.

"Vandyke and Harper," she said.

"Oh yeah. I fuck around over that way myself on Badger," I told her as she smiled.

"Stop lying," she said excitedly. "Who told you about Detroit?"

"Pull in right here P," I told Pinky.

We got out of the car and as I got the bags out I said to Penny, "The same people who told me about California told me about Detroit." She just looked at me. "Stick around baby you fucking with a man now. I'ma show you some things you never knew existed."

I got in the room and took off my shirt. The homie Capone knew the life I lived so he gave me a pistol this time without asking. It was a .45 auto like the last one. It became clear that the Crips must have had boxes of them. With my shirt off and this big ass .45 hanging out my pocket, Penny was just looking. Pinky was already aware of how I did shit plus muthafuckas in the city kept trying to tell her stories about me.

I sat down and started eating some pizza and Pinky asked me to get in the Jacuzzi with her. I couldn't turn her down so I ate a couple of slices of pizza, rolled up a blunt and grabbed the bottle of Remy. I headed to the Jacuzzi and all the time Penny is sitting on the bed flicking through television channels. I took off my pants and put everything on the side of the Jacuzzi including the pistol. I got in the Jacuzzi butt naked. Penny was sitting on the bed with her mouth wide open. Me and Pinky was smoking the blunt, passing the Remy when Penny walked over in a purple and white neon thong with no bra on getting in the Jacuzzi. She was thick, too. She wasn't as thick as Pinky but she was probably like 32-23-39. I was very impressed.

The Jacuzzi wasn't made for many people so Pinky straddled me and started kissing me. I knew exactly what she was doing. I laughed on the inside. So I went along with it. I passed Penny the blunt and began sucking Pinky's titties. She put her hand in the water and put my dick inside her. She gave out one of the sexiest moans I'd ever heard on video or anywhere.

"You love this dick don't you?" I said to Pinky.

She tried to talk but just ended up shaking her head yes. I saw Penny hitting the blunt looking at the facial expression on Pinky. She was looking so intently it made me look. Pinky was clinching her teeth. Every time I made love to her I tried to kill the pussy because she was so thick. I didn't want her thinking nothing other than this is the best sex I ever had. I was trying to put my nuts and everything in her.

Penny got out of the Jacuzzi naked. I guess she took of her thong when Pinky and I were going at it. I looked up at her and she just came and put her pussy on my face. I started licking that fat muthafucka all over.

Pinky stopped riding me and busted out laughing. "Okay then, let's take this to the bed."

I got straight up and started kissing Penny. I told Pinky to lay down and I bent Penny straight over in front of Pinky's pussy. She already knew what to do. She started eating Pinky's pussy. She tooted that ass up for me and I slid in that pussy like I was on ice. Her pussy was so wet and good I busted a nut after maybe five minutes. But they kept going at each other. They began to sixty-nine and I was right there drinking the Remy, smoking a cigarette and enjoying the scene.

When the fuck fest was over, we all laid in the bed together. I thought Penny would be uptight laying in the other bed watching me and Pinky fuck like animals but she proved me wrong.

The next morning I woke up around 9:30 and went into the bathroom to get myself together. I was brushing my teeth when Penny walked in the bathroom naked. I immediately got back hard. I thought it was going down early, instead she sat on the toilet and started pissing. I guess she felt like fuck it, I done saw, felt, and tasted her whole body so there was no reason to get shy now. After she grabbed some tissue and patted her pussy she said, "Tra, I wanna make some money."

"What! When we get back home?" I asked her.

"Naw, I'm talking about out here in California," she said.

My mind began clicking. "What kind of money Penny?" I asked.

"I will do whatever you tell me!" she said.

I smiled. "Look baby girl, don't tell me that cause I know a thousand ways to get it and you may not be ready for my choices."

She grabbed my hand and put it on her pussy. "Tra. I'm serious."

"Alright. We will see," I told her.

Penny walked out and I just stood there thinking about what had just happened. I had plenty of women who would bend over backwards for me but I had just met Penny and she was ready for whatever.

"You straight in here?" Pinky said peeking her head in the door.

"Yeah, I'm good baby. As a matter of fact, come on in here," I said. Pinky had on her panties and bra looking like one of them females out the men magazines.

She held her hand over her mouth and said, "Hold on daddy." She reached for her toothbrush and toothpaste.

I really thought that was sexy. She reminded me of Nisha when she did that. I began thinking about whether I should call Nisha or not.

When she finished, she washed her face. "Now, what's up daddy?"

I pulled her close and hugged her. "Baby, what's up with you?" I asked,

She gave me a shy smile. "You showed yo' ass and brought Penny right out the closet. She really fucked me up last night. But I liked it daddy. I remember saying I would never do a threesome with another female."

I told her that life is full of surprises. Sometimes we gotta take chances, especially if we are hoping to find happiness.

"You right," she said.

"Pinky, do you trust me?" I asked her.

"If you gotta ask then I guess I need to rethink my position," she said.

"Baby, I'm never gonna assume anything. I keep telling you I'm a man. I believe in being upfront and honest," I told her.

"Well since you put it that way Tra, yes, I trust you," she said looking in my eyes.

"I was just asking baby," I said as I kissed her. We walked out and Penny was sitting on the other bed.

"I just know y'all wasn't in there fucking early this morning," she said. "I gotta get myself together now." Penny walked to the bathroom and Pinky started shaking her head smiling.

Pinky said she was hungry so I told her and Penny to go get some breakfast. But Penny said she wanted to get in the shower first so Pinky went without her.

"Behave you!" Pinky said pointing at me as she walked out the door.

I was already thinking about what I would be doing while she was gone. I returned the favor and walked right in the bathroom while Penny took a shower.

"Is P gone?" she whispered."

"Yeah, she just left," I said.

"Oh, what's up then?" Penny asked.

"Step out the shower right quick," I told her. "I thought about what you said and I don't believe you ready."

"What do I gotta do to become a part of your life?" she asked.

"You say you want some money well tonight we gone go out and get some. So let me know, are you down or what right now."

"I'm down with you," she said.

I walked out the bathroom and she got back in the shower. My first thought was to get some more of that pussy but I knew I had to show some restraint and let her see I'm far from a chili dick ass nigga out here.

Later on that day I left the girls at the room and shot to Capone's spot. I told the O.G. about Penny's money getting ambitions and like a true big homie he told me my options to choose from. I knew whatever I decided to do, I had to be smooth about it. But the shit was weighing heavy on me because I knew how important the opportunity was.

When I made it back to the room, the girls were talking about going to the mall because Penny didn't bring any clothes. I went with them. The mall in Watts was decent. But I learned after going to the Mall of America in Minneapolis, with my baby's mama back in the day, I compared every mall to that and there was no comparison.

While we were walking through the mall I began to wonder how could Penny afford to buy any real outfits when she only had one hundred and ninety left of her money cause I gave her three hundred to get a plane ticket. But I said fuck it. I really didn't care either way.

We went in several stores and we stopped at a store called, *Top Flight* where they had all the top of the line designers from Red Monkey jeans to True Religion. I had no intention of spending any money but I couldn't resist this pair of True Religion jeans. They were jet black with a blue and black True Religion shirt. It hit me for a couple dollars and as I look back that was too much for two pieces of clothing.

Penny stopped in some ladies' stores and bought four sun dresses. They were relatively cheap, maybe thirty dollars apiece. She stole some panties and bras out of Victoria Secret. I was looking at her walk out of that store. *Fuck Victoria, you gotta secret that only if they knew, yo' ass would be going to jail.* Pinky bought some lingerie a red laced thong and panty set that she said was for me.

On our ride back to the room we all laughed at Penny's larceny adventure. I was beginning to see that she was a real east side Detroit girl at heart. My phone rang and it was Nisha. I looked at it and pushed the ignore button. I definitely wouldn't try trusting them females with being quiet while I talked to her. I had to call Nisha anyway to have her wire this money to Capone, but I could wait til I got to the room for that.

I noticed that I spent close to two thousand dollars in only a couple days and now was the time to make some cash.

Me and Pinky took a shower together and all three of us sat back watching television, calling home and getting fucked up. I stepped in the bathroom and called Nisha. After three rings she finally picked up.

"Hey baby, I've been waiting for you to call," Nisha said.

"Yeah, I see you called me earlier. I missed your call and wanted to make sure I call to let you know I love you," I said.

"I love you too, baby." She sounded so sweet.

"Look, I'ma need you to go downstairs and get twenty racks and wire it to the homie out here. You remember the name I gave you?" I asked.

"Yeah, I got it in my purse. I gotta find it but I will do it first thing in the morning," she said.

"Take care of that for me," I told her.

"I will," she said. "So how is everything going out there?" she asked.

"Everything is cool. I'm just trying to get shit right. I was thinking about buying you something nice while I was out here but I don't know if you deserve it how you been acting."

Nisha got heated. "What do you mean you don't know if I deserve it? Tra, don't start now!"

I saw where the conversation could end up going and I had other shit on my mind. I told her I would call her back.

"I know!" she said hanging up the phone.

Me and Nisha was bumping heads like never before. I didn't understand why either. The only thing that was stopping me from correcting us once and for all was I knew she was a rider and she knew too much of my business. Plus, I loved her for real.

"Hey Tra!" Penny was yelling for me in the living room.

"What's up?" I said as I stepped out of the bathroom.

"I need you to take me somewhere."

"Why you didn't ask Pinky?" I asked sounding like I didn't want to do it.

"I did," she said. "But she talking about she not going nowhere."

"Alright," I said. "You ready cause I'm tired. I'm ready to come back and finish watching T.V. I'm waiting on a phone call."

I grabbed my shirt and walked out the door leaving it opened. Penny came out shortly after that. I sat in the car flicking through the California radio stations. Penny sat down in the car and put her hand on mine.

"I'm ready Tra," she said.

I started up the car and just started driving. "Where are you going Penny?" I asked.

"I'm hoping you ready now. I hollered at you early what's up? I'm trying to get this money."

"Okay," I said. "You wanna get this money, fuck it. Let's do it."

Capone told me about this club like spot where the female Cripettes went to turn tricks when they were putting money together to buy work. Capone said the girls were making anywhere from fifty to five hundred dollars a pop. It depends all on the john and the woman. So I put Penny up on game how these were lawyer and doctor type muthafuckas. Mostly white boys who just got off work all she had to do was sit there and see what happens.

When I first said it she said, "Tra, how did I know you would be on some shit like this?"

I kept my eyes on the road. "Look, we gone get this money but I gotta make sure you just ain't talking. As bad as I want to keep that pussy for myself, you think I wanna let you do this?"

"Well stop at a store so I can get some condoms and some liquor."

She was down. "Now that's what's up," I said.

We pulled up to this hood ass store with graffiti on the side of it. There was a couple of cats standing outside. I guess they were hustling. This neighborhood was grimy looking so I put the .45 on my lap and told Penny to go ahead in the store and I would wait right there. I gave her five dollars to get me a pack of Newport's and she went in.

I'm sitting in the car listening to the radio when I looked at one of the cats outside the store and he threw up some gang sign. At first I paid it no attention until he came out of the shadows and stood in front of the car and did it again. Penny was coming outta the store when he walked up to her and before he knew it, I was out the car busting. I let off two shots at his manz. I wasn't trying to hit him. I was just trying to make him get the fuck on which he did. The clown muthafucka ran also but he was busting back.

Penny was screaming like crazy. The dude got behind a van and kept shooting. I was ducked off beside the Charger as Penny got in the back of me. I began counting the clown's shots. I saw the pistol. It looked like a nine millimeter or .380 auto. I figured he shot already nine times. He either had four, six or eight shots left. I had the nine shot .45 and I knew to walk my shots down from past shoot outs.

Eleven, twelve, thirteen…click. I heard his gun empty and I got on his ass. I ran around the car and he was sitting there fumbling with the clip of his gun. I assume he was trying to reload it.

"Get in the car P!" I yelled to Penny.

This clown had his hands up in front of his face in a position to where, I guess, he thought they would shield him from the bullets. He kept saying he thought I was someone else. He started crawling backwards and I let off four shots. I walked back to the car not knowing whether he was dead or not but all my shots were face and body. I assumed if he was not dead, he wished he was.

When I got in the car Penny was smoking a cigarette. She remained calm and didn't mention the situation. I told her we would have to see what's up on that money situation tomorrow.

She said, "I understand. I think that's what's best right now."

Penny was one of the downiest chicks I had ran across in over ten years. I made a detour from the hotel and stopped at the parking ramp.

"Where we going now?" Penny asked.

"Just sit back and ride P. I need to holler at you." I went about three floors up and backed the car in.

"What's up?" Penny said.

"I know that Pinky probably back at the room waiting on us. I really wanted to talk to you. It's been a minute since I ran across a woman like you. I can tell you've had some cats who had a lil' game about themselves but they didn't know what to do with you," I explained. Penny was sitting next to me smiling rolling up a blunt.

"I want you to be a part of the family I'm building. You know the kinda guy I am. I want you to always have a man that you can depend on, the same way I can expect to have a woman I can depend on. Pinky knows I have a woman at home and you should, too. There's no question about it, she's number one in my life but that does not mean I will neglect you in any manner. I'ma take care of you and I gotta have you do the same for me. So what you want to do," I asked Penny.

Tra, to be honest, I had every intention on stealing you away from Pinky. She's my girl and everything but once I started feeling you out, I thought to myself, I gotta have him," she said looking at me in my eyes. She was blushing like crazy. "Tra, I'm feeling everything about you. You got me baby forever. Whatever you want, whatever you need, you let me know."

I shook my head and started up the car. Penny cut off the engine. I looked at her.

"I wanna give you some pussy right now," she said.

I started laughing. "Man, you wild as hell. We gotta get back to the room," I said starting up the car.

I didn't get down the street good before she had her hand down my pants jacking me off. I pulled up to a stop light and just looked at her. She was into it. Then she unbuttoned my pants and pulled it out. She was stroking my shit slow and it was killing me. I was so thrown off I didn't realize the light had changed. The car behind me blowed the horn. I tried to get her to fire up a cigarette for me because I knew she had to stop but she told me no!

When I got to the next light she started giving me head. My head went back as I started squirming in the seat. I pulled over on a side street and she was still putting in work. The pressure was killing me. I kept telling her to stop but I really didn't want her to. I was so glad when I started cumming cause if I stayed in that position, I would have fucked her right there in the car. Penny sucked and sucked my dick swallowing the cum. After she was done she put my mans back in my pants, button my pants back up, and then sat there like nothing happened with a silly smirk on her face.

I could only imagine what was going through Pinky's mind. I'm sure she knew something probably happened between us. What I found out later was she didn't care.

Chapter 18

Two days before she was scheduled to leave, I took the girls over to Capone's after much thought. At first they refused to come in the house because of all the homies and home girls standing out front. Finally one of the Cripettes talked them into coming in the house. This Cripette was beautiful. I was surprised to find such a good looking young lady involved in gang-bangin'. In Michigan we banged just because, while in California it was a lifestyle from birth and many had no choice.

I was laughing like crazy when the girls finally came in. I was sitting on the couch hollering at Capone when they walked in looking all scary and shit. They stood there right beside me and would not move. They wouldn't smoke any weed or anything.

Capone tapped me and asked, "What's up with them loc?"

"They just shocked cuzz. Its fifty muthafuckas in this lil' ass house," I said.

Finally Capone came up with a situation. He got up and let them sit down next to me. They were a little relaxed then. I told them numerous times to lighten up. They began to once I passed them some cans of beer and the blunt a couple of times. They started talking to Capone and even a couple of the homies. I could tell the homies were trippin' off of them. A couple of the Cripettes were a bit jealous because Pinky and Penny were getting all of the attention.

Capone asked me which one is talking about she's ready to get this money. When I pointed to Pinky he said, "Oh yeah loc, she cold too cuzz, I wouldn't mess that up?"

"Hey girl, you wanna be a Crip?" Capone asked Penny.

"Naw, I'm straight," she said.

I told Capone to chill out. Laughing he said, "You know I'm just bullshitting cuzz but I had to try."

We chilled with the homies for a couple of hours then I took the girls out to eat. These weren't no cheap girls. I spent some money that night. We laughed about how scared they were at Capone's house and then I broke the news to both of them like a straight G.

"Dig ladies, I'ma be straight with both of y'all. I'm feeling y'all like crazy but I don't know if you can understand and accept the position you are in. Both of you are beautiful women with a lot of potential. When I see you I can't lie, I see that diamond in the rough that other's notice but don't know what to do with."

Pinky and Penny sat there like school girls anxiously waiting for their homework.

"I been out here in this game for a minute. I done did a lot of wrong, and a lot of right. But at this moment I see two beautiful queens that I honor, love and respect to the fullest. I want both of you to become a part of my family."

"What family?" Pinky asked.

"Bitch if you shut the fuck up and listen you will see what family I'm talking about," I said.

I could see the expression on her face that she knew I was serious. I had never called her a bitch but Capone told me when you talk to females that way they either love you or hate you. If she hates you she will get up and leave but if she loves your dirty boxer shorts, she won't move. You got her then.

With that in mind I kept going. "The family consists of a few muthafuckas that understand the importance of loyalty, love and unity. No one in the family goes a day without the shit they need. We all moving out in the spirit of progress and I'm the head muthafucking honcho. I gotta know what its gonna be tonight before we can move forward. You fucking with a man now. I'm not one of them lil' niggas driving Escorts and messed up Grand Ams. It's all on y'all to tell me what you wanna do. If you ain't ready, I won't be mad. I can put you on a flight back to Flint tonight. But say yes, and I'ma change yo' life. I promise," I told them.

I went back to eating my food. The girls sat there for a minute, then like a echo, they both said they wanted to be a part of the family. I was going hard.

I knew that if I wanted to create something it had to start at that very moment. For years, the only family was my immediate, J.B. and Teresha but his was the beginning of a new day.

There was no time to waste so I began the job of putting together something to see if these girls could move under my pressure. I was going to give them their first assignment.

The next day J.B. called me on the three-way with Teresha. It had been almost two weeks since the last time I talked to my right hand man. I hoped for the best.

"What' up boy?" I said.

"You man. You always doing the fun shit when I'm not around. You all out in California and shit," he said.

"Yeah, I'm out here fucking with the O.G. Capone with his crazy ass. Just trying to get shit together."

"Well we gone have to shoot back out there real soon cause I'ma need to holler at the homie," J.B. said.

"No doubt," I said. "He keep asking about you, too. He just remember the young crazy nigga I came out west with." We both laughed at those words because back in the day when the big homie would say, "Hey y'all, it's time to go out west." I knew J.B. would get a laugh out of that one.

"Yeah though my nigga, I should be out next week. The judge said he would throw my case out next week if these people don't come up with some witnesses," J.B. said.

"Hell yeah!" I yelled. "I can't wait either. Do you remember the last time we talked I was telling you about that new toy I got? Well, I got me another one. This bitch out cold, too. I been fucking with it every since I got it."

J.B. was dying laughing. He was laughing so hard he put the phone down. Teresha kept saying, "Damn, it can't be that funny."

The shit had me laughing hearing him enjoying himself. All of the time Pinky and Penny sitting next to me watching television floating a blunt.

"Hey, which one of y'all going to get us some food today?" I asked them.

"Tra, who you talking to?" Teresha asked.

"Oh, one of the homies," I said quick.

"Yeah though, by the time you come back to the city, I will be going to court a couple days after that," J.B. said.

"You know I will be there my nigga," I told him.

"Well I'll see you then my nigga. Be safe out there, one," J.B. said as he hung up the phone.

By the time I hung up, Pinky talked Penny into going to get some food. I really didn't care who went as long as we were preparing to eat sometime in the next twenty minutes. I assumed Pinky wanted to talk to me and that's why she didn't go get the food. She was my number two girl and Nisha was number one.

"So what's up P?" I asked.

"Nothing just chillin', thinking about some things, that's all," she said.

"What happened to that lingerie you bought that day you claimed was for me?"

"I still got it," she said with a smile.

"So I guess I'm not going to get to see you in that huh?" I asked.

"Yeah, you know you can see me anyway you want to. I told you I bought that for you. We just been chillin' and you been ripping and running. So I planned to pull it out at the right time," she said.

"Oh, don't let me interrupt your plans then baby. Matter of fact, come here," I told her.

She came closer and I tongue kissed her. Then I put my hand down her pants. Her pussy was soaking wet. It made me wonder how her shit got that wet so quick. It was like she was sitting there all that time thinking about some freaky shit or something.

I told her to take off them pants and she was smiling so hard and looking so pretty that I began to get excited. She had on some yellow and white striped panties with hearts on them. I laughed when I saw them.

She said, "Don't be laughing at my panties," in a sexy girly voice.

I kissed her passionately and slid her panties down slow. I guess the anticipation was doing its job cause she pulled them down all the way by herself.

I just laid my head on her pussy. She had to be fucked up because I wasn't doing anything but laying there.

"Come on Tra. Quit playing games," she begged.

I hadn't fucked either of them since that first day. Penny gave me some head but that was it. I knew that if I had fucked one, I would have to fuck the other as well. I started kissing on her thighs, then her titties, then her neck and ears.

Pinky continued to beg, "Please Tra, come on before Penny comes back. I don't want to share you right now."

So I started sucking on that pussy and she was gone. I opened her pussy lips and licked around the rim of those pretty muthafuckas. Then I sucked and licked gently on her clit. She grabbed my head.

"Let my head go," I said.

She busted out laughing. "Baby, that shit feels so good. You ain't playing no games," she said.

When she let my head go I freaked her all the way down. I flipped her over and kissed her ass cheeks then slid down the crack of her ass with my tongue. When I got to her ass hole I licked around the rim of it and blew softly. Her body started shaking and I could see chill bumps on her booty. I pulled of my clothes and got behind all that ass. Her pussy was so wet, she grabbed both pillows. I started pounding that pussy like crazy cause I knew it would be busting soon. The pussy was just so good and wet. Then Penny walked in.

I turned and looked at the door, there was Penny standing there smiling with two bags of Long Jon Silvers. Me and Pinky are but naked on the bed and I'm hitting that muthafucka doggy-style. So I just kept going.

Penny stood there like a big baby talking about, "Why y'all didn't wait for me?"

"Come on baby. I got you," I said.

She put the food on the table and stripped off her clothes like she was in a house fire or something. I told her to sit on me and Pinky could ride my face but Pinky said she was straight.

"I done busted me two or three good ass nuts, y'all go ahead," Pinky said getting off the bed, that big ass booty shaking with every step she took.

She went to the table and started pulling out food eating. I made it up in my mind that I'm about to fuck Penny so good that Pinky gone wish she didn't leave.

"So you just gone get up like that?" I asked a full mouth Pinky as she sat there smiling. "That's alright. Come on Penny."

I grabbed Penny by the hand, took her in the bathroom and shut the door. I posted her up against the bathroom wall and slid my dick in her. She wrapped her legs around my waist and her arms around my head. I was digging deep in that pussy, laid her on the floor and spread her legs. I slow stroked her then sped up, then slow, then fast, when she came it was chunky white. I got down in her and started sucking her pussy while fingering at the same time. She started beating on the floor of the bathroom. Then she lifted my head up and told me to sit on the toilet. When I sat down, she rode me reverse, cowgirl. I was trying to put a dent in her pussy. Pinky started knocking on the door.

"Are y'all done yet? I need to use the bathroom!" she yelled.

"Naw, we ain't done yet, hold up," Penny mumbled back.

I told Penny, "Alright, let's go in the front room so she can use the bathroom. I grabbed Penny by the hand and took her back in the front room passed Pinky. I was trying to teach her a lesson and as bad as I wanted to cum, I didn't. I put Penny on the bed doggy-style. I looked back and there was Pinky. "I thought you had to use the bathroom," I asked her.

"Naw, I just wanted y'all to come out of there," she said.

"Well, now we back out here and we still ain't done so…"

I crawled up behind Penny slow and teased her with the dick for a minute. I flicked the tip of my dick between her pussy lips. Her shit was so wet it looked like I had Vaseline on my dick. Finally I put the whole thang back in her. We were fucking like crazy. I looked up and Pinky was climbing on the bed trying to kiss me. Then I busted a nut.

Penny was so much of a souljah and so freaky. She told Pinky to "watch out" while she sat there and sucked all the nut outta me. I was drained and too tired to even eat.

I woke up a couple of hours later hungry as hell. I tried to eat some of the Long John Silvers but it didn't taste as good cold. I really wish I had a microwave. I jumped in the car taking both girls with me. I had to get something to eat. I pulled up to this lil' moms and pops soul food spot to see what they were working with.

When we walked in they had pictures of old freedom fighters all over the wall. They had Malcom X, Martin Luther King Jr., Booker T. Washington, and numerous others. There was music playing and it gave the place that old southern feeling. I went down south with J.B. five years ago for a family reunion and the vibe was the same as this restaurant. I'd always loved to hear and read history, especially concerning my people. The restaurant's menu was straight, too. They had the typical things like ribs, chicken, coleslaw, spaghetti, collard and mustard greens. After a few minutes, a older black woman came to the counter.

"Hey baby. Can I help y'all?" she asked.

"Can you give us a minute please," I responded.

"Y'all take as much time as you need," she said sounding country as hell. Finally the girls were ready.

"Miss, we ready!" I yelled.

I got three fried chicken breast, mac and cheese, fried green tomatoes and some collard greens. Pinky got five fried chicken wings, mac and cheese, and a slice of apple pie. Penny got five fried chicken wings, some collard greens with hot sauce and apiece of peach cobbler. I guess the food was smelling so good, Penny kept looking at the menu.

"Ain't no use in you looking up there. It's a done deal," I told Penny.

"Oh, I'm just looking. They got chitterlings, turkey, roast, and ham. This is a real soul food restaurant.

I said, "Yo' lil' ass can eat."

The lady brought the food out and we left. Pinky offered to drive and that was cool because I wanted to eat. While she drove, I started digging into my food. I told Pinky to stop over Capone's house on the way to the room.

I called Capone and when he picked up the phone it was noisy. I told him I was on my way over there for that then I hung up. I bought two birds of heroin for the low-low but the trick was I didn't have a way to get them back. I figured now was the perfect time to see was my ladies' ready.

Pinky parked in front of Capone's house. In Watts, in the Crip neighborhoods, they knocked out all the street lights so it was dark as hell. The girls were trippin' because all you could see was white tennis shoes on the porch. All you could hear was dice clicking and the words, chip cuzz, cu cuzz, and loc.

Then one of the young locs came to the car and handed me the work. I passed it to Penny in the backseat and told Pinky to take us to the room.

I was trying to figure out how I could ensure that the girls got back to Flint safe with the dope. I knew that the bus or Amtrack but then the police frequently brought dogs aboard them. I wasn't going to believe they got caught unless they were locked up and I didn't want to risk that. I decided to sleep on the idea and the next day spring it on them.

I woke up the next day determined to come up with something cause we were leaving in the morning. Capone blessed me with a deal I couldn't refuse. He gave me two bricks of heroin for $125,000. I didn't have to pay him up front, money was on my mind. One thing about them gang-bangin' ass niggas in Cali, they had plugs on plenty of drugs. I was always amazed at how they managed to gang bang and get a couple of dollars at the same time. But the only ones with the real money was the O.G.'s. They had put in enough work and now they just sat back and watched the young homies. I decided to strap a brick on each girl then place a girdle on them.

As I was telling them the news, the phone rang. It was Nisha. I looked at the number and kept talking. I then pushed the ignore button. Minutes later, Nisha called back. I knew it had to be something serious so I picked up the phone and walked in the bathroom.

"What's up?" I said answering the phone.

"Hey, I tried to call you," Nisha said.

"Yeah I know. I saw your number. I'm in the middle of something, what's up?" I said.

"Well, Teresha just called me and told me to let you know that J.B. said he needs you to come home today," Nisha said.

"But I leave tomorrow. He must have forgot," I told her.

"Naw baby, I believe he does know. I think you should call Teresha. I think it's something important from how Teresha was saying it."

"Well I will call her," I said and hung up.

Something was telling me it was some bullshit in the game but I called Teresha anyway. After a couple of rings she finally picked up.

"Hello."

"What's up though Teresha?" I asked.

"Hey Tra, you must have talked to Nisha," she said.

"Yeah I did what's up with J.B?" I asked.

She said, "J.B. said the two witnesses are supposed to come to court in three days and he said you know how to get in contact with them."

"Oh yeah, I do. Tell the homie I'm leaving today.

I will be there tonight."

"Okay," she said and hung up the phone.

I walked back in the living room sick. My facial expression must have been apparent because Penny asked me was I alright.

"Yeah, I'm straight," I said.

"Who was that baby? Not trying to be in yo' business but your whole demeanor changed," she said.

"We gotta leave today. I got some shit on the floor and the family needs me. So start packing y'all shit. Pinky, baby I need you to go to the store and buy two girdles. You gotta get a size that fits tight so the work is hidden good," I told her.

"Okay daddy," she said.

"Penny, I need you to get the phone book, call the airport and book a flight for three to Flint."

"Alright," she said.

I sat back and began contemplating the situation waiting in Flint. I thought those witnesses had lost their memories but I guess the police forced them to find it. I jumped up and started packing. I had food and shit everywhere. When I saw the blunt wraps I stopped dead in my tracks and started rolling a blunt. I walked around the house smoking the blunt while throwing shit in the suitcase. There was so much I had to do. I called Capone and told him that J.B. needed me and I was leaving in an hour but I would stop by and drop of the pistol he gave me. Capone understood how we lived cause once upon a time, we did the shit for him.

"Oh yeah, I went and got that situation yo' lady sent from yo' city," he said.

"No doubt. These hoes gone take care of business that's for sure," I said.

He started laughing. "So when you think you gone make it back to Chicago for that one situation?"

"I think we might have to let folks take the trip this time and I will cover their traveling upon arrival, you feel me?" I told Capone.

"Yeah, just hit me up when you ready for them to come on down," the big homie said.

"I'll see you in about thirty minutes big homie," I told him and hung up the phone.

Pinky walked in with the girdles and I told the girls to take their shirts off. Pinky didn't even had on a bra.

"Come on baby you gotta put a bra on," I said. She let out a giggle.

I strapped one of the bricks on Penny and luckily there was some electric tape in a dresser drawer in the hotel or we would be using shoestrings. She slid the girdle on and I told her to turn around so I can see how it looked. She was ready.

I did the same thing to Pinky. Her titties sat on top of the girdle so pretty in her little designer bra.

Both girls said they were comfortable and everything was straight. They could walk normally without any problems. They got the rest of their shit and we jumped in the ride headed to Capone's.

I told Pinky don't be speeding cause we were too dirty, two bricks of heroin and a pistol that had probably a dozen blood members bodies on it. We got to Capone's and I hollered to one of the Crips to come here. It just so happened to be the one who tried to holler at the girls. I told him to give the O.G. the pistol and tell him I will holler in a few days. He grabbed the gun and ran in the house. I told Pinky to head to the airport.

Chapter 19

As we walked through the airport there were so many police everywhere. I was seeing the tension on both of the girls faces.

"Hold up," Pinky said. I stopped and turned around. "Hold on, let me sit down for a minute."

"Aw shit," I said.

"Come on girl. We finna do this," Penny said.

I looked at Penny and she looked just like a girl scout. It tickled me to see how tough she tried to be but I was happy. I told them to just walk through the metal detectors normal and act like they don't have anything. They'll make it.

I had watched enough U.S. Customs reality shows to see how people were getting caught to recognize it was facial expressions and intimidation that usually caused the police to suspect you of anything. I shared my game with the women and it made them relax. We made it passed.

Once we got on board Pinky sat next to me so excited she squeezed my hand hard as she could and just kept kissing me. All I could say was, "I told you."

The stewards on the plane was making rounds every five minutes it seemed like. I looked a couple rows up and saw why. There were two Arab women with their religious attire on arguing with each other in Arabic.

"What the fuck is wrong with them bitches up there?" Penny asked from behind me. I just shook my head.

For some strange reason when I was on the plane with them I was straight. The only fear I had was getting caught with the heroin. The women must have been my nerve angels.

The plane glided into the Bishop Airport like a paper airplane being thrown in a classroom full of sugared up children. I was glad to be home. Usually, I would have Nisha or my mother to come and pick me up but today was a different story. I had the girls with me and it would be a bunch of nonsense if they saw these girls.

Now Pinky was bad. She was five feet nine, one hundred fifty pounds with 32-34-40 measurements. She had brown skin and long hair. Penny was five feet five. She had a Halle Berry haircut with a banging body. These women were the center of attention everywhere I took them. I called a cab and we all went over Pinky's house.

When we pulled up, Penny's car sat in the driveway with a broken window. She flipped out.

"What the fuck?" she yelled as we pulled up in the cab.

Before the cab could stop, she jumped out and ran up to her car. Penny dropped everything on the ground and started crying.

"I betcha that lame Flez did this shit. He probably thought this was Tra's car," Pinky said.

Penny had an '85 Cutlass with some twenty-two inch rims on it. *She was lucky no one stole it.*

"These lames y'all be fuckin' wit be trying to get killed around here," I told them.

I grabbed Penny and hugged her. I whispered in her ear, "I got you."

It was hot as hell in Pinky's house. I started turning on the fans, opening up doors and everything.

Penny said, "Come on boy and take this stuff off of me."

"Take yo' clothes off," I said.

"You mean my shirt?" she said smiling.

When she pulled off her shirt the girdle was good but the tape was on its last string and the brick was about to fall. I was lucky and so was Penny.

Pinky walked into the living room butt naked with nothing on but the brick and the electric tape. I started smiling.

"Damn, that's when you know its hot in here," I commented.

"Hell yeah. Plus I wanna just take a nice, hot bath," she said.

I took the work off Pinky and watched her walk to a room in the back. Her ass was talking to me with every step.

"Tra, do you want me to drop you off?" Penny asked.

"Yeah, I do," I said.

We walked out the house and stopped. We both looked at the big ass whole in the front window and when I saw that, I changed my mind.

"Naw P. I can't chance that one. The police may want to pull you over just to ask about the window and my house is too far from here," I said. I told her to holler at me later on. "I got something for you."

"Oh yeah, I forgot about the window til now. Alright," she replied.

I started walking to the store with my suitcases in hand. I was trippin'. I looked at the suitcases and turned around. I called Pinky and she came back to open the door. She was still naked. I guess she jumped out of the water cause she was drippin' wet. I just stood there.

Pinky laughed. "Boy, come on in and shut the door."

I wanted to fuck her so bad but I knew that business was on the floor, all around the board. I called another cab. I walked in the bathroom where

Pinky was and sat down on the toilet seat cushion. She was washing up looking so pretty. I told her I had a couple of minutes so I began washing her up.

"Tra, I have never met a man like you. You a straight up killa but then you are also so romantic and generous," she said.

"I'm just being me, baby and when it comes to you, you are someone who deserves so much. I just wanna be the best I can be for you," I told her.

After around ten minutes, I heard a car horn. I got up to see was it the cab and it was. I opened the front door and told him to give me one minute. I went back in the bathroom and kissed Pinky. I told her I would see her later on that night.

"I love you," Pinky said.

I was ready to lay in my own bed and most of all I was ready to see Nisha. Despite all the wrong I did in the streets, Nisha was my rock. Our recent disputes could not sway my love for her. She was definitely number one. Before reaching the house I called her.

"Hello," she said sounding like she had an attitude.

"What's up?" I said.

"Nothing, where you at?" she asked sounding concerned.

"I'm in Cali where I been at. Why, what's up?" I asked her.

"I thought you were supposed to be coming home today, that's all. I got all dressed up and cooked hoping you would be here," she said.

"Damn baby. I wish I could have made it. Teresha and J.B. gone have to understand. I'm trying to get this money. I got a baby on the way."

She said, "But Tra, you got money already."

"You can never have enough sweetheart," I shot back.

"Aw man. This is fucked up." Nisha started sounding like a spoiled kid who was looking forward to going to the candy store.

"Hold on baby," I told her and put the phone down. "Turn right here mister. It's that white house with the armor guard on it, right there," I said to the cab driver as we approached the house.

I gave him twenty dollars even though the meter was only at thirteen dollars. I really was just happy to be coming home to see my baby.

"Yeah though, I'm back," I said picking up the phone. "I miss you though baby and I wish I could come home. Do you know what I would do to you if I was there?" I said as I walked up on the porch.

"Man Tra, I need you inside me so bad and you ain't even coming home today. You sure there ain't no other planes leaving out tonight?" she asked.

"Nope," I said sadly. I opened up the door and looked around. She wasn't downstairs.

"What are you doing?" she asked.

"Shit, I'm laid up at this hotel smoking a blunt, watching television thinking about you," I told her as I approached the bedroom.

"You could be home watching television with me. I sitting here looking like Teresha was before you left."

I stood in the doorway of our bedroom looking at Nisha laying on the bed with some red Monkey jeans on and a white t-shirt with my necklace on. Her ass was sitting up like a Charger on twenty-six inch rims.

"You ain't looking shit like Teresha was," I said.

Nisha jumped up screaming and ran to me. I dropped my bags as she jumped in my arms.

"You play too much boy. I missed you so much," she said. She kissed me with so much intensity that all I could do was tell her I love her.

The thing that distinguishes Nisha from Pinky, Penny and even my baby's mama was she

217

possessed a wifey quality and ability to bring her home to mama and feel content with her in my mother's presence. Now Pinky, from the little time we spent together was okay but I had not known her long enough to say for sure. I was determined to make Pinky a part of the family with Nisha being aware of it, and cool with it. I just didn't know how.

"So where's this food you cooked baby?" I asked.

"I wasn't lying Tra. It's downstairs. Go wash your hands and I will fix you a plate," she said.

I brought my bags in the room and grabbed my two bricks of heroin and put them in the basement. I was excited. I knew the money I could make was at least a good three hundred thousand dollars and with that I could lay back and start some kind of business. I always wanted to have a hair salon where there was nothing but beautiful black women who braided hair all day. I would also send Nisha back to school or something. I was planning big.

I came back upstairs to the dining room and Nisha had the candles lit with the music playing. She had Luther doing his thang and she was in the kitchen fixing my plate when I came in to wash my hands.

"You still have not washed yo' hands?" she asked.

I went back in the dining room and sat at the table. It resembled those dinner tables shown in pictures of ancient Rome where the king and queen sat in those huge chairs. That was probably the second time I sat at the table since buying it because me and Nisha usually ate upstairs in the bedroom. Nisha brought my food into me and I was speechless. She actually cooked a full course meal, steak, mashed potatoes, green beans and mac and cheese. I was impressed.

Nisha hadn't cooked like this since the days at my mother's house. I wondered did my mother have anything to do with it. We sat at the table and talked about the trip and the time she spent with my mother. Nisha was excited about the baby all of the sudden. She said that she began thinking of names and I knew she was in a different place mentally. I had to let her know though I'm picking the child's name. She looked at me at first, then she said, "Okay, you can name it."

I said, "Cause my baby gone have a Afrikan name."

"Afrikan," she repeated the word like she didn't hear me.

"Yeah Afrikan. Oh yeah baby, I went to this soul food restaurant with Capone and everything was right. The food, the service, even the decorations inside the restaurant was right. Baby they had pictures of African American heroes, people like Malcolm X, Marcus Garvey, it was out cold," I told her.

"Baby, I have not seen you this excited about anything other than weed, cars, or somebody on the news. I really never heard you speak on black history," she said.

"Well, I'm trying to change," I told her.

Nisha started laughing. I looked at my watch and it was getting late. I told Nisha I had to take care of some business and I would be back later.

"I thought you were going to stay home with me tonight." Nisha said.

"I am. But I gotta see what's this stuff J.B. got going on. You know my brother needs me," I explained to her.

"Oh yeah. I forgot all about that," she said.

I ran downstairs and grabbed a couple thousand dollars out the shoe box and shot out the house. I got out the National and fired the engine up. The pipe hollered as I gave it gas. Nisha had a female singer in the CD blasting. I turned it down and listened to the words as I sat there rolling a blunt. The woman sounded like she had been hurt by a man and she just couldn't deal with the situation no more. I actually liked the song. Every time I heard it from then on, I thought of Nisha.

I went over to J.B.'s to holler at Teresha so I could know what the hell was the scoop on these witnesses. I pulled up and Teresha had those damn dogs running around the front yard in the fence. I really did not feel like fucking with them wild ass dogs jumping on me and shit, but I said fuck it. I reached under the car seat and surprisingly the .45 was still there. I grabbed it and got out of the car.

When I got out the car, all the dogs stopped and started barking at me. I thought they were happy to see me or something and I paid it no mind. When I walked in the gate, all of them ran up to me and smelled me. But one of them tried to bite me. I hit him on top of the head with the .45 and the dog ran under the porch.

Teresha opened the door. "What just happened?"

"That hoe ass dog tried to bite me and I popped 'em on the head," I said walking in the house.

"You shot her?" she asked sounding more concerned about the dog than me.

"Naw, I didn't shoot it," I said as I inhaled the blunt. "But I should have," I said blowing the smoke out.

"I have never saw her do that," Teresha said.

She was killing me how she kept referring to the dog like it was a human being. "Man fuck that dog, what's up with my dawg J-Murda?" I asked.

Teresha reached in her bra and handed me a piece of paper with two addresses on it. I looked at it and put it in my pocket. I wondered did she know what was going on. I could only assume that she did because she had known us for so long. I looked around the house and everything was neat and in order.

"I see you feeling good now that yo' boo-boo is coming home," I said.

"Yeah, I am. Oh yeah, Tra please, I would appreciate it if you didn't tell him how I dealt with him being gone," Teresha said.

"I got you. And Teresha, I think you better check on that dog cause it might be dead," I told her.

"Aw shit Tra. Don't say that."

She ran outside calling the dog's name. I came outside and Teresha was bent down on the side of the porch talking to the dog. I walked past her.

"Alright T. Stay up," I said.

She didn't even look at me. I just laughed. When I got in the car I called Pinky.

"Hello," she said sounding sexy as hell.

"What's up baby? What you doing?" I asked her.

"Cooking something to eat," she said. "Are you hungry?"

"Naw baby. I just got done eating."

"Oh," she said sounding disappointed.

I noticed the change in her energy and asked her what was wrong. "Why you sounding sad baby?"

"It ain't nothing. I just wanted to sit down and eat with you," she said.

"Baby I know. But I'm about to come over there right now. Is that cool with you sweetheart?"

Her energy came back. "Yeah, you can come over here any time you want to Tra. As a matter of fact, this yo' house," she said.

I gave a chuckle. "Oh yeah."

"Hell yeah, this yo' house. I'm yo' girl and this is yo' pussy!" she said sounding demanding.

"Well I'm pulling up in yo' driveway right now so come open the door," I told her.

When I walked in the house, Pinky had it smelling good. In fact, I never knew she could cook like this. She was cooking roast, rice and gravy.

"Damn baby. You got it smelling good," I said.

Pinky was standing over by the stove. She turned around and said, "You sound surprised. Is that how you feel about me?"

"What are you talking about Pinky?" I asked.

"You think I can't cook. Well you thought I couldn't cook," she said looking at me sideways.

"I just didn't know baby and I apologize if I offended you," I said.

I knew Pinky cooked a good fuck game and she boiled a dick out cold but her capabilities in the kitchen really made me look at her in another light.

"P, where Penny lil' thug ass at?" I asked.

"I don't know. I haven't talked to her since earlier, why?"

I pulled out the money and counted five thousand dollars. I looked at Pinky and her eyes were as big as bottle tops.

"Here, this is for you," I said. Pinky looked confused and kinda just stood there.

"Here, this is for you," I said again.

"What's me?" she asked.

"The money is yours," I said. "Now quit playing games."

She was smiling all teeth. "Thank you Tra," she said as she reached out to hug me.

"You earned it," I told her.

She said, "I earned it how? What did I do?"

"You brought that situation back plus you been riding like a souljah since the day I met you. I told you I would take care of you," I told a serious looking Pinky.

"But Tra, I would have brought that back for you any way. I didn't do it looking for anything in return," she said pushing the money back towards me. "I'm straight baby."

She was making me mad. "Look, I'm not going to tell you no more this is yours. Take this and put it up. You never know what can pop up. Plus, if I'm yo' man as you say, let me take care of you."

She grabbed the money and walked in the back with it.

"Hey Pinky, call Penny, too!" I yelled to her.

When she walked back in she said, "Pinky said she will be over here in a minute."

"Pinky, do you got plans for tonight," I asked.

"Nope. Why? What's up?" she asked.

"I need you and Penny to do something for me," I said.

"Oh, okay," she said.

225

I looked at Pinky and she had on a white t-shirt, some white stretch pants, and some all-white Air Force Ones looking good as hell. Ass was everywhere. She fixed her a plate and sat down next to me to eat. I leaned back and fired up a cigarette. Pinky fed me a couple of pieces of roast and I had to tell her stop before I got fat. I was getting tired of waiting so I called Penny myself.

"Hello," she said.

"Man what's up? Don't you want to see me or something?" I asked her.

"You know it ain't like that Tra," she said.

"To be honest, I don't know. You got me sitting here waiting on you and I'm like damn what the fuck," I told her.

"I'm pulling up right now baby. I'm in the driveway."

"Oh, come on in," I told her.

When I opened the door for Penny, I noticed that she had the front window fixed. "I see you got your window together," I said.

"Yeah. I was upset my car wasn't in the condition where I could have took you home," Penny said.

"Aw baby I appreciate the concern but you know I'ma make it happen even if I gotta call baby girl at home," I said. Penny chuckled.

I threw the money in Penny's lap and she looked like I was her long lost father.

"What's this?" she asked.

"That's yours from that situation on the plane and the help I'ma need tonight," I said.

"Tra, I didn't do that for you earlier looking for something in return. I did that because I want you to be in the best position to win. I want to take care of you. Is that cool?" she said.

"That's cool but at the same time I want you to get yo' situation together so that we can grow as one unit. I told you that I would make you rich and I'm a man of my word. This is only a token of appreciation to my lady. So take that, put it up or spend it. Whatever you want to do. It's yours," I told her.

After I called Pinky in the living room, I told both of them what I needed them to do. It was 9:30pm and time was flying by so we had to go right then. I was hesitant to leave the National in Pinky's driveway for fear of coming back seeing it look like Penny's car or completely gone. But I stepped out on faith with the intent to kill every muthafucka Pinky thought could have done it.

The two ladies were in the front seat and I was in the back. The last time I was in the backseat was when I got arrested. The police backseats were like being in hell compared to Penny's.

I looked at the addresses and directed to the house while smoking on some of the killa Cali green. When we arrived at the first address it looked like no one was home but I sent Pinky up to the house anyway. I told Pinky if the guy comes to the door get him to come out of the house and I could take it from there. Pinky was so down for me. When she knocked on the door, the dude didn't answer but a female did and Pinky hit the girl. Pinky was in the doorway of the house on the ground fighting with the mystery woman and me and Penny jumped out the car and ran up there. By then the dude was pulling Pinky off his girl. I was fucked up like how this gone play out?

I ran up and hit the dude in the face with the pistol knocking him unconscious. Then I dragged him in the house. His girl started screaming and Penny put her hand over the girl's mouth while Pinky tried to kick the girl who was on the ground looking so helpless. The girl bit Penny's hand and Penny hit her in the face. I then punched the woman knocking her out. I had to push Pinky to stop her from trying to get at the unconscious woman. I told Pinky and Penny to get in the car and go park five blocks over. I would be there in a minute.

The only reason why I didn't kill the witnesses because the girls had made too much of a spectacle outside the house and the whole scenario was screaming prison time. I took them both in the basement and tied them up. I figured after the court date the police would come looking for them but then it would be too late. The idea that they could starve to death was good, too. Either way, J.B. would be free.

I ran out the house and got ghost. I hopped a couple fences and then started walking. The girls were sitting in the car waiting patiently. I knocked on the window and Pinky jumped. The fear in her face was something I would end up getting used to and she would end up getting rid of.

We had one more address to check out now. This time I told the girls don't do nothing unless I tell you to.

Pinky said, "I'm sorry Tra. I just wanted to hit that bitch. She had the nerve to roll her eyes as soon as she saw me standing there. I guess she thought I came to see her man for real, with his weak ass. He kept trying to get me off that bitch."

Penny was laughing so hard that she started swerving. "Come on P2. Keep your eyes on the road," I said.

"Who the fuck is P2?" she asked.

I said, "Man, fuck that shit. Just drive Penny damn. You got me in the backseat with this pistol and you swerving. If the police pull us over I gotta push Pinky seat up and try to run so come on baby, just drive. As a matter of fact, turn right here. This is the street. Hey Pinky, the address is 548."

"I think that is the house right there where that

blue Malibu at Tra. You see it?" Pinky asked.

"Yeah baby, I think that is it. Penny pull down the street and park. I'ma do this myself," I said.

I got out the car and put the .45 in my back pocket. As I began to walk towards the house, three people came out, a guy and two girls. I wasn't sure if that was the dude or not because I never saw him before. So instead of running up there killing all three of them, I turned around and walked back to the car.

Once they left I decided to go back to the house to double check just in case he was still in the house. When I knocked on the door, I thought I heard someone but no one came to the door so I left. When I got back to the car I told the girls the lame left with the females.

"Penny said, "Baby, it looked like they were going out to the club or somewhere."

I asked them what was jumping on a Tuesday night. Pinky said the only club she knew of was a new club called The Spot. I told Penny to drive over there.

The Spot was a lil' rinky dink club between my hood and some rappers hood. I knew it would be trouble going into the club because I rode passed a couple times and saw some old enemies going in. I always knew if I ever wanted to relieve some stress I could come right to that club.

While driving through the parking lot, Pinky said, "That car looks like the one that was at that house baby, don't it?"

I looked and it sure did. I told Penny to park right where we were at. We sat in that parking lot for hours smoking and talking about all sorts of other stuff. Penny talked about how her old boyfriend in Detroit used to beat her and that's one of the reasons she moved to Flint. I felt sorry for Penny. I have always disagreed with a man putting his hands on a woman. I assumed this gave Pinky a lil' emotional courage because she began to talk about how as a child her father sexually assaulted her and every time she tried to tell her mother, it fell on deaf ears. She said at times she felt suicidal and a couple of times ran away but was forced to come back because she had nowhere to go. She then tried to play it off by laughing saying that shit was crazy.

It was now 12:40am and I knew the club didn't let out until 2:00am. I was tired of waiting and I had ran out of blunt wraps. I asked Penny did she have a screwdriver or a knife. I grabbed the knife and got out of the car. I looked around the parking lot and there were a couple of cars full of people but I said fuck 'em and put two of the car tires on flat.

On the way back to the car my phone rang. I looked at the clock at it was 12:55am. It was Nisha calling.

"What's up baby?" I said answering the phone.

"Hi, I was just calling to check on you. Is everything alright?" she asked.

"Yeah baby. I'm good. Just waiting to come home. Is everything good with you?" I asked.

"Yeah. I'm up just waiting on you and watching television."

"Oh yeah baby. I should be home in thirty minutes to an hour," I said looking at my watch.

I hung up the phone and got in the car. The girls were talking. I said, "Let's go to the store right quick. Matter of fact, go through the drive thru on Pasadena. What was y'all sitting in here talking about though while I was gone?" I asked.

"Nothing," Penny said.

"I asked Penny had she ever seen yo' woman at home," Pinky said.

"Oh yeah. Well have you?" I asked Penny.

"Nope. But I hope that she is pretty," she said.

"I have not seen her either but a friend of mine said she saw y'all in the club together before and the girl was okay," Pinky said.

I started laughing. "Who is these people you keep saying know me, or think they know me?" I asked.

"Apparently a lot of people think they know you. I am the only one late coming to the party. I feel a

lil' jealous," Pinky said.

"Alright, here you go Penny." I gave Penny a twenty dollar bill as we pulled in the drive thru. "Get me two six packs of Budweiser and a pack of strawberry wraps, and a pack of Newport shorts. What's up? Do y'all want something?" I asked the girls.

"Naw, we straight Tra. We got money," Penny said.

"Oh yea. I forgot y'all ballers. I should have been asking y'all to pay for my stuff."

I cracked one of the Budweiser's as we headed back to the club. Penny started talking about how fucked up the dudes are in Flint and why a lot of females in Flint like dudes from Detroit.

Aw shit. Not this story again.

Penny said, "See men from Flint be players and although most don't believe in giving females money, there are some who are good dudes. It's just so hard to find them. Now in Detroit, when guys come down here they are looking for that female who lives by herself, maybe with one or two children. See the niggas from Detroit is looking to open a crack house down here using the female as his way to get into the Flint scene. He will take care of the woman and her child for a while and the Flint girl will think she has a real man. Then one day, the Detroit dude is up and gone."

We pulled in the parking lot just in time to catch the people going to the car. I told Pinky to lift up her seat so I could get out. I told Penny to park around the corner in the church parking lot and I would be there in a minute. As I walked away I heard Penny and Pinky say be careful.

There was only the dude and one female now. They were both outside the car looking down at the tire. I walked right up and shot the dude once in the head and once in the chest. The female started screaming and then she took off running. I let off four shots. I later found out I shot her in the

234

back, once in the back of her thigh, and once in the right shoulder.

I walked for a minute and once I got a distance, I started running. Penny and Pinky was in the parking lot waiting. She had the door cracked with the engine running. I got in and Penny pulled off.

Around 2:45am, I walked in the house fucked up. I don't know how I drove home but I guess something or somebody was looking over me. I used to refuse to even think like that. I was doing so much dirt I felt like I was cursed and no one was so merciful to protect me. However I got home was truly a blessing. When I stumbled in the bedroom, Nisha was still awake flicking through channels on the television. I felt kinda bad because I knew she wanted to fuck but I was so high, drunk and tired, I wasn't feeling it.

"Baby, you still up?" I asked.

"Yeah baby. I told you I was gone wait for you," Nisha said.

"I'm sorry baby for having you waiting so long but J.B. had me going everywhere and people kept putting me on hold," I told her.

"I'm just happy you are finally here. You have been away from me for two weeks. I know you can stay in the house for the next couple of days," she said.

I looked at her.

"Why you look at me like that?" she asked.

I sat down on the bed and began taking off my stuff without even responding to her. "What you watching?" I asked trying to switch the subject.

"Some old ass movie on fifty-eight," she said.

I got in the bed next to her and she had the nine millimeter under the pillow. One thing about Nisha, she knew to keep that pistol close by. I believe it was due to the lifestyle I lived. I put the gun on the nightstand and propped the pillow up. Nisha laid her head on my chest and started picking at my chest.

"I missed you daddy. You can't be leaving me alone like that. I need you laying next to me every night," she said.

Nisha brought out the best in me and our relationship was based on love and commitment so I always tried to make her happy.

"Alright baby but you know I gotta do my thang out here. That's how I take care of home," I told her.

"Well all I'm saying is you gotta be right here at night. All the other shit you doing is irrelevant to me. I just care about you and our relationship," Nisha said.

I held her in my arms and fell asleep.

Chapter 20

The next day I woke to my ringing cellphone. I looked at my clock and it was 8:30 in the morning.

"Hello," a voice said on the other end. "What's up boy?"

"What's up? Who is this?" I asked.

"This T-Mac cuzz. What you doing sleep?" he said.

T-Mac was my crazy ass gang-bangin' cousin from Atlanta. I hadn't heard from him in two years. In fact, I was even confused on how he got my damn phone number.

"Hell yeah I'm sleep. Its eight thirty in the morning!" I yelled.

"My bad cuzz but I had to call you. This shit is important," he said.

I tried to sit up in the bed but Nisha was sound asleep on me. I was surprised she didn't wake up after all the talking I was doing and how loud my cousin was on the phone.

"What's up cuzz? What you done got into now?" I asked.

"Naw cuzz, not what I have got into mane. The question is what you done did nigga? You got muthafuckas all the way down here talking about you and J.B. stupid ass," he said.

"What nigga?" I yelled.

"Mane some Michigan niggas down here talking about y'all up there killin' everybody in Flint and its money on y'all boys," he said.

"Well cuzz you can't believe everything you hear. I ain't killed nobody in my life and J.B. is too scary to do shit," I told him.

I didn't know what the fuck T-Mac was working out of. I hadn't heard from him in years. Then he pops up calling me talking about murders and shit. I wasn't going to get caught up like that.

He said, "You uppity niggas think everybody stupid. You must have forgot I lived with you for a year nigga!"

"Look," I said. "I don't know what you talking about cuzz. I'm going back to sleep," I told him before hanging up the phone.

I was so upset I was unable to go back to sleep. I just laid there and tried to put together the reason for his unsuspected call. I was frustrated and wondering what the hell just happened.

"What's wrong baby?" Nisha asked.

I had awakened her. "Oh nothing baby. I'm just thinking," I said.

A crusty-eyed yet still beautiful Nisha mumbled, "What time is it?"

"Its 8:40," I told her.

"Come back to sleep, it's too early. We just went to sleep," she said.

I couldn't though. I got up and went to the bathroom. After pissing I put the toilet seat down and sat there with my hands on my head. Then

Nisha came in the bathroom and kneeled down beside me.

"Tra, what's wrong?" she asked again.

I never liked telling the women in my life about shit like that because being the man of not only my family, but my different relationships, I didn't want to worry them. Plus, I knew how dangerous pillow talking was. I lifted my head and looked at Nisha. I got up. Nisha grabbed my hand and led me back to the bedroom.

I sat on the bed and Nisha sat next to me and said, "Now what's up?"

I told her how my cousin called talkin' about people in Atlanta were talking about me. I didn't mention J.B. or the allegations.

"Oh, I see now," Nisha said.

I laid back on the bed and Nisha cuddled up with me. I started kissing her and whispering in her ear that I loved her. She began sucking on my ear and I grabbed her ass. Nisha climbed on top of me stretching my arms out wide and kissed me like we just met. My nature began to rise. Nisha never wore panties or a bra in bed with me because I didn't allow it. To me, wearing clothes under the covers was bringing germs in the bed. Nisha reached down and slid my dick in her wet, tight pussy. I was all the way awaken then.

I used to kill Nisha lil' pussy. She wasn't no hood rat type of girl so everything she knew, I basically taught her, but she was a quick learner. Nisha bounced on my dick like a pogo stick with facial expression that porn stars got paid thousands for. I told her let me get behind that muthafucka and she put that fat ass in the air for me. I got in there and put my thang down. I must have busted a nut after five minutes.

Nisha got up and I was confused. She came back with a towel and started cleaning up the mess. I was used to Penny making sure no nut was being wasted on a towel and not getting that treatment made me think about her.

I woke up around 12:30pm and Nisha was walking in the bathroom naked. I smiled at the sight. I began thinking about what I had to do today. I thought about Nisha's request for us to stay in the house together.

"Hey baby. Run me some bath water with a lot of bleach," I told her.

I was so fucked up the night before that I couldn't get in the shower or nothing. I knew I couldn't go anywhere until I took care of my business and that was erasing any evidence of gunpowder. I went downstairs to get a blunt wrap so that I could roll up and something told me to look out of the window. I saw white dudes pull up in a black Crown Victoria and one of them jumped out and took my garbage can off the street. My mouth dropped and I had to blink to make sure I wasn't trippin'. Luckily, nothing was in the trash. Them stupid muthafuckas didn't know what day we put our garbage out. I grabbed the wraps and ran back upstairs. Nisha was in the bathroom pouring the bleach in the water.

"Hey Nisha, don't take no garbage out. Put it in the basement and I will take it to the school down the street," I said.

"What's wrong? Why you say that?" she asked.

"I just saw the FBI or some detectives take our trash can off the street and drive off. Luckily there was nothing in the can," I told her.

"That's crazy baby."

After seeing that, I didn't waste any time getting in the tub. I barely could stand the hot water but I definitely couldn't stand a life sentence all because I was scared of some hot water. I scrubbed and scrubbed. The thought of the Feds knowing where I lived meant that I had to get my house in order and quick.

I got out the tub and put my clothes on. I had on some black velour pants, a white t-shirt, and some white and black Air Force Ones. I got the bricks of heroin and put them in a school back pack. I went in the basement and got all the money I had which ended up being $64,000.00. I put the shoe boxes in a Foot Locker bag.

I pushed the remote control start button on the Grand National and told Nisha to grab the Foot Locker bag. I got the back pack and we jumped in the Grand National. I dropped Nisha off over her mother's and told her I would be back to get her after I sold the bricks.

I slid through the hood and stopped at one of the big homies' house named Harpo. The big homie was a true O.G. from the hood. He was one of the only older cats from the way that me and J.B. had respect for. The homie was a money getting muthafucka so I had to see what was good with him. As I walked on the porch, he was coming out the front door.

"What's up Tra nigga I ain't seen you in months?" Harpo said in his raspy voice.

"What's good folks?" I said to him as we showed each other love.

"How is the homie J.B. doing? When is folks getting out of there?" he asked.

"Oh, that nigga straight for the most part. As a matter of fact, he supposed to come home tomorrow," I told him.

"Oh yeah. That's what's up. So do y'all got something planned for G or what?" Harpo asked as he fired up a blunt.

"We might do something. I don't know. He may just want to lay up with Teresha," I explained.

"You right," Harpo responded with a smile.

"Anyway though folks, what's up with you? I got a slab of raw from out west I'm trying to get off," I told him.

"What's the ticket?" he asked.

"For you folks, give me 110 a gram. I paid 105 but there has been so much extra expenses I had to come off. I gotta at least break even," I explained to him in my car salesman pitch.

Harpo looked in the sky as if he was counting and then repeated the price, 110. Where a pound of weed would cost $500 in another city, in Flint, it was $1200. All our prices were higher than other cities.

"Damn," he said as he passed me the blunt. "I need that shit, too. I got like seventy right now. Let me think who I can call," he said.

I stopped him. "Look cuzz, come on with the seventy but I need that other forty in at least a week.

I gotta take care of my ticket out west," I told him.

"No doubt baby. That's love. Look, today is Wednesday, shoot back through here on Sunday. I should have it all together for you," he said.

I gave him a brick and he took it in the house. I sat in the front yard listening to the radio when Harpo came out to the car with a pillowcase full of money. I emptied the pillowcase out in the backseat and began counting. He had all the money separated in thousand dollar stacks, so it didn't take long. Harpo stood on the side of the car as I finished counting.

"Everything there folks?" he asked.

"Oh yeah. It's all there. I was just thinking," I said.

I showed Harpo some love and told him I would holler at him in a minute. Harpo went in the house and I sat there putting the money back in the pillowcase. Harpo's house wasn't too far from Pinky's. I wasn't about to ride around with all that money in the car and still have a brick of heroin, too. Pinky's house was the best choice.

I parked in the driveway and called her. After a couple of rings, that sexy voice was in my ear.

"Hello," she said.

"What you doing?" I asked.

"Nothing just sitting here in the window watching you," she said.

"What!" I looked up and Pinky was in the window waving at me. "You play too much," I said to her and she started laughing. "So you gone let me in or what?"

"I don't know yet," she said. "It all depends."

"It all depends on what?" I asked.

She said, "All depends on whether I can have some dick or not."

I busted out laughing. "Come open the door."

I put the brick in the pillowcase with the money and I went in the house. When I walked in, Pinky had on a t-shirt and some panties.

"Damn baby. I'm starting to think you be doing that on purpose."

She said, "Doing what?"

"Being naked every time I come over here," I said. I gave her a hug and gripped her soft ass. Pinky started laughing.

"I probably do."

I shook my head and sat down on the couch. Pinky came and sat next to me and put her legs on my lap.

"What's in there?" she asked.

"Oh, this money and one of those bricks. I need you to show me where your attic is at?"

She said, "Come with me." With every step Pinky's ass literally shook like jello.

"P," I said.

She looked back at me smiling. "What's up daddy?" She asked sounding so damn sexy.

"What am I going to do with you?" I asked her.

She said, "Fuck me and get me pregnant."

It was the exact same thing I was thinking but I didn't want to let her know. "You trippin," I said.

"There go the attic up there." She pointed to the cut out box shaped compartment.

I told her to grab me a chair so I could get up there. I looked in one of her bedrooms and there was nothing in there, no television, nothing.

"What you gone put in here?" I asked her.

"Nothing right now. Maybe when I have a child I will turn it into her room."

"How do you know it will be a girl?" I asked her.

"I just know," she assure me.

After finally getting the shit in the attic, I went in Pinky's bedroom. It was straight. She had a nice king sized bed, a sixty inch flat screen television mounted on the wall, and a oak dresser with a big mirror. She had pictures stuck around the mirror and I started looking at them. They were mostly club pictures, her with different people, her and Penny looking drunk as hell, her and some lames and then I saw one that looked familiar.

"Who is this right here?" I asked her.

"Oh that's Sleepy. He's from the eastside. We used to talk a long time ago but he's dead now. He got killed about six or eight months ago."

It was the same dude who killed my cousin from Chicago and who shot me. The dude J.B. was in the county for fighting that murder case. I played it off and kept looking at the pictures.

"Where is P2?" I said laughing.

"You crazy with that P2 shit. You know she called me talking about that? You really hit a nerve when you dropped that bomb. Anyway, I haven't talked to her since earlier."

I sat down on the bed and told Pinky to come here. She stood in front of me and slid her panties down. Her pussy was so hairy and fat. All I could say was "Damn."

She started laughing and said, "You like that."

"Hell yeah," I said.

For some reason Pinky excited me when it came to sex sort of how Nisha did when we first met.

My dick immediately got hard when I saw that pussy.

"Let me hit that muthafucka from the back," I told her.

Pinky crawled on the bed on all fours and turned her head back to me and asked, "Like this?"

I almost busted in my pants. I snatched off my shirt and pulled my pants down half way. The .45 fell on the floor. I pulled her to the edge of the bed and went to work on that pussy. Pinky was throwing that ass on me, too. When I did bust I shot all the nut in her.

"Did you put nut in me?" she asked.

"Yep," I said.

Pinky was something else. She wanted me bad as hell. And if she could have things her way, she would move in with me and Nisha. I knew her and Penny resented Nisha though because they felt I deserved better. They believed they were as good as it got.

After leaving Pinky's, I saw Tye's son walking home from school. *He's growing up.* I hadn't seen him in months and I wanted to holler at him but his mother wasn't right and I was too hot already. I had $135,000 and I owed the O.G. Capone $125,000 of that. I wanted to make sure the big homie got his money first, plus, I still had one hundred pounds in Chicago to pick up and that was good money. I would rather be caught with the hundred pounds of weed than the brick of heroin any day.

One hundred twenty-five thousand was a lot of money. In fact, it was the most I had ever sent on the wire. A few years ago me and J.B. put together $150,000 to cop twenty bricks of cocaine from a cat in Canada, but he came to get his money. It would have been cheaper if we went to Canada.

I began making preparations to send Capone his money. I told Nisha to go to Western Union to see how much it would cost to send forty-five thousand to someone. She said the clerk said any money exceeding five thousand had to be reported to the IRS. My mouth dropped because over the past couple of months I had Nisha send Capone over forty-five thousand dollars. It probably was twenty thousand dollars here and twenty thousand dollars there but it was always over five thousand dollars.

Right then my mind began to click. I figured that was probably part of the reason the feds were looking in my trash. My granny used to always say, "Travon, our people are destroyed for a lack of knowledge." I was too young to understand her words then but today they were very clear.

I didn't trust the phone so I didn't call Capone but I had Pinky do it. I told her to tell him about the money transfers and the feds and that I had another plan to get that bread out west. On one of my tours in the county jail, there was this older brother named Turtle, at least that's what we called him. He was already doing a bit in prison and was back in the county on appeal. Turtle told me and some other young cats how he was getting all this money in the 1980's. He had money coming in from all over, Chicago, Atlanta, Texas, he was everywhere with it. He said his money came via airplane through a independent airline called Airborne that had no ties with the government or any of its agencies. I did my research on them through the internet and they were solid. I told Pinky to call Capone where to pick up his package and I sent him his money using Airborne.

I felt broke. I had sent Capone all his money which only left me with nine thousand dollars on hand. I knew I had to hit the streets.

Chapter 21

The autumn winter always brought the ultimate hustler outta me and that day I was determined to get my bread. After shooting a couple moves, I finally found someone to purchase the other brick but I had to split it in half, eighteen and eighteen. I had to push it to the limit. I smashed the first eighteen on a young money getting nigga named L.G. I practically raised him. He followed the motto me and J.B. laid down about gang-bangin'. He said fuck that stupid shit and began focusing on his chips.

I put that eighteen on him for sixty thousand dollars. I kinda got upset when he gave me the money to buy the whole thang and I felt he was being cheap. I ended up selling the other half to this nigga from Detroit who move to Flint a couple years ago. Back in the day me and J.B. usually saw guys like him as golden opportunities. We were heavy on out of town niggas. That's one of the reasons that lame ass nigga, big homie used to have us kill them muthafuckas, we were known for it.

But this city nigga was all right plus he was folks. Everybody called him Country. He also

252

dropped sixty thousand for the eighteen ounces. I was all the way together again. However, I knew I couldn't continue having large amounts of money in my house without a source of income. After much debate with myself, I had Nisha open a bank account.

The next day me, Nisha and Teresha sat in the courtroom patiently waiting for J.B. to be escorted in by the sheriffs. Teresha sat there looking so helplessly anxious that I held her hand. I began to think about all her friends I had sex with over the years, and how she must see me at times. I looked at Nisha's hand and she had on the diamond ring I bought her awhile back. She had the ring on her married finger.

J.B. walked out looking like a straight gorilla, face hair everywhere and it looked like he put on a couple pounds. My nigga was all smiles. He threw his head up in a nod manner and I threw up the hood. I looked at Teresha and she was telling him she loved him. To see her so happy made me proud. J.B.'s lawyer came over to Teresha and told her he was bringing J.B. home today. Teresha said, "Thank you."

I looked at Nisha and told her, "Baby, I'm bringing you home today."

She busted out laughing and the people in the courtroom looked over at us.

When the proceedings got started, the prosecutor told the judge that the witnesses had both been killed and he believed J.B. had something to do with it.

"Objection Your Honor, this is ludicrous!" J.B.'s lawyer yelled.

The judge took of his glasses and told the prosecution, "If you don't have any witnesses then the case is dismissed." The judge pound the gavel and I exhaled. My brother is coming home.

Me, Nisha and Teresha all stood up. Nisha and Teresha hugged and I saw tears coming out of Teresha's eyes. The sight of her crying made me think of how much pain she must have endured up until that point.

As much as we would have liked to see J.B. walk right out of the courtroom that just wasn't possible. He had to be taken back to the county jail and processed. I knew Teresha would be outside the county jail waiting on him the entire time so me and Nisha left.

I was hungry as hell so we stopped to get something to eat. There was a car dealership next door to the restaurant. I figured why not go over and look at some of the cars after we ate. Me and Nisha sat down and talked over breakfast. She was mostly talking about the baby and how she couldn't wait to have it. I shared her sentiments.

I looked out the window and saw a car drive up.

It was a Cutlass. It stopped behind my car like it was looking at the license plate or something. I looked at the car but paid it no real attention and focused my attention back on Nisha. Next thing I know, I looked up and there were two niggas coming into the restaurant guns in hand, with bandanas on their faces looking dead at me. I jumped up and let off five shots. The first two striking the first dude in the door. Nisha was on the ground next to me. I let off two more shots, grabbed Nisha and ran to the back. I couldn't let her get killed like that. Especially not with my baby inside her. The second bandana bandit kneeled down to check on his homie and when I saw that, I started busting again. Then the second dude starting running. I was relieved.

That was one of the first times I was scared. I looked at Nisha and she was looking so pitiful. I stood her up and walked out the restaurant. I had the pistol in my hand as we left. When I saw the cashier on the phone, I knew the police would be there is seconds. I couldn't get caught up so easy especially not like that.

We jumped in the National and peeled off. I was so mad for the simple fact that I had Nisha with me and we were in the presence of so many people. I knew the National could be hot so when I made it home, I pulled it in the backyard and put the car cover over it. The next time I drove that it would be another color.

I had my mother take me to get a rental car. I was not about to allow that small bullshit to stop me from moving around. When J.B. got home he called me.

"Hey, what's up Tra nigga? Why you ain't over here?" he asked.

"I was trying to let you and Teresha do y'all thang and I was gone bring Nisha that way later on," I said."

"What else is up though," J.B. asked.

"Shit," I said.

"Same ole Tra. Boy you still can't hide nothing from me. Don't you know that shit was all over the news?" he said.

"What the fuck you talking about?" I asked trying to play it off.

"The shootout at the restaurant with the black male with corn rolls and the black female…"

"Man chill out. I gotta holler at you about something! As a matter of fact, come over here," I told him.

J.B. was unaware of the feds watching me so that's why I stopped him from talking. I assumed since the feds were on me, they surely had my

256

house phone tapped and maybe my cell phone. All J.B. had to say was something about the color of the Grand National and the feds would have known it was me.

The conversation I had with my crazy ass cousin, T-Mac came to mind. I wondered was that shit he was saying coming true. *That muthafucka is bad luck.*

There was just too much shit going on and I told Nisha that we would go out of town for a month or two. Her eyes lit up when I told her.

"Where we gon go though?" she asked.

"I don't know baby. Somewhere down south," I told her.

I gave Nisha the car keys and told her to go over my mother's and let her know that we are going out of town for a while.

"If she asks you why, tell her we are going to see your father's sister," I yelled as Nisha headed down the stairs.

When J.B. finally got there, I was on the phone smoking a blunt. I heard a hard knock on the door. I knew it was his heavy handed ass.

"Why you didn't ring the doorbell nigga?" I asked his crazy ass as he stood there red-eyed, still with that county jail look, perky, hair wild and need a shave.

"Who you talking to?" J.B. asked as he walked in.

"I'm talking to my mans who painted the National. He supposed to be coming to pick it up," I told J.B.

"Oh hell yeah. You definitely gotta paint that," J.B. said.

"Yeah, I will be here. Alright. Yep. In a minute," I said to the painter as I hung up the phone.

"What you was saying nigga?" I asked J.B.

J.B. sat down on the couch and hit the blunt super hard. "I said, yeah, you definitely got to paint that fool."

He made me realize how aggravating he could be at times. My nigga had been gone for a nice little while and I almost forgot.

"So what the fuck happened at the restaurant?" he asked.

I told him the whole story. Then I told him about Pinky, Penny, Capone, the feds, and T-Mac.

"Nigga you wanna have all the fun when I get locked up. When I was out here, all you wanted to do was layup with Nisha," he said laughing uncontrollably.

"Man fuck you! Speaking of, Nisha's pregnant. You about to be an uncle and a Godfather!" I told him.

"It's about time. I thought she couldn't have children for a minute. So now Janiah gonna have someone to beat up on," J.B. said.

"Yes she will," I echoed J.B.'s thoughts.

I had a lot of things going on. I still had to get my weed from Chicago. I could not go anywhere with that business unfinished but I had to figure out how I would play the situations. So I called Capone so that I could get that weed en route.

"Hey loc what's up?" I said.

"What's up cuzz I got that letter you wrote me," Capone said. Pinky had put the homie up on game and he knew there was a chance the feds were listening so we had to talk in codes.

"Yeah though my girl sister having a baby in New York so we gone shoot that way, but I can't leave until cousins from the land come down here. So once they get here everything is straight," I told him.

"No doubt loc," Capone said. "That's gotta be handled ASAP!" he said.

Oh yeah, that nigga J.B. beat that case. His crazy ass sitting right here blowing like a muthafucka," I said.

"Oh yeah, let me holler at cuzz," Capone said.

"What's been poppin cuzz?" J.B. yelled.

"Nigga you know I been asking the loc about you. Shit that nigga done came this way twice this year already when you bringing yo' crazy ass out here loc?" Capone asked him.

J.B. started laughing. "Aw shit loc. I'm definitely coming out there we gotta talk for real cuzz. I just beat this case so once I get my shit together, I'll be there. You feel me?"

"No doubt," Capone yelled. "You gotta stay out of that cage cuzz that shit for blood niggas. Ain't no locs ever supposed to be in there!"

"But I'ma be to see you real soon cuzz," J.B. said. "I'ma give this nigga Tra his phone back. He looking all crazy at me."

"Hell yeah!" I said as I grabbed the phone. "Y'all gotta talk on yo' phone. My shit for money and hoes."

I heard the door slam. "Tra, what you in here saying?" Nisha walked in. "No hoes bet not be calling yo' phone."

"Anyway, in a minute Capone," I said.

"Yeah cuzz, I'm out on top of that," he said before hanging up.

J.B. was laughing at Nisha so hard it made me

laugh. "Nisha you better sit down some where coming in here listening to my conversations," I said.

"You shouldn't be talking so loud. And what you laughing at J.B. Don't make me call Teresha," Nisha said.

"Yeah, don't make her call Teresha," I said to J.B. echoing Nisha.

"Man, I missed y'all crazy ass," J.B. said as he relit the blunt.

"Tra! This tow truck outside!" Nisha yelled.

"Oh yeah, that's the painter," I said jumping up.

I ran outside and grabbed the few little odd things still in the car and hollered at the painter dude as he loaded the car on the truck.

"Hey, take care of my baby my mans," I told him before he pulled off.

Me and J.B. sat around the house kickin' game and getting high. I guess he was on a mission to catch up on all the days he didn't smoke in the county. After the fourth blunt, I told him I was straight.

"Aw, you ain't gangsta Tra no more nigga?" he said trying to get under my skin.

"Fuck what you talking about nigga. I done

smoked so many blunts already today, I feel like a swisher sweet."

"I'm just fucking with you my nigga. I'm glad you straight that means more for me," he said looking at the weed reaper.

I needed to talk to T-Mac but I could not talk to him on any phone so I told J.B. to take me over to Pinky's.

"Nigga don't be trying to holler at my hoes I'm telling you right now," I told J.B.

"Tra, don't nobody want your tired ass hoes. I know you like 'em fugly." J.B. busted out laughing after he let that bullshit fly out of his mouth.

I was kinda cautious about carry my pistol with me. I feared the police would be coming to get me if the feds didn't come first. But I would not feel right if a nigga got another chance to get off on me. I had made it up in my mind that the next time some shots go off, I will be the one doing all the head hunting. That nigga J.B. just had to ride through our old stomping grounds. I mean I loved the hood, too. but them niggas wasn't there when J.B. needed them and they never will.

"Come on cuzz, you just had to ride through the hood," I said.

"Hell yeah!" J.B. said. "Ain't no place like home."

"Man, muthafuckas trying to kill me and you driving through here. These nigga ain't talking about no money, no hoes, no drama, nothing!" I stressed to him.

"Sit back and ride nigga!" J.B. said turning up the music. I wanted to punch his ass but he was driving. When we got to Pinky's I called.

"I know you don't got on any clothes, so put some on. Me and my brother in the driveway," I told her.

"Okay," she said.

"Man, all the shit you been talking about, these girls betta be laying like that. Plus, nigga you been cheating on my home girl Nisha with this chick. I hope she worth it," J.B. said.

"You finna see in a minute my nigga," I told him.

When we got out the car J.B. started looking around. "This is a alright neighborhood, too." he said.

As we walked on the porch, Pinky opened the door. "What's up baby?" I said as I walked in and gave her a G hug. "This my nigga J.B., I been telling you about."

"Oh hey, what's up J.B.?" Pinky said as she walking in the direction of the bedroom.

J.B. hit me with his elbow. "Cuzz, she bad as hell. She strapped too nigga, damn! I can't lie you wasn't

lying she cold." he said smiling.

I already knew what he was going to say but I enjoyed hearing it anyway. Pinky came back in the living room and sat down.

"So I finally get to meet Ms. Pinky? This nigga been telling me about you the entire time I was in the county and I see why now," J.B. said. Pinky was smiling like a muthafucka.

I jumped straight in. "Man fuck that shit. Pinky I need to use your phone. I gotta make a call to Atlanta right quick." Pinky reached over and passed me the phone.

"Hey Pinky, where is Penny at?" I asked her. I could tell she was probably a lil' jealous because I always asked about Penny when I came over.

"She is supposed to be on her way over here. I thought you were her when you called," she said.

"Who is Penny?" J.B. asked as he begin rolling a blunt.

"Oh, Penny is my girl," Pinky said.

While they talked I made the call.

"What's up mane?" T-Mac answered the phone with his country ass sounding just like a muthafucking farmer.

"Man, what's up? This Tra nigga!"

"Oh, what up cuzz. I thought you would be calling me," he said with his hoe ass.

"Now tell me what the fuck you was talking about yesterday cuzz?" I asked.'

"Mane I'm higher than a kite cuzz. Yea though mane these Michigan niggas down here talking about you and J.B. stupid ass up there killing niggas left and right. These bitches be talking mane, you know how these niggas be running they mouth. The shawty tell me how these Atlanta niggas left from here on they way up there to kill a nigga name Tra and his boy J.B. I called yo' dumb, stupid, scary ass, and tried to tell you. Hey, them niggas might be outside from where you at right now," he said laughing.

When he started laughing I got so mad. "Cuzz you a hoe ass nigga and the next time I see you I'm fucking you up!" I told him and got off the phone.

"Tra, what that nigga talking 'bout?" J.B. asked.

"This clown ass country bunkin nigga started laughing," I said.

"What! What did he say?"

"Oh he say somebody went down there and gassed up some Atlanta niggas saying our body count is on the rise and the niggas I got into it with at the restaurant was some Atlanta niggas hired to come kill us," I explained.

Pinky sat there looking as I told J.B. what T-Mac had said. I wondered what was going through her mind. Pinky reminded me so much of Nisha it was crazy.

There was a knock at the door. I pulled out the .45 and peeked out the window. Pinky was looking scary as hell.

"Oh, it's Penny," I said.

"Thank God," Pinky said sounding relieved.

Penny walked in looking good as hell. She had on some black jeans with a burgundy t-shirt.

"Hey, what's up y'all?" she said as she walked in.

"Hey Tra," she said walking right up to me and planting a passionate kiss on my lips.

"Where you been at?" I asked sounding like a concerned father.

"I just came from the grocery store with my sister and her kids. What? Have you been looking for me?"

"Girl, he is always looking for you. That's the first thing he says when he comes over here. No, hello Pinky, how you doing, nothing. Just have you seen Penny," Pinky said sounding jealous.

Penny looked at me and I winked my eye at her. I saw J.B. looking her up and down so I introduced him to her.

"Hey baby, that's my right hand man, my brother, J.B."

"Hey, how you doing?" She said to J.B. while giving him a girly wave. "So this is your manz J.B. you been talking about you gotta get out of jail."

"Yeah, that's him," I responded. "Man, fire that blunt up J.B."

"Oh, I just don't be smoking in people house unless I get they permission," J.B. said trying to sound like he had some type of manners.

Pinky said, "You straight. But just to let you know, this is Tra real home, and you his brother so this is your home as well. Whatever you need just holler."

"Alright," J.B. said as he fired up the blunt.

We stayed at Pinky's for a while then left. When I told them I was going out of town for a while they were telling me to come live with them.

"What about Nisha?"

They both said in unison, "She gotta mama don't she!"

I cherished the fact that they held me in such high esteem but they had a reason to. I was a real nigga and ain't too many of us left.

The next day the folks from Chicago made it to Flint and I was happy to be getting my shit. These Chicago niggas represented the same thing me and J.B. used to back in the day so we always felt comfortable around them plus they were Capone's cousins.

Around 1997, me and J.B. was coming from Cali doing a job for the big homie and he told us to stop in the Windy City he had something for us to take home. We were wondering what the fuck could it be. At first I thought it was some female or something, then I thought some pistols. Me and J.B. started making bets on what it was. Back then Capone's family lived over near 79th and Vincene Street and when we pulled up they stood out in front of the tall house maybe eight to ten deep, nothing like the Crips in California. The streets in Chicago were crazy and the way traffic moved out there was different from Flint and even in California. One of the older folks walked up to the car with Capone on the phone. He told us to pop the trunk then brought out fifteen pounds of weed.

J.B. said, "Hell yeah!" He was extremely excited because back then we were just really starting to see real money.

That was a long time ago. I was getting real money now. We met the folks from Chicago at a Wallis Restaurant and they loaded the pounds in the rental car and J.B's Caprice. I definitely could not take one hundred pounds of weed with me out of town so I gave J.B. thirty pounds and told him to give me $18,000 off it and the rest was his. I looked at him and he was rubbing his hands together looking crazy. I knew then he was going to get his smoke all the way on. I smiled on the inside. I figured he could sell eighteen of the pounds for a grand a piece and have twelve others to get his money and smoke on with.

I took thirty pounds over Pinky's and had Nisha put thirty-eight pounds in her mother's basement when she went to work. I decided to take two pounds with me just in case I got somewhere and started selling it.

It was only Saturday but I stopped by Harpo's spot because I needed all my money before going out of town. Niggas got a habit of acting like they forgot about the money they owed you. I decided I wasn't gone give the O.G. a chance to pull that on me. To my surprise the homie was in the front yard hooking up some sounds in his Tahoe truck. I thought I was going to have to look for him but again, Harpo was one of the solid ones. As soon as I got out the car he started smiling. I initially thought his smile was *damn I almost got it…*but it wasn't.

"You early folks but I got you," Harpo said as he showed me some hood love.

(For the unconscious reader: Hood love is a sign of demonstrating unity of the same nation.)

Harpo headed in the house to get the bread while I looked in his trunk at the sound equipment he had.

Harpo had six twelve inch JL Audio speakers with two five thousand watt amps. I knew his shit was going to be pounding especially with the three fifteen inch speakers he already had in the trunk.

My hood was crazy. We had Crips, Gangstas' and even Breeds running around. Every other hood said we were the gang-bangers of Flint outside of some ole rinky dink ass hoods that were the opposition.

When Harpo came back outside, I noticed the big homie had a flag hanging out of his back pocket.

"Boy, you gone rep that thang till you can't no more," I said.

"Ain't no secret Tra. Nigga I'ma rep this shit til the casket drop," he responded, as he passed me the forty thousand dollars.

270

Our hood suffered the most out of every other neighborhood in Flint. We had lost two of our youngest G's to the opposition so muthafuckas didn't give a fuck about anything other than the nation.

Chapter 22

There wasn't too much action going on with me for the next couple of days. There was no more news coverage of the shootings and I for sure didn't see any more Feds looking through my trash.

I decided instead of going out of town for a couple of months I would take Nisha down south to Covingtonville Tennessee where I had family. Being a street nigga from a small city like Flint made me stand out in Covingtonville. The south has always made me think of slavery, the lynchings, and the struggles for equality.

We lived with my Aunt Ernestine and her husband Willie. They were older but they were cool. My uncle Willie opened a afterhours joint that was popular in Covingtonville and it became one of my main hang outs. Nisha and Aunt Ernestine became close and Nisha learned how to cook a bunch of old down south recipes. We were blending in good.

When we first got down there I was fucked up. Aunt Ernestine's house looked like a old slave plantation. When we walked in she already had a big meal already cooked for us. I heard stories about southern hospitality but to experience it for yourself is something different.

After eating, we were shown our room. Everything was perfect besides all the plastic on the furniture in the bedroom. I was tired but I wanted to get out and see the city. Uncle Willie told me about all the ghetto areas and what to look out for. I appreciated that because I didn't ever want to wander off into the wrong neighborhood and end up getting killed by mistake. Although the house showed its slavery roots, the land was beautiful. It sat on at least thirty acres of land which had a small pond and a nice size garden in the backyard.

I took Nisha outside and she sat on a homemade swing that hung from a tree while I rolled a blunt. My people didn't mind me smoking in the house but I wanted to spend a intimate moment with Nisha.

"Baby, I like it down here," I told Nisha.

"For real!" Nisha said excitedly.

The look in her eyes were so beautiful it caught me off guard. I began to cough. The smoke went down the wrong pipe.

"Yeah, I'm for real. This is nice down here. The only thing is I don't know how I'm gonna make money and the money I have now is going to run out eventually," I explained to Nisha.

"Tra, I can get a job and I am quite sure that you

can get Uncle Willie to hire you if it came down to it," she said.

I kinda hated that I came outside with her then because everything she was saying was right. I just wasn't ready to make a big step like that and leave everything and everyone, especially my mother, daughter, Pinky or Penny.

"Baby, we are definitely going to do something. It's just at this minute, I don't know exactly what it is, I said.

Nisha looked at me and she began to swing back and forth on the swing. I allowed the weed to take me to another place mentally. I was ready to find something to get into.

When we got back in the house, Uncle Willie was sitting on the couch watching television. They still had a old floor model television from back in the day. It looked good but it was certainly outdated. I was ready to get my venture on though but I was not about to go somewhere in a foreign city ill-prepared. I had heard stories about the ku klux klan doing bullshit to black people in the south and how it had became the norm down there. For me, I had always said "I wish they ran up on me!" *Now is my time to perform.*

I thought now was the best time as any to crack on Uncle Willie about a pistol. I sat down on the couch next to Uncle Willie and went for it.

"So Tra, how are you and Trisha coming along," Uncle Willie asked.

"Her name is Nisha, with a "N" Uncle Willie," I said.

"Oh, oh. I been calling her Trisha all this time. No wonder she looks at me all crazy when I say something to her," Uncle Willie said laughing.

I muscled up my nerve. "It's alright Uncle Willie. I am about to drive around the town to see what's going on but I don't feel comfortable without a pistol. Do you have one I can hold onto while I'm down here?"

Uncle Willie reached into his waistband and pull out a ten shot Colt 45 Automatic. It looked like old school but in good condition, just like the floor model television.

"Here, hold this one. I know exactly what you mean. These niggas is crazy down here, too. And you gotta look out for the klan. They live around these parts so you gotta be careful," Uncle Willie said looking in my eyes sternly.

I grabbed the .45, checked the clip and tucked it in my waistband. I told Uncle Willie I would be back later on. I then went to holler at Nisha. She was in the bedroom talking on her cellphone.

"Here he is right here," she said as I walked in the room.

"Baby, who is that?" I asked.

"Oh, this is Teresha crazy ass! She keep asking me have we ate any gumbo yet." I just looked at Nisha. "Tra, J.B. is in the background yelling something. He saying something about he may need to use one of your toys while you gone."

That lame J.B. was on some bullshit. He was talking about Pinky and Penny. I started to respond but I was on a mission and wasn't about to let him fuck up the smooth pace me and Nisha was on. I kissed Nisha and told her I would be back in a minute.

I didn't know where the hell I was going but I intended on riding around until I found the black people. I sparked up a blunt and just rode around. I saw a group of kids outside a grocery store and I decided to stop and grab a couple of beers.

When I walked in the store, black people were everywhere. There wasn't a white person in sight. I was in shock. I guess I prejudged the south from the stories and movies. There was a thick ass brown female working at the counter. I smiled at her as I headed toward the cooler.

The cooler consisted of beer kegs with ice inside. You literally had to dig your hand around in the ice to put together a six pack of twelve ounce bottles. This was so country to me.

So I am standing there watching a guy next to me

dig his hand in to get three forty ounces and I'm stuck wondering should I even put my hand inside the cold ice. Then I turned around and there was the female from the counter.

"You want some beer," she asked.

Embarrassed I looked at her and said, "Yeah, I was trying to decide whether I would put my hand in there to get it."

She busted out laughing.

"Where you from?" she asked.

"I am from around here. Why you ask me that?"

"No you are not from around here. I can tell from your accent, your dress, and the way you are looking at those barrels. And, you are not a good liar," she said.

Feeling exposed, I couldn't do anything but smile. I extended my hand to her. "How are you doing sweetheart, my name is Tra," I said.

She shook my hand and said, "Hey Tra, my name is Emyra."

"Emyra. A beautiful name for a beautiful woman. It's my pleasure to meet you Ms. Emyra," I said.

Emyra blushed. Our eyes locked. I was admiring how beautiful her skin was and she was polite and sexy as hell.

"I guess I better gone ahead and go for it," I said gesturing towards the barrel.

"It's actually not that cold," she said.

I threw my hand in there the first time fishing for the first bottle. Emyra stood there smiling at me. Once I got the first bottle I was a bit relieved. The cold shock was over with and I easily got the other five bottles.

"I told you," Emyra said walking away.

Emyra had so much ass just like Pinky but the difference was that she wasn't trying to throw it when she walked like Pinky and numerous other females that I had known. She was a southern bell. A respectable woman with swagger.

I grabbed a few more items and walked to the counter. Emyra had taken her place back behind the counter and she had a nice little line of customers. I didn't want to seem desperate so I went to another clerk. This was a female, too. She was a red bone with long hair. I said little to her while paying for my things. I couldn't get Emyra off my mind though.

I stopped at Emyra's counter on my way out the door and gave it a shot.

"Excuse me Ms. Emyra. Do you know where Willie's at on Maple Street? It's a bar."

She said, "Yeah, I know the people who own it. Why?"

"Oh, that's my uncle. Anyway, I was wondering could I meet you there when you get of work. I need someone to show me around. You are the first person I met. Plus, I believe I can trust you."

"But I don't get off work until 9:30 tonight. That's six hours away," she said.

I said, "Yeah, I know but I wouldn't feel comfortable with anyone other than you."

She finally gave in. She agreed to meet me at ten o'clock at Uncle Willie's bar. I was excited and couldn't wait for my chance to talk to Emyra.

Chapter 23

"Travon come on in here and get you some of this food," Aunt Ernestine yelled.

I was lying on the bed looking at the ceiling thinking about all kinds of shit. I needed to call my daughter, my mother, and check on Pinky and

Penny. I wondered about the situation back in Flint like was the police looking for me. It was 8:54pm and I was so high and buzzing off the beer, I didn't want to interrupt my comfort. Aunt Ernestine and Nisha had it smelling good, too. I probably wouldn't have gotten up but I knew I needed to eat my high down so I could be focused for Emyra. After washing my hands I headed to the table and sat down.

"There he finally is," Aunt Ernestine said as Nisha looked up at me.

Nisha brought me a plate and we all sat down at the dinner table. Uncle Willie had already left for work so Aunt Ernestine called on me to say grace.

"Say what?" I asked.

Aunt Ernestine said, "Say grace boy. I know you can say grace."

I was embarrassed because it had been so long since I had to say grace. It made me think of my grandmother and how those southern roots began to die in our family in Michigan when she passed away.

I took a deep breath. "Alright. Father GOD we come before you tonight thanking you for strength, wisdom, knowledge and understanding. We thank you for your protection of us, our family, and our friends. And we ask that you bless this beautiful prepared food for us today. In your name we pray, Amen."

Aunt Francis and Nisha echoed my amen. Then Nisha reached over and kissed me. I guess she was surprised that I could pray or something. I began thinking I hope she doesn't think I will be doing this when we get back to Michigan.

We really enjoyed ourselves. We talked about everything. Aunt Ernestine even brought out pictures of me from the late 90s' when I was knee deep into gang-bangin'. I wondered how she got them.

It was getting late so I jumped in the shower and got ready. Nisha came in the bathroom while I was in the shower telling me to be careful tonight and that she would be waiting for me to come home.

I looked at the clock and it was 9:50pm. I felt like I was running late for a job interview or something. I mean Emyra had me gone like that. I grabbed some weed, the .45, and a couple of dollars and shot out the house. Nisha and Aunt Ernestine sat at the table watching me.

I made it to Uncle Willie's bar around 10:10pm. When I parked the car I could hear the music from outside. They were playing my homies from Flint, Gloc Gaim Entertainment. I was surprised and wondered how did they know about Gloc Gaim. When I walked in the bar there were people everywhere. I walked up to Uncle Willie who was behind the counter.

"Hey Unc, I see its' poppin' in here," I said through the loud music. He shook his head and turned down the music then got on the microphone.

"Hey everybody, listen up. This is my nephew Tra from Michigan. He down here visiting so y'all show him how we do it down here!" Uncle Willie told the packed bar.

In unison, everyone in the bar yelled, "Hey Tra."

I couldn't help but smile. I looked around the bar for Emyra but I didn't see her. I shook so many hands and gave out so many hugs that I couldn't wait for her or somebody to save me. Uncle Willie called me into the back office and I was relieved.

"What's up man?" he said sitting down on top of the desk. "Is everything alright?"

I told him I met Emyra and he confirmed he had known her since she was young. He said she was a good girl and if I got her to come to the bar he would be surprised because she didn't hang out. That was the last thing I wanted to hear.

Uncle Willie patted me on my back and said, "Come on, let me get you a drink."

When we came out the back, there was Emyra sitting at the counter looking good as hell.

Everything inside of me lit up as I walked over to her.

"Hey, I am glad you could make it," I told her.

Emyra looked straight passed me and spoke to Uncle Willie who was bringing me a Remy on the rocks.

"Hello Uncle Willie," she said.

"Hey Emyra, how are you doing?" he responded sounding surprised she was there. I looked at him and nodded my head.

"I'm doing fine," she said as she looked me in my eyes. When Uncle Willie walked off I knew it was time to represent.

"So," I said. "Are you going to give me my official tour of Covingtonville?"

"You ready," she said.

I swallowed the glass of Remy and said, "Yep."

Emyra shook her head and smiled as we walked outside.

"I think I better drive," she said. "Here's my car right here."

Emyra had a platinum Infiniti, like a 2007 model. It was clean besides the specks of mud from the dirt roads. We talked the entire time. She showed me her old high school, the Covingtonville

Mall, the police station, all the best places I could get the best fast food, and even where the klan had killed a female friend of hers in the late 1990's. That made me mad.

"Do y'all have any beaches down here?" I asked.

"Yeah, we got beaches," she said.

"Let's go to the beach then," I said.

She looked at me sideways with a smirk on her face and said, "Okay."

When we made it to the beach, she said, "No one comes to the beach at night time."

"Yeah, I know," I said.

"Is all guys from Michigan like you?" she asked while turning off the engine.

"No sweetheart I'm one of a kind," I shot back. Emyra had the biggest smile ever on her face.

"Come on," I said opening the car door.

"Where are we going?" she inquired.

"Nowhere. I don't want to smoke in your car. Plus, it's nice out here."

We sat on the hood of her car talking while I smoked a blunt. The way she looked at me was crazy. I guess it was different to her. She told me she had boyfriends who smoked weed and she even smoked with them at times.

The whole scene had me feeling romantic. The weed plus the shot of Remy didn't make it any better.

"Come here," I told Emyra. She looked at me confused but came closer.

I held her hand and said, "You are beautiful." She smiled and turned away."

"No, don't turn away," I said. "Why you don't want me to tell you the truth?" She turned back to me and looked in my eyes.

"I'm serious," I said. "I think you are cool. You are the only person down here I know and to be honest, after meeting you I don't need to meet anyone else."

"You are just talking," she said.

"I promise," I shot back.

"Why are you saying this to me? I have a boyfriend."

"That's cool cause I have a girlfriend but what I'm saying is still true," I told her.

She looked at me and I kissed her passionately. Emyra was all the way in and then she pulled back.

"There go a car. We better go," she said.

I turned around and saw the bright lights coming. "They not about to say anything to us," I said.

Emyra yelled, "That might be the klan!"

She got inside the car and started the engine. I hesitantly got in the car. I was so mad I didn't know what to do. When we pulled off I looked in the other car and it was some white people. It looked more like some young horny college kids instead of the hooded klan.

I didn't say much on the way home. I knew she could tell I was pissed because she pulled over.

"Tra, I'm sorry if you are mad but down here we can't take any chances," she said.

"Emyra, all that is good and dandy but I'm not down her for nothing. I will never let anything happen to you. Where I'm from, white people can get killed as quick as blacks. In fact, maybe even quicker," I told her.

I wanted to fuck Emyra so bad but I knew that

wouldn't happen that night so she dropped me back off at the bar to get my car.

"Are you going to make it home safe?" she asked me as I got out of the car.

"Yeah baby, I'm okay," I told her.

The bar was empty when we got back. I looked at my watch and it was 12:15am. I was trippin' how early everything shut down.

When I made it back to the house, Nisha kept her word, she was still up waiting on me. Uncle Willie and Aunt Ernestine were so old fashioned they did not have televisions in the bedrooms so when I came in, Nisha was playing a game on her cellphone.

"Hey baby," I said walking in the room.

"Hey, did you have fun?" she asked.

Nisha was looking sad as hell. I figured that she was bored down there with nobody she knew but me and I kept ripping and running around town. I knew I couldn't continue to allow her to suffer like that. We made sweet love that night.

The next day I made up my mind that we would only stay down south for three more days and that I wouldn't leave Nisha at home by herself anymore. I took her shopping and everything. Even though the clothes stores they had were not like the ones in Flint or Detroit for that matter, we were able to find some stuff.

I had to put Emyra out of my mind. I didn't call her or go to her job. I liked her but I really wasn't in the mood to chase her.

People from down south carry on so many traditions from the past that, just like my mother and granny did in Michigan. Aunt Ernestine cooked fish and spaghetti on Fridays. I decided to do the family thang and help out in the kitchen and show them a man can carry his own weight. Me, Nisha and Aunt Ernestine were in the kitchen cleaning and frying fish while talking shit and chewing bubble gum.

I had went through a six pack of beer just cleaning the fish and my bladder was telling me it was time to release some pressure. As I got to the top of the stairs, I heard someone knock on the door. I was headed back down the steps when I heard Aunt Ernestine yell, "I got it boy. Go use the restroom."

That was music to my ears. I walked past Uncle Willie's bedroom and he was laid out on the bed sleep with his mouth wide opened. All I could think about was one of them big ass dragon and horse flies that kept me away from the garden, landing in his mouth.

When I made it back downstairs, Emyra fine ass sat there in the kitchen with Nisha, and Aunt Ernestine. My mouth just dropped. Keeping my fronts up, I played it off like it wasn't nothing because it actually wasn't. I was going home in two days and Emyra would still be down here with her boyfriend.

Introducing us Aunt Ernestine said, "Tra, this is Emyra Jones. Emyra, this is Travon Turner my nephew."

"Oh, I met him in the bar the other night. Uncle Willie introduced him to the whole bar," Emyra said as we all busted out laughing.

I couldn't help but look at Emyra. I wanted to fuck her so bad. She had that look, that one where you know she had some good ass pussy.

"It's beginning to be too many of y'all in this kitchen. So I'ma go back here in the bedroom until the food is done," I told them.

"Okay baby," Nisha said.

The situation was just too intense for me and I didn't want Nisha to start putting things together in her head. I always felt she knew I was fucking other females but she never caught me or had a confrontation with one so she never said shit. To get my mind off of that shit, I called Pinky. I hadn't talked to her since I left and I knew I better check on her, my weed, and my money.

"Hey baby," a excited Pinky yelled through the phone.

"Hey, what's up?" I said playing it off in case Nisha was standing by the door listening.

"I miss you so much," Pinky said.

"I do, too. That's what's up," I responded.

"When are you coming home daddy?" Pinky sounded like a little girl.

"In maybe two weeks. I got some other little things to put together down here and I'll be on my way," I said flat out lying. Although Pinky was my number two, I never knew whether somebody was listening to our conversation or someone paid her to set me up.

"Tra, Tra the food is done!" Nisha yelled from downstairs.

"Well I just wanted to check on you to let you know I haven't forgot about you and that I will be there soon," I told Pinky.

"I'm glad to hear your voice and I can't wait to see you daddy," Pinky said.

"Alright then, I'll see you soon," I said ending the call.

Thinking about Pinky, I couldn't help but think how mad Penny would be that I didn't call her. When I got back downstairs I looked around and Emyra was gone.

"Where did the little girl go?" I asked them.

Nisha said, "Little girl nothing. That girl is older than us but anyway she left, why?"

When Nisha asked me why I immediately got mad and if Aunt Ernestine wasn't sitting there, I would have checked the shit out of Nisha. I guess she got a lil' jealous because I asked about Emyra but I didn't give a fuck about her jealousy. The only thing I could think was she is out of pocket questioning me period!

"Shit, I thought she was gone eat with us," I said. "But anyway, what the fuck is wrong with you. Don't be asking me why I asked about somebody. You trippin'."

"Hold on now Travon Turner. Don't you be talking to that girl like that boy! What's wrong with you is the question!" Aunt Ernestine injected.

"I'll be out back," I said as I walked out of the house.

"Yeah, I think that would be a good idea," I heard Aunt Ernestine say.

I allowed my emotions to get the best of me. I was doing fine until I saw Emyra. I had tried to put her out of my mind because my situation was difficult already and pursuing her would only make Nisha and my family suspicious. I'm quite sure Aunt Ernestine knows that I have some sort of feelings for Emyra by the way I behaved. I just wondered did she tell Nisha.

I sat out by the pond and looked at the fish swim back and forth in search of food. After sitting out there smoking my life away, Uncle Willie came out with a plate of food.

"Boy, I heard about what happened in there," he said. I remained quiet. "When you find yourself in a situation like the one you in, you got to be smart. Now you done came down here with this girl and from what I see, you finna have a baby. Then you meet Emyra but you can't have her because ya' old lady in the way. You can't be acting crazy," Uncle Willie said with his mouth full of fish.

"Have you ever been in this situation Unc," I asked.

"Shit yeah, man. Any muthafucka who's gotta old lady has been down that road. But the trick is again, being smart. You can't jack yo' shit off on a one night fling. Now Emyra is a good girl and a damn good catch but ya' timing ain't right. Now what you gotta do is go apologize to ya' old lady in there crying her heart out to my wife," Uncle Willie said.

Uncle Willie gave me some real stern game and he was absolutely right. If I wanted to fuck with Emyra I had to be on point. I had to go make things right with Nisha first though.

"You right Uncle Willie. Let me go talk to this woman," I said.

Uncle Willie nodded his head and continued eating his fish. "Hey Tra, tell Ernestine to come out

here," he yelled as I walked in the house.

When I got in the house, Aunt Ernestine was in the kitchen washing dishes.

"Auntie look, I just want to apologize for being disrespectful. I was wrong and it won't happen again."

Aunt Ernestine turned around and said, "I hope it doesn't happen again Travon, but you don't gotta apologize to me, you need to say that to Nisha."

"Where is she?" I asked.

"Back there in the room," Aunt Ernestine said.

"Oh yeah. Uncle Willie out by the pond, he said come here."

Nisha was laying on the bed playing sleep. I just laid down next to her and started talking.

"Baby, you sleep?" I asked.

"Nope," she said flatly.

"Turn around and face me then," I told her.

When she turned around I could tell she had been crying. I kissed her softly. "Baby, I'm sorry."

Nisha tried to talk but couldn't. I guess she was beginning to get emotional again.

"You know I love you," I told her.

"Yeah, I know," she said softly.

"Baby, I apologize for snappin' at you. But don't be questioning me about asking about a female. I told you about that jealousy shit. I love you so much. I never meant to hurt you," I told Nisha.

I was hungry as hell but I was too tired to get up and get some food. I laid there with Nisha and eventually fell asleep.

I woke up a couple hours later to the growling of my stomach. I knew I had to eat. After getting my hygiene together, I headed for the kitchen. I looked in the backyard and Uncle Willie and Aunt Ernestine were still by the pond but now they were cuddled up. I fixed me a plate and put it in the microwave then sat down at the kitchen table. I was ready to get back home.

While eating my fish and spaghetti, my cellphone was vibrating in my pocket. When I pulled it out and looked at it, it was a text message from Emyra. She was telling me to meet her at the place her friend got killed in an hour.

For some strange reason I was excited to get her message. I guess more than anything, I was surprised. I looked at my watch and it was 6:30pm.

I had to come up with a reason to go out that would sound reasonable considering that I didn't know anyone down there. I decided to go down to the bar with Uncle Willie at 7:00pm and wait until around 7:15pm and head to my destination.

Nisha woke up around 6:50pm. I walked in the room and told her I was going down to the bar for a couple of hours and I would be back. A crusty-eyed beautiful Nisha laid her head back on the pillowing saying, "Alright."

When I finally got to the spot, Emyra was there waiting on me. I wondered how she could come to such a place that held so much pain. I parked the Charger there and got in the car with her. Emyra started the car and we pulled off.

"How are you doing sweetheart?" I said as I got in the car.

"I'm fine," Emyra responded.

"So what's up? Is everything okay?" I asked sounding concerned.

"Yeah, everything's alright. When I was talking to Aunt Ernestine and your girlfriend mentioned that y'all was leaving Sunday, I figured that's less than forty-eight hours. I wanted to see you before the last day to avoid the awkwardness," Emyra said in her sweet girly voice.

"It's been cool down here though but I'm ready to go back home," I said. "Then meeting you Emyra hasn't made it any better. I really like you. You represent the qualities in a woman that I need and look for. But then, like me, you are in a relationship."

"Your girlfriend was nice and pretty. I can't lie, I was surprised when I met her because I didn't know you brought her with you," Emyra said.

We drove around until she pulled up to a house. This house was much smaller than Uncle Willie's and I was confused.

"Who's house is this?" I asked.

"It's mine. Come on in," she said.

I guess my killer instinct was putting me on alert cause as we walked to the door, I eased the .45 around where I could grab it easier. The inside of the house was beautiful.

"Who lives here with you?" I asked.

"Nobody, just lil' ole me.

"Ain't nobody else in the house?" I asked.

"No, why are you asking me like that? Do you think I live with my boyfriend or someone is going to come out the back or something?"

"Where I'm from, you never can get too comfortable. The women up there will bring you home and there will be a house full of guys who were waiting on you and I've been one of those guys on more than one occasion."

"You just a gangsta ain't you?" Emyra said in a sarcastic voice.

"Naw, I ain't a gangsta but I am a survivor. My lifestyle gets crazy at times. To be honest, I need to stay in a environment like this because no one knows me and the chances of me living to become an old man is greater."

"Well, here you can relax," she said. "Oh, I usually don't let nobody smoke in here but since this seems like the last time I will ever see you, I guess I can break my rules."

Emyra is the truth. I pulled out a blunt and began emptying the weed inside of it. Emyra came and sat next to me.

"I always wanted to know how this was done," she said.

I started laughing. "You play too much Emyra," I told her.

"What!" she said. "I'm serious. I always see people smoking blunts but I never seen someone roll it up. I thought people used glue or some type of tape to hold it together."

I couldn't control myself. I laughed so hard I nearly spilled the weed. I couldn't even finish rolling it.

"Come on baby. You gone make me mess it up," I told her as I slowly licked the blunt.

Emyra was paying close attention. "Damn," she said.

"Damn what?" I asked.

Emyra said, "Nothing, never mind."

After a couple of minutes I caught on to what she was saying.

"Come closer, let me tell you something," I told her.

"But I'm right next to you," she said.

"But I want to tell you in your ear."

"Tra, ain't nobody here though," she said trying to reassure me no one was there.

"So what. Come here," I told her. When she did I whispered in her ear, "You know I'm gone miss you right?" Emyra shook her head yes.

Then I kissed her softly on her lips and pulled away. I grabbed the blunt off the table and lit it. Emyra sat on the couch next to me looking stuck but she could have been watching television. I grabbed her hand and kissed it. She looked at me in my eyes.

"Can I make love to you tonight?" The words came out of my mouth.

A shy seeming Emyra said, "Yes."

I continued smoking my blunt. When she stood up

I thought she was going to the kitchen or the bathroom. She grabbed my hand and said, "Come on."

I put the blunt in the ashtray and followed her into her bedroom. It was beautiful and very girly. She still had teddy bears and shit in her room. I sat on her bed as she stepped into the bathroom. I took off my shirt and laid back on the big comfortable bed.

Emyra came back out with a laced panty and bra set on looking cornbread thick. The light of the bathroom showed the beauty of her shapely body/

Emyra walked over to me and said, "Let's move this."

Grabbing the .45 from my waistline and placing it on the nightstand. She straddled me as we kissed intently. I was so hard I thought the .45 was pressing up against me. Emyra stood up and unbuttoned my belt and pants. I took them off as she removed her bra and panties then climbed into bed. The clock on the wall said after 10:00pm but I didn't give a fuck.

I kissed Emyra's soft lips then sucked on her ears as she wiggled. I placed two fingers inside her wet pussy as I sucked on her nipples. They were just right. She moaned like a cow as I worked my way down her body while still stroking her with my fingers. When I got to her pussy, I took her beautiful pussy lips and lifted them up so I could get to the clitoris. Still stroking her, she squirmed and begged for me to stop. I licked the rim of her pussy then slipped my tongue inside her. By now I had my arms cuffed under her legs so the pussy was right there and she wasn't able to move. I sucked on her clitoris and continued dipping my tongue inside her wetness. Emyra grabbed a pillow and covered her face. She was crazy with ecstasy.

I removed the pillow and whispered in her ear, "Turn over baby."

Her shaky legs were so beautiful. There was not a mark or bruise anywhere. When she turned over, her ass was shaped like an apple. I thought about that rapper's jeans on her.

I spread her ass cheeks and let my tongue walk up the crack of her ass.

"What you doing Tra, damn!" she said.

I didn't respond. I was so into it that I wanted to make the night something we both remembered. I opened her cheeks wider and got to that secret spot and licked it softly and blew on it.

"Oh shit!" she yelled.

That was the first time I heard Emyra use a cuss word. It was funny but I held my composure. When I started sucking on her she jumped and said, "No, I can't take no more." She turned back over.

"Baby, let me show you how to be made love to," I said as I moved closer to her. I grabbed her legs putting them both in the air. I slid my dick in her tight, wet pussy and just as I thought, it was good. I long stroked her until she wrapped her legs around me to get me to stop. I shook my head no and she let her legs go.

"Turn over," I said.

I thought Pinky had a cold spread on her, Emyra was killing Pinky shit. I slid my dick up and down her pussy lips and then slammed it in her. She hollered and then snatched the top of the bed off. Emyra started throwing it back on me and I knew she was cumming again. I wanted to pull out because I felt myself starting to cum but I couldn't. I busted all in her. My dick was going soft but I didn't want to come out of her. Emyra had some of the best pussy I'd ever had. She was still trying to throw her ass back on me when my dick just fell out of her. I was sweaty as hell and I laid there next to Emyra kissing her.

"Oh my God," she said.

"You alright baby?" I asked.

"Yeah, I'm alright. I just can't believe this," she said.

I was starting to trip. "You can't believe what?" I asked her.

"I have never had that done to me before. I mean I've heard stories and even rappers talking about it but to experience it is breath taking," she said.

"What?" I asked. "Having sex?"

"No, I'm not a virgin. I'm talking about what you did to me with your mouth. I can't even describe it." She was holding her sheet over her mouth.

I said, "I wish I could take you to Michigan with me. I would marry you."

"You shouldn't say things like that when you have a girlfriend."

"Why do you hate when I tell you the truth? You are so much of what I want that its going to be hard to leave you," I told her. She just looked at me.

I looked at the clock and it was 12:09am. I knew I had to go. I told Emyra I had to leave because it was getting late. I could tell that she was thinking about not seeing me again cause she kept saying damn. I got my stuff, grabbed my blunt out the ashtray, then we left.

"So will I ever see you again Tra?" Emyra said while driving me to my car.

"I definitely hope I can see you baby," I told her.

"I wish you weren't leaving so soon," she said.

"Emyra look, I would like to stay longer too but I have a lot of things going on back home and I know no one is going to take care of my business like me."

"I understand," she said.

"So tell me, if I sent you a plane ticket will you come to Michigan to visit me?" I asked.

"Yeah, but what about your girlfriend?"

"I have more than one house. She will be at one and we will be at the other," I told her.

"Yeah, I would like to see you again. If that's how I gotta do it then okay," she said sounding so sad.

When we pulled up to my car, I grabbed Emyra's hand and she didn't want to look at me.

"So you gone do me like that?" I asked her.

"Tra, this is painful enough as it is. We just made the best love I ever thought possible. I know I won't meet another man like you. How can I be happy?"

"Come here and give me a kiss," I said. "All you have to remember is this ain't the end. You have a place in my heart. You have my cell number so if you ever need me just call. I will be there, I promise." I held Emyra's hand as I spoke to her. "Don't forget me baby," I told her as I got out the car giving her another kiss.

Sitting in my car I looked at my watch. It was 12:48am. I knew it would look suspicious but I could work with it. I sparked up my leftover blunt and headed home.

I drove home smelling like pussy and weed. Emyra was the truth and her pussy was the bomb. I couldn't wait to see her again.

When I got in the house Nisha was sound asleep. I went into the bathroom and washed up. My cellphone was vibrating and it was another text from Emyra.

YOU ARE SPECIAL AND I WILL NEVER FORGET YOU I PROMISE! I LOVE YOU EMYRA.

I smiled at her message and erased it. I was tired as hell. I climbed in the bed with Nisha and went to sleep.

The next morning I woke up to the smell of breakfast. Aunt Ernestine had the whole house smelling good. The people down south didn't play when it came to cooking. Everything that they prepared was full course meals. Every day we spent down there our breakfast was lavish and our final days were no different. Aunt Ernestine cooked bacon, ham, eggs, grits, toast, and sausage. I miss those breakfast meals. Anyway, Nisha laid next to me sleeping so peaceful. I kissed her lips and she began waking up.

"Hey," she said looking super tired.

"Baby, wake up. I'm horny," I whispered to Nisha.

"What! Boy you betta go back to sleep talking about you horny!" she mumbled.

I usually made love to my girl every day but since being down south, I didn't because I didn't want to seem disrespectful to my elderly family members.

Unfortunately, Uncle Willie and Aunt Ernestine never had children of their own so they treated me and my crazy ass cousin, T-Mac like we were their sons.

Nisha tried to stay laying down so I put my hand under the covers and begin caressing her pussy. She moved.

"What are you doing Tra? You know Aunt Ernestine is right there in the kitchen. Why would you start something we can't finish right now?" Nisha said through her hot morning breath.

"Because I can. This is my pussy and I can do what I want with it," I said while still stroking her.

Nisha didn't say anything. "Come on let's get in the shower," I told her.

She said, "Let me brush my teeth and stuff. As a matter of fact Tra, you go brush yours and I'm coming in after you."

"What you trying to say?" I asked her while heading to the bathroom.

"Tra, turn on the shower while you in there,"

Nisha said.

I got my situation together and decided to go ahead and get in the shower. The water was hot as hell. I thought the water in Michigan was a muthafucka. The water down there was unbearable. I mean literally you couldn't stand there. I know why Nisha told me to turn it on now. I was already naked. I got out the shower and sat on the toilet seat flap naked as a new born baby.

"Watch out baby, I got to pee!" Nisha said as she walked in the steamy bathroom. I moved out the way so Nisha could do her thang.

"Why you ain't got no boxers or something on Tra?" Nisha asked.

"Cause I'm here waiting on you," I told her. Keep them panties off too when you get done."

She looked at me crazy. When she got off the toilet she left her panties on the floor. She started brushing her teeth and I got behind her. My dick was rock hard. I pressed it up against her ass then whispered in her ear, "Baby I need to be inside you."

Nisha looked back smiling with a mouth full of toothpaste. I bent her over the sink and lifted up her t-shirt so that I could get to the pussy. I slid my dick in and she was soak and wet.

"Damn!"

Nisha spit all the toothpaste out her mouth as I slammed the massive meat stick in her. Nisha hollered as I put every inch of me in her.

"Tra, please, please!" she begged. But I turned a deaf ear to her pleas. The pussy was too good to stop.

There was a knock on the door. "Travon, are you alright in there?" Aunt Ernestine yelled.

Damn! "Yeah. I'm alright Auntie. The shower water is just a bit hot," I yelled back.

"Alright, be careful now. I got your breakfast out here waiting on you."

"I told you," Nisha whispered.

I couldn't do nothing but laugh. "Man, come on and get in the shower," I told Nisha.

After getting dressed, our breakfast table experience was awkward. Aunt Ernestine was looking crazy at us and Uncle Willie had his head in his plate smiling. I busted out laughing.

"What' up with y'all this morning?" I said trying to settle the mood.

I knew they were on to us when out of nowhere Aunt Ernestine said, "Have y'all thought about baby names?"

Nisha said, "Tra is going to name the baby. He wants a boy though so we got our fingers crossed."

"Oh yeah, that's good Tra. You can name the baby after your Uncle Albert. He would love that," Aunt Ernestine said.

"That ain't gone happen," I said flatly.

Uncle Albert was her dope fiend ass brother that went on a crack serial smoking spree and ended up getting killed over a couple of dollars. He came up to Michigan and stayed with me and my moms and that lame ended up stealing some money I was saving up to get my first car. Luckily I didn't catch his ass because he would have just been a regular cat off the street in my eyes. Aunt Ernestine knew what he did to me. I couldn't believe that she even said that lame name. I had forgot him, period.

"You gotta learn to forgive Travon," Aunt Ernestine preached. "How can you expect God to forgive you and you have not forgave your uncle?"

"Auntie, I still have not forgiven myself for not getting on a bus and coming down here to put my hands on Uncle Albert," I told her.

"Who is Uncle Albert?" Nisha asked.

"Nobody," I interjected.

"He's my brother baby. He was murdered twelve years ago in Atlanta," Aunt Ernestine told Nisha.

Me and Aunt Ernestine never agreed on Uncle Albert and although my conscious was sensitive to that being her brother, I often thought about how him stealing my money got me doing my first paid hits.

The rest of the day went by smooth. Me and Nisha would leave at 2:00am so that we could be back in Flint around 9:00am. That way people wouldn't know I was back in town.

Aunt Ernestine decided to prepare a big dinner for us. While her and Nisha did the cooking, me and Uncle Willie did some runs and laid around the house. Aunt Ernestine needed some brown sugar so I went with Uncle Willie to get it. I guess he called himself being funny because he went to the store where Emyra worked. I knew there were others because I went to them myself to avoid Emyra. I just looked at Uncle Willie as we pulled up. Uncle Willie kept his eyes straight and wouldn't even look at me. I knew he was on some bullshit.

I entered the store with so much anxiety that I almost turned around. Just like our first encounter, Emyra was at her register looking good. At first she had her head down punching in prices with a customer so I walked up to the counter.

"Hey you," I said.

Emyra face lit up. "Hey Tra, how you doing?" she said.

"I'm alright. I just came up with Uncle Willie to get a few things for dinner. I will be leaving tonight," I told her.

"Hold on Tra. Let me finish ringing this stuff up. That will be $14.63," she told the customer. "Hey Diane, can you hold me down for a couple minutes," she yelled to her co-worker.

Diane came over to relieve Emyra and we walked around the store and talked.

"I'm happy to see you Tra. I really been thinking about you a lot. I have to be honest with you about something. I don't have a boyfriend. I know it probably doesn't matter to you but I want you to have the truth before you go."

"That's what's up. I appreciate you feeling the need to be honest with me," I said.

Emyra lowered her head. "Lift your head baby. You are too beautiful to have your head down about anything. I want you to go with me so bad. Baby, I want you to become part of my family," I told Emyra as she looked in my eyes.

"With you and Nisha?" she asked.

"Yes, and there are a few other important people in my life. That's why I just can't move down here like that. There are a lot of people who depend on me and I depend on them also, I know that you probably don't understand that but…"

"Hey Tra, come on. I'm all set," Uncle Willie yelled.

"I know this shit sounds crazy but I will treat you

like the queen you are. I know if I leave without you, we will both have regrets," I told Emyra.

I looked in her eyes and the tears began to come down.

"Give me a hug baby," I told Emyra.

I wiped the tears from her eyes and gave her a hug, a passionate kiss then walked out the store.

"Trust me, I know how you feel son," Uncle Willie said as I got in the car.

I was disgusted and it was all his fault for coming to this store. The remainder of my time in Tennessee was messed up. I was quiet during dinner and the ride back to Flint. There wasn't much to be said but back to business.

Chapter 24

"It feels good to be back home," I said as I put my bags down.

"It sure does baby. I can't wait to lay in my own bed," Nisha said.

"Well go ahead and unpack while I check the house out to make sure everything is cool," I told Nisha.

Living in Flint you never know. People will be waiting on you in your own house anticipating the right moment to kill you. I walked through the house checking windows and even closets. Everything was intact. I noticed messages on the answering machine so I pressed the button.

Beep. Hey Tra, this is Tone X down at the shop. Hey the National is ready to be picked up. The ticket is twenty-three.

Beep. Nisha this mama. I'm just calling cause I haven't heard from you. Call me when you get this message.

Beep. Pic up the phone nigga. This T-Mac. I know

you there with yo' stupid ass. I heard about you. You done went crazy.

You have no more messages, the answering machine said.

Damn! What the fuck do T-Mac want now? I assumed that he heard about the restaurant situation. I wish I had took J.B. down south with me. We could have went to Atlanta and killed T-Mac hoe ass. He was a liability. I ran upstairs and told Nisha to call her mother. I called J.B. and told him to come pick me up.

"You about to go somewhere Tra?" Nisha asked.

"Yeah, I'm going to get my car and shoot a couple moves. I gotta get my work outta these niggas houses," I said.

"Okay, well I'ma just go over my mother's house. Do you want me to get that stuff while I'm over there?"

"Naw, keep that over there unless she wants it out of her house. I will definitely understand that," I explained.

When J.B. finally got there, I was glad to see my dawg. I jumped in the car and it was smoky as hell, just like he likes it.

"There go yo bread right there but I still gotta get you five hundred," J.B. said.

"That's seventeen-five?" I asked.

"Yep," he said.

"Oh, take me to the shop on Cecil so I can pick up the National. I'm coming out hard," I said. J.B. passed me the blunt and I was back at it.

When we pulled up, there was a couple of niggas standing outside the shop. I knew one of them. He was a young rida from the rap group Gloc Gaim named, Tool Man.

"Hey, what's up Tra?" the homie Tool Man said as I got out the car.

"What's up boy? Man y'all making a lot of noise out here. I just left the south and they lovin' y'all," I said.

"That's what's up! Tool Man said. "These my niggas, Gun Man and Money Man. Hey y'all, this Tra."

"What's up homies?" I said and showed them some love.

Them Gloc Gaim niggas was some straight street niggas and I believed that's why they were loved by everybody because they were living it. Just like Skanbino Mob. I knew that if I had the time and less muthafuckas trying to kill me, I would put some bread behind them and reach out to some people.

I looked at them lil' niggas and all three of them looked like their hips were broke.

315

Walking in the shop, I asked J.B., "Man, what the

 fuck is wrong with them lil' niggas?"

"What you talking about?" J.B. asked.

"Them lil' niggas look handicap. What they got shot while I was gone or something? Cause they look like they got on back braces or something?"

"Aw shit. Hell naw. That's them extended clips," J.B. said laughing. "Them lil' niggas got at least seventy shots between the three of them. That's only one clip a piece."

"Damn," I said.

"Yeah, each of them lil' niggas carry no less than twenty-one shots," J.B. assured me.

Tone-X came out smiling ear to ear. I didn't know whether it was the money I was going to give him or the National.

"What's good TX?" I said.

"Damn Tra, for a minute I thought you weren't going to come get yo' baby. I called you over three days ago," he said.

"I had to take care of a lil' business, my bad. But you know I was coming to get it. Where is my baby?" I asked him.

"There it is over there with the car cover on it," he responded.

I walked over there and pulled off the cover. *Damn!* It was baby blue, glass house wet with the same chrome pantoes. I loved it. I gave Tone-X the twenty-three hundred dollars and he pulled the car out of the garage. I felt like it was a new car. I don't know why but every time, it never fails. The lil' Gloc Gaim niggas hollered at me and I knew I was ready cause if the young homies are feeling it, I was good to go.

All the dirt I was doing made me feel older than I was and now I look back with regrets because I rushed to get old and didn't enjoy my youthful years. I told J.B. I needed a CD to listen to and he threw me some shit called, *1000 Bars.* I threw that shit back at him and walked to his car myself. I grabbed my money out of the backseat and the homie Young D from Skanbino Mob CD. I needed some shit I could relate to and that I knew about. I didn't know shit about *1000 Bars.*

I started the National and just sat there for a minute. I hated that I didn't bring any weed plus J.B. had pulled off already. I fired up a cigarette and went over Pinky's house.

When I pulled up Pinky had the front door open. I looked at her house and noticed some bullet holes. I thought I must have missed them the other times but it was unlikely and I instantly got mad.

317

I just walked in the house. Pinky wasn't in the living room or the kitchen. I went in the bedroom and there she was with a gun pointed at me!

"What's up?" I yelled.

"Tra!" she yelled and lowered the gun. "My fault. I just heard somebody walking in the house. This bitch ass nigga done shot up my house. I can't stand these niggas."

I asked her, "Who shot up the house?"

"I believe it was Flez and his lil' cousin with they hoe ass. That lame ass nigga came over here and I wouldn't open the door so he gets mad and calls me all kinda shit," she said and laughed. "Then, about twenty minutes later, I'm in the kitchen and I'm hearing shots. Maybe like five of them. I paid it no attention because no windows were broken and I wasn't shot. I literally thought it was down the street until the next day Penny came over to take me shopping and she points the bullet holes out to me. I immediately put two and two together and came up with a bitch ass nigga named Flez."

"That's some hoe ass shit," I said. "Come here, give me a hug."

"Fuck a hug. I need some dick," she said laughing. I hugged her and squeezed her soft ass.

"So tell me about your trip," she said.

"Hold up. You smoking on something?" I asked mid conversation.

She said, "Yeah. There go the weed and the wraps are in that dresser drawer."

She pointed toward the drawer. I grabbed the shit and told her to go close the front door.

"Alright, we gotta get out in that tonight," I heard her saying on the way back in the room. "I like the color of yo' car."

"Oh yeah. I just went to pick it up," I said rolling the blunt. "Matter of fact, let's go hit some corners.

"Let me put some shorts on and get out of these sweatpants," she said.

"Well I will be in the car," I told her.

I knew I had to get my weed from over there because them clowns she used to fuck with was pussy whipped and I felt anything was bound to happen with them. I couldn't afford to take them kind of chances.

When she got in the car I told her, "I'ma get that shit when we come back. You got them hoe ass niggas going crazy and somebody is gonna get killed. Here, fire this up." I passed her the blunt and pulled out the driveway.

I began telling Pinky about the trip down south and even about my encounter with Emyra.

"Is she prettier than me?" Pinky asked in her sweet girly voice.

"Come on baby," I said and continued telling her the story. I was telling her how nice it was down there and I wouldn't mind living down there. I told her how Nisha wanted me to move down there as well.

"So you just gonna leave me up here, huh?" she asked.

"You be on some bullshit Pinky," I said. "Did I say I would leave you up here? Better yet, did I say I was moving down there?"

"Oh," she said.

I hit the blunt and Pinky unzipped my pants.

"What's up Pinky? What you doing?" I asked.

"Nothing," she said. "Keep telling me about your trip."

Pinky had my dick out and in her mouth. I couldn't even focus on telling the story. I had to focus on the road or we both would be in trouble. I drove pass a strip mall and turned around. I couldn't continue driving with her doing that so I pulled up and parked. The car was smoky as hell. I leaned my seat back and lifted up Pinky's head.

"Take off them shorts!" I told her.

Pinky took off her shorts and didn't have on any panties.

"Get in the backseat," I told her as I pulled my seat back up and followed her.

"You see, its just like you like it baby," she said talking about how hairy her pussy was. I sat down in the backseat and she straddled me like a real cowgirl.

"Oh shit, daddy, damn, I missed you," she said. "Damn, I missed you."

Pinky had some good, tight pussy. Every time we got together it was always special.

"Daddy I want you to hit this muthafucka from the back." I had to follow her instructions.

When we got back to her house, there was a dude walking through her driveway towards the backyard.

"Look Tra!" she said.

When I saw the dude I parked right there and got out. I didn't know whether this was the shooter or not so I pulled out the pistol and crept around the house. This dude was in the backyard at the window taking the screen off. I shot him in the side right under his arm probably piercing his lung. He was hollering like a pig. I looked around to see was anybody paying attention then I pistol whipped him. Pinky stood at the edge of the house looking.

"Don't kill him Tra but beat his ass. That's Flez's lil' cousin.

I hit him with the heater maybe eight times and his mouth looked so bad. I made that lame get up and run. He could barely walk but I guess he figured either that or die. I knew that based on where the bullet hit him, he would never make it home but I didn't tell her.

I was in rush mode now. I pulled the car in the driveway and ran in the house. I went straight to Pinky's attic to get my weed and started loading it in the National. Pinky was helping me but I told her to stop and go pack her shit.

"Where we going?" she asked.

"We ain't going nowhere but you are. I'm taking you to a hotel until we can find you another place to live. As a matter of fact, call Penny and tell her I said to come over here and help you pack this shit up. I'ma go drop this shit off and I'll be back," I told a nervous looking Pinky.

I shot out the house and into the National. I didn't want the police to come over there and I got a house full of weed.

When I made it back home, Nisha was in the bed. "Hey baby," I said. "How was your mother? Is everything okay with her?"

"She's alright," Nisha said.

"I got the car out there but it's full of weed and I gotta shoot this move so I'ma take the rental car. Do you have somewhere you have to go?" I asked.

"Naw, I'm too tired to do anything right now. What time will you be back?" she asked.

"Its 12:30pm right now, I will be back about 4:30 or 5:00," I said.

"I want you to stay in the house with me when you come back. Can you do that?" Nisha asked.

"Yeah, I definitely can try. You know I got so much going on. But I will try baby."

Nisha focused her attention back on the television and I left. On the way back to Pinky's I called her.

"Hello!" Pinky answered the phone sounding all jittery.

"Hey did Penny make it over there yet?" I asked.

"No, she's on her way though," Pinky responded.

"Well when she gets there I want you to go get a U-Haul truck. I'ma bring some of the shorties from

323

the hood to move your shit and let them make a couple of dollars. I'ma scoop them and be right over." I was moving fast.

"Alright," Pinky said.

I was moving way too fast and I knew it. When I got to the hood and saw the shorties, I got out of the

car.

"Man, what y'all out here doing?" I said getting out of the car.

"Hey Tra, what's up nigga? I ain't seen you in a minute," one of the lil' homies said.

"Look, I need y'all to help me move this female shit out of her house. I got fifty dollars apiece for y'all," I told them.

There was four of them and in unison they said, "No doubt Tra. We will help you homie."

We jumped in the rental car and headed to Pinky's. Unfortunately when we got there Pinky hadn't made it back yet so me and the homies sat in the car and got our smoke on.

One of the lil' homies name was Dalonja. He was probably the youngest of all four. When he was like eight or nine years old, he would be out on the block with the rest of the kids. I would gather them up and catch the ice cream truck.

He always reminded me of those days when he got older. I knew his mother from the hood. She was cool as hell. I was messed up when he hit the blunt. He smoked like a professional. He reminded me of myself and that was painful because I knew what his future would look like.

Pinky and Penny finally pulled up. Pinky was

driving the U-Haul and Penny was following her. We got out of the car and I told Pinky to let me back the truck up to the door. When I got out the U-Haul, Penny ran up to me and gave me a big hug. The lil' homies were looking at the girls hard.

"Hey Tra, what's up with ole girl?" Dalonja said.

"I don't know homie you gotta shoot your shot," I said.

After I pulled the truck up to the porch, I looked back on my way in the house and Dalonja ran up on Penny and began shooting his game. I just smiled.

It took us a hour and a half to get everything in the truck. I was so ready to get the shit over with so I could go home and lay back. I told Pinky that she would have to drive the truck for a couple of days or drop it off over her mother's house until we found her a new place to stay. I paid the lil' homies and dropped them back off in the hood. I let them know how much I appreciated the love.

"Hey, tell ole girl its all good though," Dalonja said.

I assumed that she shoot the lil' homie down. I have never been a hater. I believe that any female can be knocked. I will definitely give a guy a chance to take one of mines. I just wish one shared my realness.

One time I was in the mall with Nisha. She was

getting some clothes for a party that night or something. I was walking behind her in the mall looking at her ass when a guy I went to elementary school with came up to me and asked me was Nisha my girl. I told him, "Naw, shoot yo' shot." He talked that shit like he was going to holler but I guess he froze up. Later on Nisha asked me who he was. I told her what happened and what I told him. She looked at me like I was crazy.

On the way home, Pinky called me and told me she was going to the Knights Inn hotel and if I needed her to holler. I knew what she was up to. I told her that Nisha wanted me to stay in the house today so I was going to lay back for a while.

"But what if I need something tonight?" Pinky asked.

"Well you know, I will see what's up. It all depends on what it is. My phone will be on. Just text me and let me know," I said.

"Okay. I will tell Penny what you said, too."

Chapter 25

Three months later I'm riding down Martin Luther King Boulevard, past the liquor store and it's a muthafucka stretched out in the parking lot. It was so many people outside it was crazy. I assumed it was someone with a lil' status because the crowd was so big but I was on my way to Pinky's new crib to see what was up.

Pinky ended up moving in Mountain Boy Hood on Mallory Street. I plushed her house out for her and got her a lil' whip to ride around in. She wanted a National but I couldn't see her riding around like me. I found a clean ass 1987 Chevelle and got it painted for her. Once she got that car, she was in a world of her own.

I had Pinky selling pounds of weed and Penny was selling cocaine, everything from ounces to bricks. I would give her eighteen of them and tell her if she needed more than that, she needed to call me. I knew niggas stayed looking for a easy brick lick because I was one of those guys before.

Everything was moving good. Nisha was getting big as hell. She kept my phone ringing asking for anything from food to just talking. I got her a lil' whip, too. But I got her a 2007 Camaro, brand new off the lot. A man should never put his main girl in something less or equivalent to his second or third woman.

I finally made it to Pinky's and soon as I cut the car off my phone rang. I immediately thought it was Nisha. *Damn, I know this is this girl.*

"Hello," I said.

"Tra," the small voice said.

"Yeah, what's up though?"

"Hey, do you know who this is?"

I pulled the phone away from my ear and looked at the number on the phone. It was Emyra.

"Emyra, hey sweetheart, how are you doing?" I happily asked. The thought of her made me feel a lot better. The adrenaline in me was on fire.

"I'm doing alright," she said. "I am actually surprised that you remember me."

"Quit playing. How can I forget about you out of all people? I told you that you have a place in my heart," I reminded her.

"Tra, you still make me feel like a queen. It's been three and a half months and you still have that effect on me," she said.

"What's up though baby? How's things in the dirty south?" I asked.

"Have you spoke to Uncle Willie or Aunt Ernestine?" she asked.

"Nope. I actually haven't called them since I been back but I'm quite sure my mother has, why? Is something wrong?" I asked. She was beginning to have me thinking.

"I have some bad news Tra," she said softly.

"What!" I said irritated expecting the worst.

"I'm pregnant," she whispered.

"Damn baby. I thought you were going to say somebody died or something. You got me scared. I mean how can you being pregnant be a bad thing?" I asked.

"I don't know. I just thought you would be mad," Emyra responded.

"No sweetheart. I'm not mad. You are a beautiful, smart, intelligent, and special woman. I would prefer to have a queen like you have my child," I said trying to lift her spirits. "I am going to take care of you and my child. I promise. Even if I gotta move down there."

"You for real?" she asked excitedly.

"Hell yeah. I'm dead serious," I responded.

I looked up and Pinky and Penny was standing in the doorway passing a blunt back and forth.

"Look, I'm so happy baby. I'm about to celebrate.

I got to tell everybody, even Nisha," I said.

"She is going to be mad as hell," Emyra said sounding like a little kid.

"Yeah, she sure will be mad. But hey, it's too late now. The same way I wouldn't want her to abort my baby is the same thing I feel about ours. So the worst thing she can do is leave me," I assured her.

"Well I just called to let you know. I guess I will talk to you soon," she said.

"Alright baby. I will call you soon," I said.

"Tra, I love you," Emyra said before hanging up the phone.

Pinky and Penny are some nosey ass females. They rushed me with questions of who I was talking to that kept me smiling. I knew that once I told them, especially Pinky, she would be on some bullshit. Really if I told her about Emyra being pregnant, that would start some other shit.

"It ain't none of y'all business who that was. Y'all don't never call me to let me know how much I mean to you," I told them. Pinky and Penny both looked stupid when I said that. It shut them up.

Females always do that. Even men, too. When they try to compete with another person, then the one they are trying to impress informs them of what they are failing to do, it gets' quiet. I learned that from my own experience. I had this one female named Valerie who used to love my dirty boxer drawers. I would make love to her and leave her laying in the bed. I would completely leave the house without her knowing until I was gone. I did her so wrong. Then she stopped letting me fuck her. When I asked her the reason, she said the other dude was eating her pussy. I was young back then and I thought I would never go "downtown" as that singing group coined the situation. I couldn't do nothing but be quiet, just like Pinky and Penny were.

My life always presented crazy situations. I was trippin' about Emyra, how I fucked her one good time and she got pregnant. I fucked Pinky and Penny damn near every chance I got but neither of them ever missed a period. I had knew numerous cats in my position with two women pregnant at the same time but I always wondered how could they honestly be there for both women when the babies were secrets. There was no way I could do that and I had to find a way to tell Nisha. She was going to have a fit but it had to be done.

I sat on Pinky's couch and turned on my PS2. I engulfed myself in *Grand Theft Auto* to take my mind away from my issues. Pinky came in the living room and dropped nine thousand dollars in my lap.

"Damn baby, you a baller," I said sarcastically.

"Shut up," she shot back.

Pinky sat next to me and started playing with my braids. "What's wrong Tra?" she asked.

"Ain't nothing wrong. What the fuck you talking about?" I tried to get her to believe me by getting aggressive.

"Nigga I been around you long enough to know when something is bothering you," she said.

"Yeah, I'll be over there in a minute nigga," Penny said talking on the phone as she walked in the living room.

"Naw, that was ole girl from Tennessee," I said.

"Oh, the lil' female you met down there?" Penny jumped in.

"Yeah, she pregnant," I uttered.

"What!" Pinky yelled. "She's pregnant! Damn, that's fucked up Tra. That's real fucked up! I can't believe this shit right here! So now you got a baby coming from a girl you just met, but you won't get me pregnant?"

Pinky was so heated she got up and went in her room. I told Penny to pass me the wraps that were on the table. I needed to get high.

"She's mad at you Tra," Penny said. "But you really don't understand though."

"I don't understand what Penny?" I asked licking the blunt.

"A bitch ain't trying to fuck with these lame as niggas out here after she meets you. You think ole girl you live with don't know you cheating on her? Come on Tra, you know better. There ain't no niggas out here like you. These muthafuckas are broke, gay and they looking fiend out. You know why she trippin' and to be honest, she has every right to," Penny said.

I sparked up the blunt and started back playing the video game.

"Tra, I will be back later. I gotta go drop this work off. Oh yeah," she said digging in her purse. "Here."

Penny placed some money on the edge of the couch then left. I knew I had to talk to Pinky but maybe she didn't want to talk. I know if she got pregnant by some dude, I would be mad as hell and she would have to abort the baby most likely. The situation called for drastic measures so I took my shirt off and walked in Pinky's room.

"What's up?" I said.

Pinky looked up at me teary-eyed. "Nothing."

"I mean damn, you acting like I tried to make this shit happen," I said.

"Well you sure didn't wear a condom. You never do," Pinky said calmly.

I walked over to her and stood between her legs.

"Gone Tra," she said.

"So you don't love me no more?" I asked her.

She said, "It seems like I am the only one who does in this situation."

I knew she really wanted me to get her pregnant and she had every reason to be mad. So instead of beating a dead horse, I kissed her, told her I apologize, I love her, and I left.

There were no way I was telling Nisha now. I am damn near sure she would probably try to kill my baby and I would have to kill her.

"Fuck that shit!" I said to myself while driving to J.B.'s. I had other business on the floor and females get pregnant all the time. There was nothing I could do. Me and J.B. had to go meet the brothers from Chicago with the weed. They agreed to bring it halfway. We would pick up the package in Adrian, Michigan. J.B. was hustling now. I guess he was doing hits on the side because he kept poppin' up with money. He even bought Teresha a new car that kept reminding Nisha costed $26,000.00 fresh off the lot. I was glad to see my comrade doing good. He brought $35,000.00 to the table so we both were getting one hundred pounds of weed each.

I had to pick up the homie Dalonja so he could ride with us in case the shit got crazy. That lil' nigga wanted to be like me and J.B. He was a young killing machine. The shit he was doing made news reporters cry on camera.

So after scooping the lil' homie up, we headed to J.B.'s which was a few blocks over. The Chicago niggas had the weed in a regular truck with the black top over the back. All J.B. had to do was drive the truck home. When I pulled up to J.B's, he came out the house with a bullet proof vest on looking hot as hell. I don't know if he thought he was hiding it or not but the small t-shirt he had on didn't do him any justice.

"Hey cuzz, why you got that hot ass vest on?" I asked when he got in the car.

"I got my vest on nigga for one, I'm grown and for two niggas ain't playin' right, and for three, niggas ain't playin' right!" he said sounding stupid as hell.

I just pulled off shaking my head. The lil' homie, Dalonja was in the backseat laughing at comical ass J.B. and it made me laugh.

"Dog, you be on bullshit!" I said.

"Tra, these niggas Capone's cousins these niggas ain't no kin to me, you or Dalonja. I don't trust nobody no more, fuck that! I'm wearing this vest for the rest of my life! Shit, all the work a muthafucka been putting in, yo' ass should have on two vests, and a helmet nigga! J.B. was in his element.

"Hey, y'all muthafuckas crazy!" Dalonja said so hard he could hardly breathe.

"Come on Dalonja, don't encourage this nigga with this dumb shit!" I said.

"I mean the nigga right big homie. You can't trust these niggas out here," Dalonja said.

The shit they were saying was right but at the same time, we have been taking this same trip for over ten years. *I know shit could change but damn.* My thoughts were interrupted when I looked down and saw my cellphone light up. The music was up a bit so I probably would have missed it. I picked it up and it was Penny.

"Hey, what's up?" I yelled through the phone.

"Hey, where you at?" she asked.

"I'm on the E-way. What's up?"

"Oh, I'm headed to drop this work off to this lame and at first he say bring him nine girlfriends then he calls back and say he want eighteen but I don't have it," she said.

"Well, I will be back in maybe two hours. You can give him what you got and tell him he'll have to wait for the rest or you can tell him to take the nine."

"Alright," she said. "Call me when you come back."

"In a minute," I yelled and hung up.

"Hey Tra. Where is ole girl who was at that house I hollered at?" Dalonja asked.

"That was her who I was just talking to," I said.

"Damn," he said.

337

"What, you want me to call her back for you cuzz?" I asked him. He sounded so disappointed.

He said, "Hell yeah!"

I turned down the music and called Penny then passed the phone to Dalonja my cellphone.

"What's up daddy?" I heard Penny say when she answered the phone.

"This ain't Tra. This D.J."

"D.J. who?" Penny asked.

"Damn lil' homie," J.B. said laughing.

"The lil' homie," Dalonja said to her. "I met you that day we moved yo' girl stuff for her."

"Oh, what's up lil' nigga?" she said.

I felt bad for lil' homie. He was trying and she wasn't giving him no action. I thought she better quit playing before his emotions get the best of him and he kills her ass.

"You know I told the big homie I wanted to pop at you on some shit," he told her.

"Aw shit! It's way too many niggas over here! Tell Tra I ain't feeling too good about this nigga," Penny said.

"Tra, girl said it's too many niggas where she at and she ain't feeling it," D.J. said.

338

"Ask her who is the nigga," I said trying to drive and listen to her at the same time. "Put her on speaker phone," I told lil' homie.

"It's a nigga named Val. I met him at the store a few weeks ago," she said.

"Well fuck it then baby. If you don't feel safe just keep driving," I told her.

"Okay," she said. "Tra, this nigga flagging me down on some desperate shit."

"You got yo' strap on you right," I asked her.

"Yeah, I got it," she said sounding scared.

"Well baby I think dawg you fuckin' wit on some bullshit. He asked for nine zips then he went to eighteen. I want you to put the gun under your shirt and pull up on him. When he comes towards the car roll yo' window down and shoot him in his face in front of all them niggas!" I told her.

"You for real?" she asked sounding like she needed my full assurance.

"Hell yeah!" I yelled. "And do it right now!" I said forcefully.

"I'm turning around right now," she said.

As I was talking to Penny on speaker phone, J.B. was in the passenger seat shaking his head in agreement looking crazy.

"Okay," Penny said.

Everything went silent as we waited to see what would happen. I looked in the rearview mirror and Dalonja had fury in his eyes.

"Hey, what's up?" I heard a male voice say.

There was three shots then hard breathing.

"Bitch ass nigga!" I heard Penny mumble through the deep breaths. She shot the nigga then pulled off.

"Tra," she whispered in the phone.

"Yeah, I'm right here baby, you alright?" I asked.

"What do I do now?" she asked.

I went straight into survival mode.

"Wipe your fingerprints off your cellphone with a shirt or towel and toss it out the window. I want you to go over Pinky's and run some hot water with a lot of bleach in it. Take all your clothes off and put them in a garbage bag and get in the tub. I will be there in about an hour and a half," I instructed her.

"Okay," she said.

"Go straight there! And don't forget to toss that damn phone! You hear me?" I said.

"Yeah, I hear you," she replied. "I will see you when you get back."

I turned the music back up in the car and continued on the mission. J.B. looked at me and winked his eye. I already knew what he was thinking. J.B probably thought I had just turned Penny out and how she could be trusted to do shit but little did he know I was already aware of Penny's gangsta and that was small shit to a giant like her.

Capone's cousins from Chicago had the truck parked in a grocery store parking lot. The truck was so messed up it had paint primer on the front clip and a donut tire on the back. No one would ever suspect that two hundred pounds of lime green good weed was under the black top.

When we pulled up, J.B. immediately jumped out to get in the truck. Dalonja got in the front seat with me. J.B. was looking so stupid with that tiny t-shirt on with the vest. I rolled the passenger window down and had D.J. throw him a sweater I had in the backseat.

"Cuzz, put that on. You looking crazy with that vest on. And cuzz, don't be driving wild either," I yelled.

"Nigga shut up, I know what I'm doing," he said pulling the sweater over his head.

Chapter 26

We made it back to Flint without incident. J.B. drove back to his house and when we got there, I dropped D.J. off. I yelled to J.B. that I would be back later. The only thing on my mind was getting to Pinky's to make sure Penny was safe. I called over Pinky's on my way there.

The phone kept ringing and I began to get worried so I drove faster. I was doing sixty miles per hour down Proctor Street where the speed limit is maybe twenty-five. Then my phone rang.

"Hello," I yelled.

"Where you at?" It was Penny.

"Why you didn't answer yo' phone. I just called over there," I said.

"You told me to sit in the tub and Pinky just let it ring," she said sounding innocent.

I knew she was going through it. The flow of emotion that a person experiences when you take a life is unexplainable and I could only imagine what she was going through.

"I'm pulling up in the driveway right now. Tell

Pinky to open the door," I said as I pulled up to the house.

When I saw Penny's car I knew she would have to get rid of it. We would have to find her another one. Pinky opened the door looking so good. She wore her hair in a ponytail and had on some boy boxer drawers and a sports bra.

"Hey Tra," she said as I walked in.

"Come here," I told her as she began to walk away.

I knew she was still upset over me getting Emyra pregnant so I had to comfort her. She turned around and I could see tears forming in her eyes. I grabbed her hand and looked her in the eyes. A tear fell and I wiped her eyes with my hand.

"I apologize baby," I said. "I can see that you are still hurting and I never wanted you to go through this. I promise we gonna make it right, okay?"

Pinky wrapped her arms around my head and cried on my chest.

"Pinky, is Tra here yet?" Penny yelled from the bathroom interrupting our moment.

"Here I come," I yelled.

"This water is almost cold now Tra," Penny yelled back.

I told Pinky I would come over later so we can finish talking but I needed to deal with Penny right quick. Pinky shook her head in agreement.

Penny did exactly as I told her. She sat in the tub looking so innocent. I came in and I gave her a kiss.

"How you doing?" I asked.

"I'm okay," she responded.

I turned on the hot water and sat down outside the tub. Penny had her thong and bra in the middle of the bathroom floor.

"Damn, who you wearing this shit for?" I said jokingly but serious.

"I'm not wearing it for nobody Tra. I just be wanting to feel sexy," she said with her head down.

I reached in the water to see how hot it was. It was heating up. I took off my shirt and wife-beater, placed them on the sink along with the .45 and began to wash her up.

"That nigga was on bullshit now that I think about it," Penny said.

I grabbed the bottle of bleach and poured some more in the water. I took the wash rag and soap then began to lather it up.

"You gone wash me up?" Penny asked blushing.

"Just chill!" I told her.

I took her hands and began scrubbing them and dipping them back into the water. I took my house key and scrapped under her fingernails. Penny was watching my every move. I told her she could get out of the water now. I stood up and closed the bathroom door. When Penny stood up I was reaching for my clothes. I stopped when she stepped out of the tub. Her body was so beautiful and it sparkled with the water glistening off her. I felt my nature beginning to rise.

"Man, damn," I said as I attempted to push my erection down.

Penny looked at me and smiled. Clearly she knew exactly what she was doing because she turned her ass toward me and bent down to grab her thong and bra. I couldn't help but to cuff her pussy from the back.

"Whew!" she said sucking on her teeth.

I already knew I couldn't resist. Before I knew it, I was pulling my pants down to slide in her. I hadn't fucked Penny in over a month and her pussy was so good and tight. She had that super wet. I knew that I couldn't make love to her like she deserved so after I busted my first nut I whispered in her ear.

"I'ma come get you tonight."

Penny grabbed the towel and wiped her pussy then put on her thong. I walked out of the bathroom and she followed me holding her bra in her hand. Her titties were bouncing all over the place.

I had so much stuff on my plate and I was trying to make sure everything was done right. I couldn't shake my conversation with Emyra and I knew that I would have to tell Nisha some way in order to take care of Emyra and my seed properly. I loved Nisha too much not to tell her.

"Girl, put them titties up!" Pinky yelled as we walked in the living room.

"Snap me up," Penny said as she turned around to Pinky.

"Why you didn't have Tra do it. Y'all were back there long enough," Pinky responded.

"Hey P, don't drive that car nowhere. And as a matter of fact, you might as well go get all yo' stuff out of it. And don't forget the trunk either."

"Why you say that," Penny asked.

"Because you gotta burn that car! You can take your radio and speakers out of it and everything else you care about but that car is evidence and we have to be safe. As a matter of fact, call the police and say it was stolen. I will have one of the lil' homies come and get the car," I told her.

Penny was looking so sad but I didn't give a fuck. We both would be looking sad if she got caught for shooting that lame.

"I gotta lot of shit to take care of tonight so just be patient with me. We will get you a car either tomorrow or the next day. I gotta go pick up this weed and figure some other shit out. I will be back

347

later," I told the girls as I stood up and walked out of the house.

When I got out to the car, I just sat there for a minute thinking about everything from Nisha finding out about Emyra, Pinky being upset Emyra is pregnant, the hundred pounds I had to go pick up, and Penny possibly committing her first murder. Thoughts clouded my mind so I fired up a cigarette to ease some of the tension. I sat there for about fifteen minutes just thinking about life and most of all, I was thinking about Nisha.

We don't think about shit like that happening. Although Pinky wanted to have my child so bad, and I was busting nuts in her and Penny, its crazy how things happen.

Finally, I started the car and backed out the driveway. I looked up at Pinky's house and one of them was peeking out the window. I had to get my weed so I called J.B. to see what was up. After maybe two rings he picked up.

"Hey what's up bro? Is everything good with that situation?" J.B. asked as soon as he answered the phone. I could tell someone was close to him by the way he was talking.

"Yeah, everything good bro. I'ma shoot by the house and holler at Nisha then I will be over to get that," I told him.

"Okay," he said and hung up.

I decided to call Nisha and see what she was doing.

"Hello," she said.

"Hey baby. What are you doing?" I asked.

"Nothing, just laying here. When are you coming home?" she asked.

"I'm on my way now. I will be there in about five minutes," I said.

"Is everything alright. You sound sad. What's wrong?" she asked.

I was not conscious of my actions. I knew that mentally I was messed up but I couldn't tell my voice was so revealing.

"Everything is going to be alright baby," I told Nisha.

"I will see you when you get here," she said.

Chapter 27

I was so exhausted when I walked in the house.

"Tra!" Nisha yelled.

"Yeah, it's me," I responded.

I needed to smoke so I went in the kitchen and grabbed a pack of blueberry leaf wraps and walked upstairs to the bedroom. Nisha was laying watching television. Over the past couple months, Nisha's pregnancy began to show more and more. I looked at her growing belly and smiled.

"What are you smiling for?" she asked with a grin on her face.

"You are glowing baby and I am just admiring you. That's all," I replied.

I sat down on the bed and started rolling the wrap. I was contemplating whether or not I should tell Nisha at that moment or should I wait. I flipped the wrap and walked out of the bedroom and headed down the stairs.

"Where are you going Tra?" Nisha asked.

"I'm going downstairs to smoke," I said.

Sitting in the living room smoking my life away, I kicked off my shoes and relaxed. I looked up and Nisha was coming down the steps. I just kept smoking when she sat down next to me on the couch.

"What is it Tra?" Nisha asked me looking like she already knew what was going on.

"It's just been a long day and I got some shit on my mind I am trying to work through. I'm straight though baby. How are you is the question? How you feeling?" I asked changing the subject.

"I'm hungry," she said.

"What are you trying to eat?" I asked her.

She said, "I been in this house all day. I got a taste for some Chinese food."

"Well, I gotta get my weed from over J.B.'s so we can make two trips at once. We can go get the food first, then go over J.B.'s. I got the weed in a truck so I will drive the truck back home and you can follow me in the rental," I told her.

"Alright. I'ma go get my I.D. and put on some tennis shoes and I will be right down," she said as she stood up.

"Well, I will be in the car waiting on you," I told her as I started putting my shoes back on.

Nisha walked up the steps looking good. I left the car keys in the kitchen so I went to grab them. I had to relight my blunt and as I opened the door to leave, there stood Tye!

Boom, Boom, Boom!

COMING SOON URBAN GENOCIDE 2

Made in the USA
Las Vegas, NV
15 June 2021